OUT OF THE UNDERWORLD AND INTO YOUR HEART!

Rumor has it that there is a way out of Hell, through tunnels. Of course the rumors could be disinformation direct from the Father of Lies; all the Heroes of Hell who have assembled for the adventure know that.

Though they do not know what hideous dangers they will face once they forsake the sanctuary of Julius Caesar's palace in New Hell, they are sure that boredom, the most awful fate Eternity has to offer, will not be one of them. Anything less they can handle; they are who they are, after all, and they have their army, equipped with the most modern weapons and electronics. . . .

Join the greatest Heroes and Rogues of all the Ages in the first full-length novel in the greatest of all shared universes: *HEROES IN HELL!*™

THE GATES OF HELL

C.J. CHERRYH AND
JANET MORRIS

BAEN
SCIENCE FANTASY
BOOKS

THE GATES OF HELL

Copyright © 1986 by C.J. Cherryh and Janet Morris

A Baen Books Original

Baen Publishing Enterprises
260 Fifth Avenue
New York, N.Y. 10001

First printing, October 1986

ISBN: 0-671-65592-2

Cover art by David Mattingly

Printed in the United States of America

Distributed by
SIMON & SCHUSTER
TRADE PUBLISHING GROUP
1230 Avenue of the Americas
New York, N.Y. 10020

CONTENTS

1. Basileus   1
2. Meetings   29
3. The Oracle   61
4. Passage   89
5. Hellhole   122
6. Iron Lady Down   155
7. Shadow of Wings, Shadow of Shadows   186
8. Of Pawns and Kings   225
9. Gift Horse   249

1.   Basileus

Alexander had styled himself *'basileus'* (Great King) after Darius' death to subdue further resistance among the Persians, then swept triumphant across the Kush, only to bog down in Bactria for three years so that marrying the Sogdian witch Roxane became the only way out.

He'd trekked across the desert to the Oracle of Ammon at Siwah to be declared son of Zeus, only proper for a pharaoh; he'd painted a great city black and flouted the prophets, entering Babylon from the west. Hc'd died there at thirty-three, no taller than he'd ever been, but a god who could buy salvation for his beloved Hephaistion with golden ships' prows in Babylon.

No one could take that away from him: no matter the cost, he'd found Hephaistion a place in heaven; his Patroklos had been spared this hellish fate.

And now he had a new Patroklos, the Israelite Judah Maccabee, tall and dark with rebellion, just the man with whom to raise an army to scourge Hell from sea to sea and bring the very Devil to His knees.

For that they were intent upon doing: they had

nothing but time. In life, he had said, "You, Zeus, hold Olympus, but I set the earth beneath my sway." In death, he had sworn to see if Maccabee was right—if heaven could be won by vengeance and force of arms.

This he did because his new companion craved it, and because Alexander was a hero and a man who had dwelt too long in Hell not to realize that goals, even unattainable ones, were priceless.

Madness, if it came upon him from hopelessness, would last forever. Raising an army to fight the minions of Hell was infinitely preferable to becoming like Che Guevara—a quivering wreck, a melange of snapped threads, a fallen hero.

No one knew better than Alexander that heroic temperaments such as his own were subject to excesses: as he was excessively brave and extravagantly generous, he was excessively vengeful and extravagantly passionate when thwarted.

It was, Maccabee was fond of saying, this heroic soul of his which had killed him, wearing out his flesh.

"If ever you'd known to spare yourself, perhaps the fever that killed you might have spared you as well," Maccabee had said one night when intimacy was upon them.

That night, like this one, had been long and full of both their ghosts.

Tonight, Maccabee had another thing than intimacy in mind; Alexander could see it in his narrow eyes as he brought the newcomer, no taller than Alexander but dark with a curly mop of hair, to see the Macedonian in his tent.

"This is Zaki, Alksandr—from a time beyond ours."

The little Semite nodded his hooked nose in Alexander's direction and folded gracefully into a squat on one of the strewn cushions around the carefully banked cookfire over which wine was warming.

Maccabee was always bringing him Jews, and Jews believed only in their nameless god. They never bowed to him, never showed the proper respect. But Maccabee loved them, and Alexander loved Maccabee, although what kinship the tall, Hasmonaean Israelite felt with these mongrel descendents of his, Alexander couldn't understand.

Now he said, as Maccabee came to sit beside him and both of them watched the hairy little fellow across the fire, "What news have you, Zaki, which Judah wants me to hear?"

"News?" The little Jew scratched his ear. "I don't know about news—I haven't been here long enough to hook in: we had a nuclear war in my time; I'm still adjusting . . ." The man's face tensed and calmed as memories flashed across it. Then he said: "I heard of Maccabee, came out to volunteer my services. I am, was . . . a modern Israeli; it is God's will, is it not, that we do not forget the Nazi murderers, even here? That we chase them down and plague them with their just punishments? . . . So I have heard, anyway, that you intend to do."

Judah Maccabee, shifting toward Alexander, said under his breath, "Basileus, be patient." Then, louder: "What our new friend means is that our plan to find the Germans who have found a way out of Hell, and wrest from them their secrets, is one in which cause he'll gladly labor. And he is—was—a spy. We are in need of spies."

"You're in need of the Roman empire," said the 20th century man, "and Machiavelli, and that whole crew that orbits Caesar like well-trained satellites."

Maccabee's face grew dark: he hated Romans.

But certain Germans were reputed to know of tunnels leading out of Hell.

"Germans, Romans—it matters not to me, as

long as what we do hurts the Satanic empire and brings us closer to heaven," Alexander proclaimed. "Gods—you do know I am one, Zaki—do not belong in Hell for longer than it takes to mete out special punishment to the especially deserving. But we're helpless without cavalry, and horses are scarce, not to mention—"

"With Caesar, you'll have cavalry and more; troops whose skills you know not of, here in the wilderness," said the small, rat-faced Jew. "We've reason to hate the Romans, ourselves." He bared his teeth. "But war makes new rules. If you want to go against Satan himself, you'll need me—my diplomatic skills, my modern knowledge—and you'll need Caesar and those who follow him."

"Who follow him?" Alexander repeated slowly, a bad taste in his mouth. "As a ruler? As emperor? As—"

Maccabee shook his head and rubbed a big hand along his jaw. "As a god, I've been told, Basileus. A god like yourself. But don't let that bother you, he—"

"A living god?" Alexander drew himself up straight, wrath beginning to stiffen his spine. He faced Maccabee squarely: "Are you suggesting that we need the help of some pretender to godhead? That another leader is necess—"

"No, no, Alex," Maccabee demurred. "_He_ needs _us_. As a matter of fact, Zaki says he loves you . . . loves your memory, reveres you, perhaps even tries to emulate you. You preceded him, you know. A good hero gives his worshippers a chance to worship, does he not?"

Alexander knew that Maccabee wasn't telling the whole truth, but he'd let Hephaistion manipulate him in the old days—it was one of the perquisites he bestowed on those he loved.

So he only nodded and said, "Fine. Set up a

meeting with this Caesar person, Zaki: the specifics must only meet Judah's approval."

The little Semite grinned from ear to ear and rose to make his way out, but Alexander stopped him. "Wait. I want to know about this 'nuclear' war. Have a drink, sit back down. We have all night."

And Maccabee might have mumbled, "We have a thousand and one all-nights," although, when Alexander turned to face his friend, all he saw was the soft, suffused glow of happiness that was the single reward, the only pleasure, Alexander cared about anymore.

If Maccabee had wanted Alexander to treat with the Devil himself, the Macedonian would have attempted it. But since all Judah wanted was that Alexander meet with a fellow potentate, a self-proclaimed god, and (if Judah was right), a man who revered Alexander, it was much easier to acquiesce. The only difficulty would be in this Caesar's willingness to subordinate himself to Alexander.

For the Great King never, ever settled for second place or second best. It just wasn't Homeric.

On the trail to New Hell Alexander's party consisted of forty horse, ten wagons, nearly a hundred dray beasts and twice as many camp followers. But the entire convoy was halted in its tracks when, during a night-long stopover by a wooded stream, Alexander the Great came upon a lone sojourner washing in the stream.

The man was made like a god and came up out of the water in twilight looking as if his skin were molten.

Maccabee, who had been with Alexander, had gone back to camp for body oils and a blanket; the *basileus* was alone when the vision came to him.

And the vision was, too.

In the lengthy dusk they stared at one another and Alexander felt a quickening of his heart as their glances met: this man had the look of eagles, the heroic brow, the fine features of Herakles. A Phidias might have sculpted him.

Alexander thought, *It's an omen—a specter, a sign that this plan is sanctified by Zeus*, and thus was not afraid. In fact, to prove it, he slid down the bank and put his feet in the very water in which the vision was standing.

As he did so, the naked man came toward him, wading out of the water, and Alexander noticed a sword and shield of antiquity in the cattails by the stream.

And these were of fabulous construction: the shield was fully five feet high, as tall as Alexander himself; the sword was bronze and scarred, but as noble as it was heavy. In that light, on that night, it was as if Homer himself had dreamed this dream; not Alexander, condemned to Hell and making do.

Overcome with the power of the vision, wondering what he could make of these omens when he retold his tale, the Macedonian sat on the bank, ankles in the water, elbows on his knees and chin propped on fists.

But the apparition didn't disappear—it kept coming. And the spray its massive legs churned from the mirror of the stream spattered Alexander as if in anointment.

And it spoke: "Greetings, boy," holding out its hand in an ancient, welcoming gesture. "I am Diomedes. Have you lost your way? Where are your parents?"

Alexander was too shocked by the name given to bristle at the mistake the apparition had made: he was boyish in appearance and the light was bad; others had made that error and died of it. Without anger, suffused with wonder, the Macedonian blurted: "Surely not *that* Diomedes?" But he knew in his heart that it was.

"Which?" said the big man, who seemed about Alexander's age, as he came abreast of the *basileus* and sat on the bank. "I'm the one who fought the Luwians—the Trojans, if you like. Or if you don't."

" 'Diomedes of the wise counsel?' *Homer's* Diomedes?" Alexander was so near tears that the words came out choked and shaky.

"Homer? Sometime later, that was—him and his poem, I mean. We didn't know him. As for the wisdom of my counsel, ask Agamemnon, or Odysseus, about that." He smiled and offered his hand again. "And whom have I the pleasure of addressing?"

Alexander began then to explain himself. But it would not be until much later that he managed to explain just how much it meant to have Diomedes appear to him—to guide him, to sanctify his enterprise with his presence, to join Alexander in his quest.

When a hero meets one of his heroes, it's always a little awkward at first.

The room was his again, the sawdust and the broken glass swept away, the marginal signs of damage only a mended break on the bureau leg and a carefully reassembled curule chair which had gone in a dozen splintered, burnished and precious pieces when a Cong shell took the window out. Niccolo Machiavelli inhaled the fresh paint and lacquer smell, trusted his slight, black-clad frame very gingerly to the chair (if he were to be subjected to indignities, it was certain the door was closed and the others were *not* observing).

It held. He edged back with a sigh, adjusted it to face the fragile little desk, and with a careful knife cut the ribbon on the bundle of papers he had brought back to their proper place. His. His sanctum, like himself, spare and elegant, cream plaster walls, scant but expensive furnishings, each piece carefully chosen. Dante, for instance, surrounded himself with clutter: his room was a warren, a labyrinth, disordered as the man's mind, all stacks and clutter that drove sycophants mad in their attempts to arrange it.

Here there was nothing a sycophant could do, the bed invariably immaculate beneath its brocaded spread. The bolster exactly as he would have it. The sycophants kept the floor gleaming, the sills dustless, the spare curtains just so, and woe betide the sycophant who moved the single potted geranium one finger's breadth from its proper place, who disturbed the comb from its precise angle beside the brush on the bureau, the chair from its equally precise position by the window, or who disturbed the prie-dieu (about which one did not ask) with its Bible angled just so in the corner.

For one thing, it made the sycophants extremely nervous in this place, and dissuaded them from impertinences, which was all to the good.

They never, for instance, dared the desk drawer, the lock to which he had changed himself (one of Louis' intricate toys, suitably modified) and to which he kept the only key constantly on his person.

Into this drawer went the papers, one by one as he sorted them into order.

Tap-rattle against his second storey window-glass.

He started, jostling a sheet of paper which sailed gracefully to the floor. And followed it, staying low until he had reached the wall. Then he ventured a cautious look, out past the shutters.

A man stood down among the replanted rosebushes, next the ornamental hedge. A dark and smallish fellow. Niccolo gnawed his lip and took the chance, putting himself into the window, watching the hands for unseemly moves, the whole of the landscape for movement of any kind, his eyes wide-focused while centered on the stranger.

Two things were certain: it was not the Administration, who had their ways of requiring attention; and it was not anyone who dared give his business to a sycophant.

That left one outstanding possibility, and his nerves twitched. Dying was not attractive even when his death was assuredly a day's affair: connections assured that. It *hurt*, and he had never, applied to himself, liked pain. Or untidiness. Or indignity, of which he had had quite enough to suffice in his life and his death.

But he served several causes, most of which were best served by going down the stairs and into that garden.

He was a wiry, unkept little man in 20th century casuals, with curling hair and that profile that howled Eastern, and he stood wringing an already shapeless olive-drab hat to oblivion, as if he distrusted what his hands might give away. He talked with punctuations from one shoulder and the other, a nod of his head, little shifts of his feet.

He might be playing a part. Niccolo thought not. It was too thorough, too preposterous.

"You don't say." Niccolo discovered a brown leaf on a transplanted rose, took out his knife and carefully pruned it against his thumb. "You want Caesar. Do you realize you're poison here? Utter poison. This house is very orthodox. The most orthodox."

The little man gave another punctuation. Left shoulder. "But you, but you, we know—aren't."

It was English they spoke. With an accent, a different one in either case. So a good many people who had no wish to speak the language of their factions—took to English nowadays. Particularly those who walked a zigzag path. Or crawled one.

"What do you imagine would induce him?"

"Ah." The little man held up a hand, the one with the ruined hat, reached ever so carefully into his left shirt pocket with two fingers of his other hand. Held up a gold ring. A massive one. "My man sends this."

Seal ring. Niccolo took it very carefully, kept his eyes on the man and held it up where he could use part of his vision on it. It was gold and it was heavy. In some cases you could take it with you.

"Old one, is he?"

"One of the old ones."

"And you won't give his name."

"Just say it's an old friend of Caesar's."

"The dagger-bearing sort?"

"Just take it to him. You want to set the place, that's all right. Just not public. My man doesn't—"

"—go out much in public. Of course. I'm sure he doesn't." Niccolo closed his hand on the ring. "I'll meet you tomorrow at noon. With particulars. Don't you realize half the house is watching us?"

"That doesn't matter. It's only ambush we fear. Not discovery. My man is willing to come here. He had rather, in fact, come here."

"Ummmn." Niccolo discovered another brown leaf, no longer worrying about the position of the man's hands, no longer worrying about watchers. Of a sudden it added up differently, and disinterest, not wariness, was the game. "High placed old one."

"Very."

"I'll tell you what. You have your man come to the armory tomorrow night. And you take your chances whether he'll meet with you."

"This isn't enough."

Niccolo smiled. Tossed the ring and pocketed it. "Ecco, when you come begging, *signore*, you must want a thing very badly. When you want it very badly, you take risks to have it. Therefore, you must take the risk. The armory garage. I'm sure you can find it. I'm sure you know it will have adequate protection. And Caesar may or may not come."

"He will come," the little man said assuredly, and straightened the hat out and walked away.

That was one who walked the edges too. Niccolo pursed his lips and went to trimming roses, a few more brown leaves, until he had seen the little man walk along the hedge and around it and down the street that led along the park, a safer walk for the moment than it had been. Toward the city.

Eccolo. The professional spy. A man to make a man nervous unless one was very sure that this one was only a go-between at the moment, doing a set task. He was not dangerous today. Niccolo fixed the face in his mind, the mannerisms, down to the finest details of the man's walk. He would know this one again, in any distance, in any different dress. There was a thing about hair and untidiness. When one cleared it away one could look so different.

But the way the bones fit together, the way a man walked, the little mannerisms, it took a great actor to alter those things.

He would know this man.

He took out the ring and looked at it. And drew in a very quiet breath.

Now, *perdio*, for a very little he would drop this ring, and tread it into the soft earth of the freshly spaded rose garden, and say nothing at all. Let a very great and very angry king go begging in vain, Caesar none the wiser.

For not very much, also, he would take a walk

himself, and manage to use a telephone, and secure a meeting. Or two.

But they were, he had not lied in this, watching from the windows. Certainly one could rely on Hatshepsut, who never let anything rest. And even that nuisance Dante, whose gratitude since the Rescue had thus far amounted to an embarrassing classical poem and a recitation at dinner, than which he had rather have died. Repeatedly. He wished desperately to offend the wretch, and he could not, dared not. It was not professional. If one had uncompromised and loyal connections, of whatever quality, one did not throw them away. Ever.

There was, for instance, the infamous computer. And the wretch was indisputably talented.

"Do me a favor, *Dantille*, dear friend. I'd like to find a certain record."

"*Prego*, countryman, I want to find a man, do you think if I gave you an account number, you could do a little investigation?"

He pocketed the ring again and went off around the back of the house where the Ferrari was garaged. A terrible scratch on it. Antonius' driving. It was forgiving too much to say that Antonius had been under considerable pressure at the time.

He sent a sycophant for the keys and, receiving them, backed carefully out of the drive and headed down the parkside drive.

In the other direction.

Julius Caesar turned the ring over in his hand, and looked up sharply at the Italian. "Meet him where?"

A shrug, elegant and delicate. The turn of a wrist. Machiavelli leaned against the door of the Ferrari, there in the armory parking lot, and Julius, khaki-clad and mud-spattered, stood by his waiting jeep.

The call from the armory had not come at a particularly convenient moment. Emergency, the radio message had said. It was emergency out there, too. Mouse sat with the motor running, and kept it so until Julius made a sudden and decisive motion of his hand: Mouse reached and cut it off.

Two disparate vehicles, aslant in a parking lot mostly vacant and otherwise harbor to a pair of Volkswagons, a Hudson, and an Edsel, besides a small cluster of camouflage-painted motorcycles and a slatsided khaki colored truck with a large shell hole in the driver's door.

One of Attila's lads had taken the Trip. Impressed the hell out of the new recruits.

"I set it up for here, tomorrow night," Machiavelli said. "After all—" He passed a gesture about them, by implication at the countryside beyond the armory perimeters. "You meet with worse, with fewer precautions."

"Nothing more dangerous, I assure you."

"I agree to that, *signore*. Fervently. On the other hand—you can always fail the appointment, with no disgrace, signore. I gave them to understand I had done this completely on my own initiative. Or you can equally well set ambush. This man's pride will drive him into it."

"Do you know him?"

"Only so much as you, *signore*. Which is certainly enough to caution me."

Julius slid the ring onto his finger. It was too small. He pulled it off with difficulty and settled it loosely onto his fourth. And looked up at the saturnine Italian. "You aren't playing any other game, currently, are you, little Niko?"

A quick denial, a theatrical denial flashed instantly to hands and shoulders. But Machiavelli's face sobered then. His dark, beautiful eyes got that look they had when they reckoned his own chances of life and death, and who he dared lie to. There was more truth between them than Machiavelli gave to most, and few illusions. "Not in this, Caesar, no, I swear."

"Then you don't need to know what I'll do."

There was little crueler than to leave this man in the dark. To take half his plan and shove him out. There was a little hurt on the handsome face.

But Machiavelli also had dignity. "Cesare," Machiavelli said, knowing himself dismissed; and straightened himself from his easy stance against the car door, straightened the hem of his doublet, and walked around and got in.

"My friend," Julius said then, before he could start the motor. "I trust you will be here, tomorrow night. Discreetly."

"Can one be discreet with a legion, Caesar?"

"We assume he wants this very badly."

"I didn't have any assurance his party would accept this. I'm guessing. But the less time wasted in preliminaries—"

"Yes, the less time other sides have to arrange things. My own philosophy."

"Your student, *signore*." A flourish. Machiavelli's face achieved pleasure, rare sight. Except over fine wines and the discomfiture of a rival. He flashed a grin, white, perfect teeth. And started the engine and drove off, with a little wave of his hand.

"The serpent," Mouse muttered at Julius' back.

"Oh, yes," Julius said. And came round and got in the other side. Mouse started up and geared the jeep into noisy motion. They spun past the truck with the shell-hole. Out on the drillfield, a motley group of recruits was standing inspection. Recent arrivals. They came *in* shell-shocked, some of them, and took a while to adjust.

"Meet who?" Mouse asked.

"Alexander."

"Of *Macedon?*" Little got to Mouse. Julius looked askance at him, saw distress. And shrugged.

"He's with the Dissidents," Mouse said.

Julius shrugged, and felt of the ring. The very, very old ring. And stared at the dirt road ahead, the way that led through secure perimeters to what was not secure.

He was afraid. Afraid not even in the way that a seventeen year old kid had been able to get to him, arriving to make himself a part of the household. Brutus he could adjust to, even a Brutus who loved and worshipped him. This Hell business was punishment for the likes of Machiavelli, but it was only afterlife, and not even a bad one, for one of the Old Dead like himself: he had figured out that much of the system. He was comfortable, mostly. Except for the fools and the bureaucrats who annoyed him beyond the grave. He had none of the ailments of the New Dead. None of their disabilities, for which he thanked the dubious gods his ancestors. Everyone in the house was immune. Everyone in the district. He spent his death doing what he did in life and with a certain lack of haste about it too, a wisdom painfully acquired.

But this. This insanity, so close after Brutus. Of a sudden he suspected malign and ill-disposed agencies, a turn in the Luck which was his only sincere deism. His own Luck. The Luck that had made Caesar synonymous with god.

Brutus idolized him. And followed Mouse with similar worship. That was one liability which worried him. He distrusted extremes of passion. Even devotion from a bastard son.

Second and greater liability: his other son Caesarion the fool had gone off with the rebels. Not enough that the young lunatic had lodged with Antonius over at Tiberius the Butcher's villa, rejecting any filial gratitude, but of course Caesarion had to commit the most injurious treason he could think of. Lunacy was not from his side of the family. He had forgotten, when he got a son with Kleopatra, just who her father was. The Fluteplayer. The idiot.

Then, annoyance and liability, Administration lost its precious boy-molesting Supreme Commander and replaced him with Rameses—Rameses, who lost the battle of Kadesh when the enemy ignored the appointment and the proper battlefield and ambushed him on his lunch break, a flagrant breach of then-existing rules. (And damned smart of the other side, Julius reflected.) But Rameses, surviving the debacle, straightway marched home, proclaimed the war a victory and had it engraved that way on his monuments—first and present master of the Big Lie. His promotion to Supreme Commander evidenced that. Somehow he had convinced Administration he had succeeded in Doing Something About the Situation, even if Hadrian was mincemeat and the war department a shambles and the war department computers a disaster area. The crisis was over. Rameses stroked Adminstration and prevaricated with such a straight face no one would be so ill-mannered as to doubt him.

Ho basileus. Great King. *Ho wanax.* High King.

Could a king of such reputation, indeed, lie? Have feet of clay?

Well, there *was* always the king of Bithynia.

Indeed. But this man. This god.

Julius looked at the ring, the gold seal reflecting back the hell-light of the sky, while the jeep bucked and bounced back down the dirt track that led to their current area of operations, a little matter of Cong spillover. Last mop-up, hoping the computer in Assignments did not *twice* blunder and drop the Cong *back* into Decentral Park.

He did not believe it would *not* happen. In fact, he rather expected it, as he expected most things, except such turns as this.

Mouse asked him no further questions. It was not a thing even Mouse was close enough to him or contemporary enough to understand of him, nor would he explain. Klea might understand. He winced at the thought of Klea. Of the look in her eyes.

He tried the ring on the index finger again, stubbornly. But the flesh and bone would not accept it, would not be that shape. To get the damned thing stuck would be humiliation upon humiliation.

The Established Order had sent him Brutus, his own son and murderer.

Now it sent him Alexander, who was (intelligence reported and Mouse faithfully reminded him) consorting with the enemy at best, very possibly one of them and high in their councils. That in itself was enough to set the fine hairs rising. Julius walked a fine enough line with Administration, and kept his own hands pure, and meant to keep them that way. He had a profound wariness of plots, a prudence learned in a reckless youth and a subtler old age. He had died old, had Julius. Wiser than his murderers, and too tired to be what he had only in that year learned to be, what he might have been if he had had his life to do over again, with the insight of the week of his death, combined with the vigor of his thirties.

Here, he had it. Had it all. He had forever, to do things the wise and the prudent way. Augustus knew it, and feared him, Augustus having reigned long and having died much the same death, of a weary disbelief in the energy and the persistence of his killer. Augustus and he were very well suited to each other. And from his side, he kept a certain truce: they were too wary and too wise to raise certain specters. So, even was Kleopatra, who in her middle years had mothered Antonius along with all his quarreling brood (and fool Caesarion). They were all too canny to be young fools all over again.

Only this ring, this man—

He had *been* this man. He had been Alexander of Macedon, three centuries before he was born a Julian. He had been Achilles. Then Alexander. He always feared he had been others too, in his worst nightmares. But a man only had three souls. He had accounted for all of them.

Kleopatra reckoned herself Alexander's great-great-granddaughter. And had reckoned herself once his new incarnation in his female principle, his *anima*. "No," Julius had said to her, when they stood hand in hand before Alexander's glass sarcophagus, there in Alexandria, this shrine, this only *place* Kleopatra had ever venerated—"No," he had insisted again, in bed, on a calmer night, there in the garden house near the Tiber, with his death only days away, and himself well knowing it. "The gods only send a soul back three times." Tapping himself on the chest. Head on pillows, musk in his nostrils. "Here. It's here. In this old man, Klea. I never lived to be old before. But I have. Third time, Klea."

"Who said that? Is that Roman?" Kleopatra's voice in the dark. Kleopatra's smooth skin. Young then as she was forever. And as beautiful. "Three times."

"Once for each of your souls. A human being has three souls." He counted them off on his fingers. "The ancestor-soul. That's the *manes*, the Good Spirit. The guardian that stays in a house with the *lares* and protects it from the bad ones. Then there's the Shade, the ghost that we pray to in February.

Hangs around the tombs as long as people remember to visit it."

"The *ka*, the old Egyptians said. And the *ba* that comes and finds you if you fail the rites."

"See, they knew. And finally the *anima*, that gets reborn again and again and brings them all back together. But three, three, Klea. A human has three souls. And I think—myself, only myself, I think mine was special. Split three ways, never finished. I'm the third. Here, tonight. Alexander thought he was Achilles. I *know* I was Alexander. So I was both. I know that I was. And I never lived to get old before. Maybe somehow I'm complete. Maybe I've finally got done what I was supposed to do."

"Don't talk like that!"

Laughter then. He knew. And she did not. Sad laughter. "You have to forgive me what I did, finally. You have to understand. I *was* there. I couldn't bear my own mortality. I refuse to accept it. Even yet." For a moment he did refuse. And was quite calm. "You forgive me."

"What you did?"

"That. Yes."

A small shiver. "Alexander." She clenched her fists, arms stiff as she lay across him. "Alexander. Then we were fated. Don't you see? I'm your other half. The philosophers say we come divided into this world. *Antonius* was never your Patroklos. *I* am."

He felt exposed in that small fiction. The partner. The partner he had supported in all his weaknesses. His alcoholism. His damaging extravagances. Antonius his personal and irretrievable flaw. "Not my Roxane." Mocking her fantasies. "Not my Briseis." The image of Klea in armor instead of silks was ludicrous.

"Patro-*klos*. *Kleo*-patra." Her small body was all

atremble and tense. He shivered, himself, caught
by the similarity.

"Hephaistion," he said. Pattern broken. Omen
averted.

"That's why. *That's* why I felt that way when I
would go there. Into the mausoleum. That it was
another part of me lying in that coffin. My other
half. The one I was waiting for. My god and my
king."

Patroklos. Hephaistion. Kleopatra.

Tiber damp. Hell-sky.

Face of a dead god beneath Alexandrine glass,
sere and golden.

Kleopatra: *You don't believe in gods.*

Himself: *I believe in my Luck. I believe in a god.*

And it was *me* in that casket. So I destroyed it.
With my own hand.

The armory garage was great and cold, forbid-
ding with the baleful light of Paradise, rufous and
taunting, spilling over its rafters and the halogen
brightness of modern illumination, evil and cold,
glinting off the macadam of the parking lot and
the chrome of the red Ferrari and the mud-hole
camouflage of the big tank sighing on its air cushion like nothing so much as a beached whale.

A *physeter*, perhaps, Diomedes thought, in the
habit of making connections with his own acquaintance—a sperm whale changed by Athene, his patron, into a juggernaut of war.

But the tank, with its air intakes and its hatch
and its long gun-snout, was like the wooden horse
they'd built once—a thing in which men could
hide, in which mischief could be disguised.

The tank made the Argive son of Tydeus nervous—
no less when the little Jew Zaki went rapturous
and danced about it, spouting gibberish:

"A hundred-seventy tons or more," Zaki gloated,

cavorting round it with upraised arms as his ancestors had over torahs and lamps that burned too long, so that Maccabee shaded his eyes and turned away, on pretext of hunting hostiles in shadows (though the possibility of ambush was real enough, and clear enough to the man who'd raided the Trojan camps with Odysseus and, in the same company, murdered Palamedes).

Ambush, Diomedes thought, was the least part of their worries—travelling with Alexander of Macedon made Diomedes fully expect to turn around at any instant and see the little party transformed into birds.

But all that happened was that Zaki danced around the tank, singing his litany: "Twenty-centimeter main gun in turret; two-centimeter three-barrel Gatling cupola; anti-personnel charges around the skirts; air cushion; fusion powered fans; iridium armor; steel plenum-chamber skirts; and, thank God, the rotating tribarrel can be slaved!"

Startled at the concept of enslaved weapons, Maccabee turned his attention from the shadows and Alexander, who was running his hands over the parked Ferrari, to the little Israeli.

"What's this?" said the ancient Israelite. "How is it that a noble juggernaut such as that can be a slave?"

Diomedes had been sent by his genius to guide this mismatched threesome he-knew-not-where, but he knew a trap when he smelled one.

His arms were pimpled with gooseflesh and his ears strained to hear the snorts and stamps of their horses, tethered beyond the parking lot where a chain-link fence enclosed the armory garage.

Had it not been a heroic impulse, but some vile, devilish one? Diomedes was no longer certain. The pretty, boyish king before him was no Odysseus. In fact, he was addled: any man who thought Achilles the best of the Achaeans hadn't been paying attention even to the poets' versions of the War. Diomedes still thought of it as *the* war even though he'd been in others: he'd been part of the Epigoni excursion against Thebes; he'd restored his grandfather's honor and brought him back to the Peloponnesus, after his throne had been usurped, by killing all but two of the usurpers. But it was the birds who haunted him: brothers and comrades, bewitched and beating with raven wings off into the Italian sky. It could happen again.

And there was the tank, on the nearly empty lot under the awful lights men made and Paradise shed. The light had been awful in Troy that day—awful because the Luwians had lost their battle to the gods, not to men.

Athene had been on his right too many times for Diomedes not to know fated times when he was bound up in them.

The horses were too quiet; the tank smelled hellish and made horrible noises like some dying thing in a land where everything was already dead.

And the Achaean was wracked with memories of other wars and other tricks, even though his patron goddess couldn't find him here to make him sure. He didn't need surety—he needed only instinct.

But it had been a specter met on the road, a bird which turned into a man and told him: "Go find you Alexander the Macedonian. Promise him Achilles' acquaintance if he distinguishes himself."

Thus had the ghost spoken, and then disappeared. A ghost that looked like an old comrade but couldn't have been—Achilles had never become a bird.

Birds were evil and so were great breathing hulks of metal with killing snouts.

Just as Diomedes was about to stride forward and give good counsel, suggest leaving this awful, too-quiet place and seeking other Romans, if Romans must be had to find Germans, or other feats of valor more likely of success than going up against the masters of metal, breathing beasts so vast, the machine before him gave a heart-rending *squelch*. Its top came up, and a head, then a second, peeked out.

Diomedes drew his sword in an automatic gesture; then, in a willful one, leaned upon his five-foot shield with as much nonchalance as he could muster: if the battle was joined here, he would fight it—fight the metal monster with the stentorian breath, its inhabitants, whomever, even should that snout point right at him and belch the Devil's own fire.

He didn't care enough about the others to intervene in their fates: it was a bird that had started all this, a bird who had used a Greek name to him: Alexander. Alexander had been Paris' war name as well. Diomedes had been attracted to the task because of the coincidence; in his time, such things had often meant more than they seemed, at first, to warrant.

And here among the Old Dead he'd never mingled, learned little, stayed to hills he could pretend were those of home—looking for Athene's shrine somewhere, to do penance, wrap the thigh of an ox in fat and say the words and make amends.

The Luwian Paris wasn't here; Diomedes' crimes were no worse; but he'd long known Achilles would be. So at the end of little Alexander's trek, should he complete it, was a meeting put off too long: among Achaeans, Diomedes had had the least use for the sulky prince of arms.

Like this child, Alexander, who walked with hands on hips, stiff-kneed, over to the giant metal dragon and spoke too boldly, Achilles hadn't an ass's ration of common sense.

But then, the two were, if the Macedonian could be believed, kindred souls.

And the situation was, in Diomedes' estimation, one which might land the Macedonian on the Undertaker's table—after which, he would be difficult to find among Hell's teeming damned.

So, having thought the matter through and found a personal stake in its outcome, the Achaean moved forward, as casually as he might with naked sword and shield in position, and met Maccabee, who was guarding Alexander's precious rear, in time to hear the *basileus* say, "Is it really you, Caesar? Come down where I can see you."

A hand raised in desultory greeting; on its pinky a ring flickered. "It's me if this is yours, Basileus. Mount to meet me—do not fear. Use the intakes as a stepladder and set foot on Hell's finest throne—a battle tank."

The word "tank" reminded Diomedes of the little Israeli, Zaki. "Maccabee," he said under his breath, "where's the Jew?"

The Israelite shrugged, eyes roaming the distant shadows. "Gone, perhaps. But he'll be back. He's right enough—some one of us shouldn't be standing here, ripe for slaughter. Caesar is a snake with many heads."

Diomedes craned his neck, expecting, from the words, to see an actual snake slithering on the turret toward the Macedonian. He saw, instead, Caesar the Roman with outstretched hand helping the slightly-built Alexander to climb up.

The second figure in the opening, revealed by Caesar's posture, was female and Diomedes caught his breath.

She was exotic beyond measure, wide of eye and gilded, with a black and beaded wig square-cut, and a neck like a swan.

"What—who is that?"

"Egyptian." The Israelite spat the word. "They all look alike to me. Probably Hatshepsut ... or Kleopatra—both queens: one collected the penises of her enemies and strapped a stuffed member on when she lead her troops to battle—against my people, among others; the other fucked her way to glory. Don't lie in with Egyptian bitches, if you want my company."

Diomedes heard the ancient prejudice, sharpened and honed deadly over millennia, and wondered how difficult this joint venture might prove to be, where hatreds he knew not of were involved.

Wars were won and lost over women, though— he'd slain his own wife when he'd found her in another's arms (no matter what the legends said); he'd seen too many die on beaches over wenches. Diomedes said only: "No women, of any blood, or I don't lend my hand to the *basileus'* enterprise."

"Tell that to the Roman with the tank," snapped Maccabee.

Diomedes then looked full at the Israelite and saw such passion as had got the man here.

Hatred, blind and foul, with good reason behind it, but the sort that made a man unreasoning. And he wondered again if he knew enough of the motives of these men to be among them.

The answer was, he knew, that he did not. But a bird had, and that bird—some soul—had turned into a man and bid him hence. So hence he was, for want of better to do. The Achaean shifted his grip on his sword-hilt then, thinking in the way of his kind that there was no trouble here he couldn't handle, if push would just come to shove.

Mounting the tank had been exhilarating; descending into its maw was terrifying even for Alexander the Great.

Being great, however, was more a matter of overcoming terror than never experiencing it: Alexander did as he was bid.

The man called Caesar, in his late thirties, was handsome—charismatic; well-spoken to a fault and smart for an Italian.

The woman, however, was a problem: she spoke of souls and spoke in riddles: "By the Egg of the Great Cackler, you *are* a little one; have you a dozen souls, or are you really part of mine—and his?"

Alexander knew what to do with women: one brought a blanket with their blood upon it back from the bower to display among the men; if not, share them out.

"Klea, mind your manners: she's my . . . friend," said the man who thought he was a god.

And there followed, then, a philosophical discussion about souls—their souls, his soul, Egyptian souls and Roman souls, which made the Macedonian realize that these two, though they commanded the fiercest war machines Alexander had ever seen, were mad.

But by then he'd determined to have these tanks, finer than elephants and even warm and smelly like horses. Since Bucephalus had not accompanied him to Hell, a part of him had pined for the steed's loss.

All he could think of, while the Roman and his Egyptian wench prattled on about being descendants of his and having portions of his soul, was acquiring this particular tank immediately and as many more as possible, as soon as possible.

And, of course, Diomedes' dropped-but-pointed hint that success here would lead to an assignation with Achilles.

"So, Basileus, you see, if you and your Israelite friend can put aside factionalism long enough to sneak into Che Guevara's camp and help free Hadrian, a prisoner there—or determine that he's *not* there—then my obligation would be to you ..." Caesar's eyes twinkled with humor at this infernal joke. "And the Administration would understand that I must honor it—grant you a wish, help you in a task ... whatever you desire. ...."

Even the little, birdlike woman was silent now, and two pairs of eyes stared steadily at him in the dimness of the tank—close quarters for lying, for fighting, for anything but frank discussion.

Waiting for him to state his business, they were.

And since he'd come here to do just that, Alexander said, "I want to raise a levy of cavalry—and tanks—and, with your help, track down these Germans who are reputed to know a way out of Hell through tunnels. Once I find them, you need not concern yourself further. But Maccabee thinks I need your help. He's a good friend and wise; thus I came to—"

"Yes, yes," Caesar soothed like a seeress finally having divined the fortune her client wants told, "for your friend's sake—and not because you need help, although tanks are hard to come by. Just how large a levy would you want? We're fond of New Weaponry ... Klea especially ... but we can do without it. And when would you want it? Is Maccabee your first lieutenant, then? And the other, the Jew-spy my people say is with you, what of him?"

Once the questioning started, once they were down to logistics and specifics, Alexander relaxed. He felt a certain uneasiness among these mad Old Dead, preoccupied with bits of souls and ancient feuds, but he understood command and its necessities: Caesar was willing, on receipt of Hadrian, to give the Macedonian what support he needed.

Alexander had dealt with too many governments and levied too many armies to doubt his ability to get exactly what he wanted while giving little in return. It was what had made him great.

And since the matter of godhead and qualities of kingship hadn't yet come up, he didn't worry about it. Years of campaigning had taught him that you handled matters one at a time.

If Caesar needed Hadrian, Hadrian he would get. If this painted whore must come along, and other menials of the household, he'd deal with that. With whatever he must, now that he had not only Maccabee, but Diomedes on his side and somewhere, beyond journey's end, lay a meeting with Achilles himself.

2.   Meetings

The household was in turmoil, secret conferences proliferating between Julius and Kleopatra and Augustus; Julius and Sargon; Niccolo and the furtive and nervous Dante Alighieri; and Niccolo and Sargon, Niccolo and Kleopatra, and even (there was strong reason to suspect) Niccolo and Antonius (not a friendly pair), *the* Marcus Antonius, *magister equitum, dux et triumvir,* who lived over the hill and past the tennis courts and a great deal of manicured meadow, in crazy Tiberius' villa. Such intrigue was ordinarily meat and drink to Hatshepsut.

But not to be on the inside of it, to be, in fact, systematically excluded from such conferences, *that* was insupportable.

"Madam." A youthful voice overtook her on one sullen stalk down the stairs. "Hatshepsut." She stopped. And in a patter of rubber-shod feet a teenager overtook her—Marcus Brutus in tennis shoes, t-shirt and faded denims. It was uncommon attire for Augustus' villa. But so were boys uncommon; *"Perdi,* let the boy wear what he likes," Augustus had said, when the sycophants filled Brutus' closet with 1970's denims. And: *"Perdio",* Niccolo had aped that statement, with a little flourish of the wrist, "the divine Julius would just as soon pry the lad out of old Rome, wouldn't he rather? I *wonder* where the sycophants got the notion."

The house's private timebomb, young and full of innocence, blackhaired and with exquisite dark eyes ("If I ever hear," Julius had said directly to Hatshepsut, "that you've been at him—") arrived on the steps beside her, all earnestness. "Hatshepsut, *what* are they doing up there? What are they talking about, *tanks* and *launchers* and that?"

"Large ears indeed, kitten." Hatshepsut had taken particular pains with her appearance: her pink 25th century jumpsuit glittered and flashed, tight and virtually transparent in interesting places. The boy struggled to look instead at her face, which was itself a marvel, glowpaint on the eyelids, the left eye having a series of dots over to the rather remarkable magenta tinted plastic of the device that swept up over her sleek black bob and incidentally insinuated a little magenta tendril into her ear, where it whispered at will with others' voices; and another tendril against her skull, where it picked up her voice and carried it elsewhere. She was virtually unarmed, in the casual peace of her own home, only a little gray box clipped to her left boot and a lovely ring that Niccolo had given her, one of her only antiques.

"Is it the Cong again?"

"No," she said, and started off down the steps again, Brutus trailing. He overtook her again at the bottom. "Listen, kit." She turned and he stopped short. "Do you talk to people?"

"Talk to—"

"Do you know how to keep a secret? Do you *want* a secret?"

He had his mouth open. He shut it and gulped,

and she put her fingertips gently under that clamped jaw.

"There's a bright lad. No, a boy in this house doesn't *want* secrets, not the sort that might put him at crosspurposes with people who know far more secrets. That's always your danger, isn't it? Don't take Niko's path; don't take Dante's either. Be your charming, naïve self."

"I'm not—"

She let fall the hand. "You're exquisite, but Julius would have my head, kitten. You are naïve. No boy ever wants to think so, but a smart boy who wants to learn had better know that about himself first and foremost. Now I want you to do a thing for me, just carry a message."

"I'm not sure I want to." His face had a charming blush. His nostrils flared with outrage and confusion. "I'm sorry I—"

"Kit, kit, kit, just go to your papa and tell him something from me."

"What?" *Father* was a trigger-word with this boy. He adored Julius, feared him, and worshipped him with a fervor which had nothing to do with godhood.

"Just tell him I've overheard a magic word. And I really want to talk to him. There's a dear lad. Go. Go."

He fled, poor young Republican. Royalty daunted him. His father daunted him. So did most everything in the house, when it came to that, even Dante Alighieri, with his cyclopic machine and his arcane wizardries; and Dante flourished in that respect. Brutus was still new, a mere seventeen. He did not remember the reason he had come to Hell or why he was famous; he did not know that he *was* famous. His worldly life had ended on a road in Italy, in his seventeeth summer—or at least his memory ended there.

Now he went running up the stairs to do what Hatshepsut asked him to do.

And Hatshepsut went off her own way. Wispy sycophants whisked out of her path, and made themselves invisible, which they ordinarily were: flunkies and lackeys in life, their existence somehow worked on points—and points were in decided jeopardy when Hatshepsut had that look on her face.

"H-h-holes?" Dante asked, as Mouse propelled him along a hallway.

"I've absolutely no idea more than that," Mouse said, Decius Mus, who had died of stubbornness and sanctity, and who was very difficult to refuse when he was working on his commander's orders. "Niko's going to drop you at Administration and you'll find a man waiting for you, and you just use your talents as you see fit."

"But—"

Augustus, Caius Julius Caesar Octavianus Augustus, *Pater Patriae, Tribunus Plebis in perpetuum, inter alias,* scratched behind his left ear (they stuck out, and his face was lightly freckled, which always gave him the look of a schoolboy, not an emperor, least of all a god) and stared bleakly out toward the building in question, beyond the library window a good several miles away. A monster skyscraper, Administration, the Hall of Injustice, rose up and up and lost itself in cloud. He scratched the ear and scratched at the hair, which tended to go unruly at the top, and turned a desperate face on his uncle. "I think it's some trap, that's all I can possibly think it is."

"Whose?"

"I don't know whose; if I knew whose, *prodi,* should I worry? Why should you go on this fool

venture? You have no interest at all in getting out!
No. It's *him*, isn't it? It's the Macedonian. You're
not thinking straight, uncle, and I'm not used to
seeing you make skewed decisions."

Julius chuckled and crossed his booted ankles in
front of him, sitting with elbows on the arms of
the Louis XIV chair and hands folded on his middle. Past his nephew's figure, the skies of Hell
swirled with cloud and a million little functionar-
ies functioned in the workings of Administration,
creating paper storms and crises; while off to the
side of the Hall the Pentagram and the War Department created their own brand of chaos, all in
miniature at this perspective. "Then you aren't old
enough to remember me when I was alive," he
said. "But trust me, *Augustulle*, I have my reasons."

"Well, *get* Hadrian back. Then arrest the lot of
them."

Julius lifted his eyes briefly to the invisible celestial. Only briefly. "*Auguste*, I have no personal
inspiration to get the ass back. Even having Rameses as his replacement fails to inspire me to en-
thusiasm in that cause: but Alexander is *in* with
the kidnappers—"

"What?"

"In a manner of speaking." Julius gave one of
his best wise and catlike smiles, to Augustus, who
was the recipient of more of those than Julius
vouchsafed to any other. And Augustus was so
quick on the uptake.

"My gods." Augustus also had the sense to say
nothing else. There were no sycophants at hand to
overhear this confidence. They were forbidden the
library, and Augustus took sternest precautions
about the security of this room—no easy matter,
considering the houseguests as well as the servants.

Hadrian dead, of course, was a very suitable
outcome. Dying in Hell got a resident right back to

Administration as quick as anything. And all the Infernal Authorities needed was a reasonable notion of the location: walk in on the kidnappers, toss a grenade, and they *all* showed up at the Undertaker's establishment, the kidnappers for their punishment and Hadrian—

—Hadrian landed on that same table for whatever fate Administration thought fit for a Supreme Commander who had proved to be such an ass. Probably reinstatement with back pay. Or worse, Rameses could stay on and they could *promote* the ass.

"But tanks," Augustus said. "You can't just move tanks here and there without papers, and Rameses—"

Julius gave one of his rare and dazzling grins. "My dear nephew, all the Pentagram runs on is paper. When it misses a paper some secretary just assumes it's lost the paper . . . not the tank. So we give them paper. If information *ever* gets into the system, they'll file it. When they find crossfiles they'll follow them til they disappear behind some security curtain. Or into some office just too far or too unfriendly for some little functionary to get into. Or until someone shoves it into the Finished pile to get to his lunch break. We'll manage. And they'll get their papers. Dante's working on it."

"But—"

"Trust me."

"*Edepol, absit omen!* You know what we can lose—if something happened to you, if you put a weapon in the hands of our enemies, *di nos iuvent!* What would we do? Don't tell me about papers! There's nothing that can replace you. I'm telling you, uncle, discount the hazards all you like, if you land back in Assignments, what's to keep someone from meddling with *your* papers? Gods know where you'd be sent, gods know how we'd find you again,

and what would we be without you? It's a fool
thing to do, it's damned foolish! Think of *us!* We
have everything. Do you want to risk it all, put
yourself at the mercy of gods know what enemies?
Who knows what Alexander's motives are?"

"Why, I commit myself to your own considerable skill, then, *Augustulle.* Who better? You and
Dante—I *am* leaving you Dante, with regrets, but
he's not the type for this operation. And you'll
keep him covering my ass. Won't you? It *is* yours
as much as mine. As you point out."

"Blackmail!"

"Filial duty." Julius smiled, a small and wicked
smile this time. "After all, you *are* my heir and
successor."

"You're out of your mind! It's this obsession of
yours, this *thing* with Alexander—"

The smile became catlike again.

"Di omnes! Would you betray *him?"*

And stayed.

"If," Augustus said, "if you ever credited Rameses
with intelligence—"

"Even fools have an on day. Yes. I plan with
that remote contingency in mind. Call it a whim.
A curiosity. If there is a way out of this place—"

"I'm sure I wouldn't take it if it was in my own
garden! Bombs and lunatics! I had enough of life
to last me."

"Are you *sure* you wouldn't?"

"What would we go back to? Haunt the living?
Be reborn gods know where, to gods know what
kind of circumstances? Neither one enchants me,
uncle. The world's gone beyond us, this business of
machines and voices in air and tanks and things
that blow up—Look, look around you! We're lords
forever in this place, we have influence—"

"We have it all, don't we? Wealth and access to
our enemies." Julius heaved a sigh and picked

himself up from the chair. For a moment he looked weary. He passed a hand over the back of his neck. Then he looked up and quirked a brow and smiled his onesided smile, his true and gently honest one. "I felt like this before I headed out to Gaul. I wanted to go there, I had to go. But I *didn't* want to, if you understand me. I felt my luck running. It had to go that way. So with this. I haven't any choice."

That perhaps frightened Augustus more than the rest of it did.

"Alexander's mine," Julius said. "I can't leave him to anyone else. Can you understand that?"

"I can understand it," Augustus said. "It's the same damned nonsense that got both of us killed the first time. We had too many ties to our murderers. We didn't see where our Luck could take us. So we let ourselves die, myself the greater fool—I knew what they'd done to *you* and I let them get at me."

"Why, it was our luck at work, bringing us here. To this place you swear you wouldn't leave for any persuasion."

"The dice are loaded," Augustus said.

"*Alea iacta est*," Julius said. And chuckled. "Wasn't what I said at all." He put his hand on the door. "I do expect you'll hold down the home front."

"I was a lousy soldier."

"You won. Can't quarrel with that. And as an administrator you were at least as good. If you'd only chucked all the relatives. And the hangers-on. That's the trouble with imperial courts. What you have to do is make sure the greater threats to every damn soul inside your borders come from outside. That's the way to run an army; or a government; or this little nest. You can even get courage out of Dante if you make that clear."

"Meaning blackmail."

"Never let the bastards get too comfortable. They forget so quickly."

He walked out into the hall, the spacious, terrazzo-floored upper hall of this very great villa in Hell.

And ran right into the boy.

Hatshepsut flung herself down on the couch, which a flurry of sycophantic hands materialized to dust even while she was in mid-drop, and which vanished by the instant she hit the surface. "Damned nonsense," she said to no one in particular. Her accustomed cohort, the little Ptolemiadês Kleopatra, was somewhere unguessed, the sycophants had not the least idea where she had gotten to, Julius was entirely uncommunicative, and Mouse—Horus and Isis, Mouse was incorruptible.

But *tanks* and *launchers*, the boy had said. It was only the half of what she had heard with her own spying.

Machiavelli was absent, gods knew where that jackal had gotten to, or what trail he was hunting.

She crossed her booted ankles, glowered at the ceiling, and blinked and promptly uncrossed the ankles as the door opened without a by-your-leave. She looked down her own length at the dark-bearded Akkadian who stood there in that doorway, between the aforementioned feet, and propped herself up on her elbows.

"Dante's off with Mouse," Sargon said.

"I noticed as much." She sat up, hooked an arm around one knee. "What else do we know?"

"I still have contacts," Sargon said in his deep, deep voice, and came and dropped down to sit on the end of the couch. "The way is being smoothed. Officially."

"Officially, is it?"

"All the way to the Hall of Injustice." He was a

beautiful man, dark curling hair, with long, almond eyes; and he kept to the kilts of his own time. He smelled of spices. Hatshepsut laid her foot in his lap, and the almond eyes lighted, the fine mouth curved in a smile. There was seldom an invitation Sargon would refuse. Of any kind. His big hand ran from the inseam of the boot to the shimmer of the bodysuit, and Hatshepsut sighed.

"Interesting."

"I expected nothing else." The hand drifted higher. "I tell you I have no interest in this nonsense."

"I do." She flung that leg and the other off the edge of the couch and leapt to her feet. "I tell you, Lion, give *me* Julius' advantages—"

"Tccchah, you *had* an army and an empire, woman, and neither got wider."

"I had the damned capital *and* held my borders; *and* more of it than I started with." She struck herself on the heart. "*Mine*, Lion, and it was wider when I died than when I took it. It was *civilized* and the damned provinces knew to keep their heads down."

"But you begat no heir, tsss?"

She shoved him at the shoulder, and the Lion chuckled low in his throat, evading the force of it with a shrug.

"Heirs be damned, I wasn't assassinated."

"Are you sure?"

"Oh, *damn* your impudence! *I* out-maneuvered *my* Pompey, I got him out of the capital and I sent *him* to Gaul, where he damned well stayed til I died of old age, Lion! And when that vandal Thutmose did come back he couldn't so much as find my tomb, it took them near four thousand years to do that! Assassinated, my ass! I *ruled the world*, Lion, including most of your feud-ridden empire, and by Osiris my explorers and my ministers were busy adding territory to the maps! I could have assassinated Thutmose. But I was too smart for that, Lion, he was a good general, he was a damned good general; and I used him to hold the borders; I used him for my heir because I couldn't get a better, and by Horus and Isis I left an empire after me! Let me loose in the world naked and barehanded, and in twenty years I'll have a share of it. In thirty I'll leave my mark on it again."

"Ahhh." Sargon lay back on the couch and crossed his sandaled ankles, hands behind his head. "What a great trouble, all to die again. I left my mark on the world. Can it be you aren't satisfied with your own?"

"Damn you!"

"Thutmose erased your records, claimed your deeds, ignored your explorations and threw out your science and your traders. Oh, yes, you preserved him; but did he preserve you? Did he save your accomplishments? Your successor was just like old Tiberius, sour and limited, damned limited—but don't you know, O lioness, that all successors tend to be that, when they're held off too long? Kept fruit spoils. See? We both have the wisdom to rule; but kings are long out of fashion."

"Give me seventy, a hundred years of life, and I'll make my way in these consortiums and these republics and these dictatorships—"

"We don't even know what exists, lioness. We don't know what the time *is* in the world."

"The worlds."

"Has that happened yet? Or have stranger things? Or is it yesterday still?"

"You're as crazy as Niccolo!"

"*I* have no worm gnawing me. I am a happy man, indeed, a happy man."

"You're rusting away."

A flash of white teeth in a golden, bearded face. "Now, little king," Sargon said in his deepest voice, "that's the trouble with you modernists. You hang onto the world with both fists. You have a great spirit. But think of this: what if Niccolo is right and what if you were right and you could leave this shadowland and find the upper world again? And what if you found the world—or the worlds, yes, well—exactly as you think; and what if you conquered them and ruled them; and you died again, and came down here to us, why, you wouldn't be Old anymore. You'd have all the ailments, all the torments of the New Dead, wouldn't you? You might find yourself in quite a different place. Would you trade this comfort—for the deeper hells?"

Hatshepsut flung up her hands in exasperation.

"You *would* die," Sargon said, "unless they've cured that ailment. Wait—wait, little king, until they invent immortality in the world. Or the worlds. As the case may be."

"Wait forever!"

Sargon sighed, an immense movement of his broad, bronze chest. "Little king, the priests warned us of a dim house of dust, bony-jawed ghosts, birds to eat up our souls: and lo! we eat, we drink, we make love forever and if we die we come back again. What would your new life gain you—but a span of years, a chance to win a deeper hell."

"Paradise. They say there is this paradise." She came and leaned above him, hands on either side of him on the couch, eyes looking close into his eyes. "And if I find it I will send for you, Lion. I will make you my gatekeeper."

His brows drew down like thunder as she darted back and upright. He sat up, all one fluid motion. "Be careful, woman. I'm no trained ape to be led this way and that. I know your methods, and no. I say it's a fool's choice. I won't go. And you've been here far too long to start dashing about like a mouse in a field fire, which is altogether what you're doing."

"Where is Klea?"

"Ah. You don't know."

"Would I ask? Maddening man."

"And she will not talk to you? Twice maddening. No wonder your pride is stung."

Hatshepsut threw up her hands again and walked off, headed for the door.

"With Antonius," Sargon said.

Hatshepsut whirled in her tracks. "My gods!"

"Business, I'm sure."

"*Overnight* business? Julius *knows* this?"

"He sent her."

"Gods." Hatshepsut dropped into the chair by the door, thrust out her feet, elbows on the chair arms.

"The little queen gets her way of most men. And there is a question of Germans. Of whom Tiberius may know more than we do. He has a guard of them. And the little queen wants to borrow them."

"So Kleopatra is going?" Hatshepsut exclaimed.

"I understand so."

"By Set and by Typhon!" She flung herself out of her chair again. "This won't do. This won't do at all!"

She was out the door and slammed it after her before a sycophant could catch it. The reaching hand was in the way of it; and it caught the fingers. A wail shrieked away and the thin air gave up a soft chorus of titters. Sycophants enjoyed another's discomfiture.

Sargon sighed, having hoped for Hatshepsut in a better mood. But she was working up to one of her rages; and the pharaoh in one of those was even more of interest.

*   *   *

A door closed softly down the hall and Niccolo Machiavelli took a casual look—he was not an unusual face in the Hall of Injustice: in fact he had a pass that got him through a good many doors. And beyond the bulletproof wired glass of the peep-hole was a most unlikely pair, a nervous little Israeli in workman's clothes, with toolbelts and all the paraphernalia of a telephone repairman, and further, his assistant with a brand new telephone system in its cardboard and styrofoam casing, one of the big ones, clutched in both his arms, his hands white-knuckled even from this vantage: Dante Alighieri with his long hair sticking out unkempt from under a phone company serviceman's cap.

Niccolo used his passcard and coded in the number to open the electronic lock, one eye to the surrounds, theirs and his. Sycophants were rare on this level of the Hall. In fact they were not permitted, but sycophants were occasionally daring and none too bright. He whisked the pair through. Zaki was bright-eyed and grinning, his darting and expert glance as he took off his cap and wiped back his fluff of hair to resettle it, took in everything: Niccolo recognized such a look for what it was, and admired the finesse. But Dante Alighieri looked apt to faint on the spot; and his eye-jerking glances from this point to that of the hall expected retribution, discovery upon the instant, and scanned for no detail smaller. Niccolo set a hand on his shoulder and Dante jumped as if it had been wired, turning an enormous pair of dark eyes toward him.

"Steady, steady," Niccolo said, and Dante gulped air and swallowed it. Sweat stood out on his forehead. "Steady, hear?" He gripped Dante's shoulder until the man winced. "You make a mistake and there'll be consequences I can't cover. Do you understand me?"

Another convulsive gulp and swallow. Niccolo caught Zaki's eye, gave a nod toward the open door, and the little Jew slouched into the time-immemorial attitude of a workman paid by the hour, and sauntered on his way. Niccolo left Dante to follow them and walked on after.

Maintenance, that door said; it led to stairs, and the stairs led them down and down a concrete shaft, three more levels.

Another security door. Niccolo carded them through. More stairs, the smell of old concrete, and finally a metal stairs weaving its way deeper and deeper. Dante was breathing in great gasps, clutching his box and gripping the rail at the turns with hands predictably white-knuckled while Zaki skipped along light as a boy on illicit holiday.

The stairs came down to a dim, dank concrete tunnel; and the ceiling of that tunnel was all pipes of various sizes: some leaked water. The air-conditioning duct ran through here, and over on the walls, various dusty sheaves of electrical lines on one wall and the countless communications lines on the other.

"Tcha," Zaki said, rubbed his hands and unclipped his flashlight, got over to the latter wall and peered here and there, prodded at a select wire or two with his finger before he pulled out his tools.

"They'll come, they'll come," Dante moaned, hugging his phone-box to him. "It's the lowest hell for us."

Niccolo simply folded his arms and waited, in real interest. Zaki was very deft with his hands. Every move said expertise. A man of many parts indeed, and skilled: *that* was of interest. And:

"Hsss," Zaki said as Dante started to fold down onto the bottom step.

Niccolo caught Dante by an arm and stopped him, turned him this way and that, brushed a bit of dust from his arm. "Really, compatriot, if you're to make a career of this, you must learn to watch your elbows. Do you want to walk past upstairs offices with tunnel dust, eh? No, of course not. You *really* don't want to do that."

Dante shook his head energetically, his teeth chattering. He did not. "Those locks," he said between spasms, "all t-those b-buttons—t-they're c-c-connected to some computer?"

Sharp, very sharp for a timid creature. Niccolo smiled one of his tightest smiles, *feeling* the little Israeli's attention up his backbone like a cold wind. "Trust me, dear fellow."

"It ha-ha-has a n-number—if the system is inter-interl—"

Dante Alighieri had no more notion of security methods than he had of nuclear physics, but he knew computers. "Trust me," Niccolo said again, and shot a look at Zaki, who gave him one back, and held out a phone receiver, the line of which was attached to, one hoped, the right line.

"It's ready," Zaki said. There was death in this little man: for a moment that face, with its prominent nose and its very dark eyes, had dropped all pretenses. Zaki knew exactly that there had to be someone deeper inside or that they were going to be traced and tracked; and knew also that it was possibly an ambush which Niccolo had arranged, in which case Zaki was never to walk out of this place to which Niccolo had the keys, never going to go anywhere but to the Undertaker's table after a long and intimate interview with those who would want to know all the details that *he* knew. But Zaki had taken the chance and come in on this, claiming the expertise to do the job—which was certainly not the easiest way for Niccolo to have done it; but it was the way that provided the most interesting information about this little man who was, perhaps thanks to his skill, not among the notorious or the famous dead. And who looked at him with the pretenses dropped for a moment, flatly staring at him in a way that said Zaki would assuredly try to take him first if something started to go wrong: no threat, just clear understanding.

"Dante," Niccolo said, never quite turning his face from Zaki. He gestured with his right hand. Dante came between them in his nervous, myopic way, and squatted down and set the phone box on the floor, easing off the cheerful cardboard wrapper that showed telephone system, beige, and opening the styrofoam casing.

Computer and modem. Right into the lines that ran between the Hall of Injustice and the Pentagram.

Dante squatted there and fussed and swore and dithered over the connection. His hands trembled over the keys and steadied, while arcane little machine talked to arcane giant computer.

And told it that certain pieces of equipment with certain serial numbers had been requisitioned and approved by Rameses' office, and shifted here and there. While it must forget that other pieces had ever existed. And an order from the highest levels of government had disposed certain troops to a certain mission which was already logged on as a completely routine training exercise.

Alexander had his tanks. The System had just misfiled them.

Dante shut down and gave the phone back to Zaki, who disconnected, while Dante carefully put the computer equipment back into its styrofoam and slid the cardboard back around it.

"There, there," Niccolo said then, gathering him up by the arm; he took a handkerchief and cleaned the dust off the cardboard and the styrofoam and off Dante's hands. "There. No dust, not a fleck of dust. Not an alarm." He adjusted the box in Dante's cold hands. "Now it's empty, it doesn't weigh a thing, does it, just carry it under your arm, now, there's a good man."

"C-c-could have d-d-done this—" *at home*, Dante was about to object. Niccolo heard it coming and slapped him hard on the shoulder.

"Couldn't have done it better," Niccolo said, and hugged his little countryman about the shoulder with one arm, which demonstrative gesture got an owlish blink and a stammer of deprecation from the man. Dante wanted so to be friends: he screwed up his courage with a visible and commendable effort and looked up that long stairs.

"Are you through?" Niccolo asked of Zaki, who was putting away his gear. "I hope you left nothing new down here." Meaning two things: new scars and something left behind. "I have connections I have to protect." His wildest and most horrible imaginings extended to sleight-of-hand dropping something among those wires, and this whole Alexander affair turning into a security disaster of catastrophic proportions. General rebellion in Hell. The Pentagram in chaos. But someone would be down here to check this whole area, *very* soon.

Zaki sniffed, twitched, and wiped his nose, drew out a handkerchief of his own and dusted his hands, his equipment, and checked himself over before he cut the flashlight and left them reliant only on the dim, few lights along the wall. The motions were birdlike, fussy and nervous, quite unlike the capability that had stared out at him for a moment.

Zaki had his shoulder turned to him, but never quite his back.

"Come on, come on," Niccolo said, every intonation the worried man, the man anxious of their safety, the man with something to be worried for.

And ushered them up the stairs.

"He *won't?*" Hatshepsut asked.

"No," Brutus said, hands behind him, feeling after the wall as he backed up. "He said not. He said—" He met the wall and edged along it. "He said—just no."

"You don't have to be afraid of me, kitten." Hatshepsut edged to stop him, so that he stopped along the wall. "What, precisely, did Julius say?"

"That. Just that."

"You wouldn't lie to me, would you, kitten?"

"No." An emphatic shake of his head. And in a rush: "I think *you* ought to talk to him."

"Don't fret. I never killed the messenger for the message. It's very bad manners." She patted his shoulder and smiled at him. Patted his shoulder again, because he looked so distressed. "Dear kitten."

"Is it dangerous, what he's doing? Is it—something—dangerous?"

"Don't worry yourself with it." But the boy looked outright scared.

"It is," he said. "I know it is!"

"Never you fear." She was disturbed. The boy's naïvete persisted, in this house, gods, of all houses. He was *good*, not hardened like Mouse, whom the Romans called holy: she had never seen such goodness in the world alive. Some power hostile to Julius had detained Marcus Brutus thousands of years out of time, then returned this bastard son of Caesar's youth not the embittered man he had died, but well before the hour that had led to that end. This boy was pure and he was vulnerable, waiting the one who would corrupt him. And she did not wish to be the fool who did such a thing. She had hung men and old friends screaming from hooks on the walls of Men-nophren; but that tremor of distress in this boy's voice engaged her pity. And frightened her. "Never fear," she said again, "*I'll* see to him. Nothing will happen. Only—" Pity was a narrow and specific emotion with Hatshepsut: and right in its hollow heart an idea took root that bared her teeth in a small, false smile. "I have to be with him to do that."

"You can't—"

"Welcome to reality, kitten. This isn't your City or anything you know. And we Old Dead control as much of the new technology as we can believe in. Your father believes in it right down to the day they landed on the moon."

"They? Who? On the moon?"

"Julius and I were quite different, you know. Both of us were explorers in our way: he opened up his north. He had a vision, a great vision, what that territory would mean to him: if Rome thrust him out he would open a new world and rule it, shape it—" She ceased. The boy was Roman, and Republican Roman at that: one had to be so careful with his sensibilities. "For the sake of the peace," she said. "But myself, kitten, *I* was a reigning pharaoh who sponsored explorations for exploration's sake, up the Nile, around the coasts, wherever I could. If I had known then the moon was a world I would have tried for that."

"The moon's a *world?*"

She had not had much experience with newcomers of late, and Brutus was a special case, far out of his own time. She saw terror in his face. "Dear kitten, so are some of the stars. And I'd have gone for those, if I'd had then what I have now. Julius' vision is different than mine. He's a homebody at heart. Italia, Italia is all he yearns for. He makes everywhere Rome. And I, I, kitten, sat on a very hardseated throne, surrounded by very tedious priests, and held an empire together from the center; but the world was strange and wild in those days, and I wanted to know all of it, I had a vision—" It was too hard to speak of. Of a sudden her throat tightened as it had not done in ages, and there was a stinging behind her eyes and a pain in her heart. The emotion shocked her profoundly; the fact that she stood here in a hallway pouring out her soul to a teenaged and uncomprehending boy amazed her, the more so because she had begun with devious purpose. His innocence was a rock around which all currents had to flow. And she cursed herself for a fool and a sentimental fool at that, all the while touched inside by his evident struggle to understand. No one understood. No one of her age had ever understood. She did not expect it in this place, among the Old Dead. And if she were not Hatshepsut the pharaoh, she might blurt out, simply, with tears: *I want to go*, the way she had ached when her explorers had come back to her and told of great waterfalls and strange tribes and unknown coasts and vast seas. *I want to go*, because she ruled two thirds of the known world and had no freedom ever to see those things, she could only send others, and learn about them with a longing that had been dead in this privileged section of Hell—so very long. The boy could not know. He only stared at her with his own vulnerability, seeming to know the subject had turned off into dark territory where he no longer knew what they were talking about: where there were frightening motives and where it involved his father's safety; that was all he could understand. He talked about his father and she

talked about the moon and her throat froze shut
on her, so that they stood there trapped and staring at one another.

"I'll talk to him again," he said finally.

"No," she snapped. "No." And regained her direction, straight for the opening he offered. "But
you have to help me."

"How?"

There were deeds that blackened the heart and
weighted it like lead; and if somehow she had
passed the river and the Judge (she conceived it
rather as a downward journey, and sometimes as
the elevator in the Hall of Injustice, and the Judge
of the Dead as a withered and foulbreathed old
man who had terrified her with the thought that
she had come alive into the House of the Dead,
among the embalmers with their little hooks for
the brain, which they drew out the nose—but however she had come here, so very long ago, it had
been the Judge and not the embalmers; and she
had answered the right answers to the great Monsters and the Guardians and the Judges)—if somehow, then, she had passed these things, still the
thought niggled at her that there were indeed the
lower hells that Sargon named, and that there
were ways to go there even having been judged
once blameless.

And she named Marcus Brutus certain steps he
would take—for reasons of his father's safety, how
he would keep a constant eye on his father and tell
her instantly if Julius intended to leave the villa.

It was surely why Caesar's enemies had sent this
boy . . . not that Brutus was himself and presently
a danger to Caesar, but that someone of Caesar's
friends or Caesar himself would someday make
him so.

It was the whole house this boy was intended to
destroy.

She feared it altogether, the appearance of the boy, now the sudden appearance of this Macedonian by whom both Julius and Kleopatra set such great store. She saw foundations crumbling, and everything they had known in jeopardy.

Most of all she saw Julius taking the offensive. He was never wont to defend. She had studied his methods and the methods of generals like this Alexander and others uncounted. She saw patterns.

"Fools," she muttered when she had left young Brutus in the hall, his instructions specific; and she struck out at a luckless sycophant who chanced into her path.

The smell of age and incense permeated Tiberius' halls. Set on a cliff overlooking the Lake, where light and breezes should have gone through it, had the builder been thinking of light and breezes, it enjoyed the advantage of its location only on the uppermost tiers. Its lower ones had no true windows to the outside, only the ventilation of the garden-court and the dank, small-apertured atrium, in which the stench of incense and smoke always seemed to predominate, where lascivious statues alternated with grim portrait busts and (Kleopatra shuddered at the sight) the lifelike statue of Tiberius' brother Drusus sat enthroned at the end between two always-smoking braziers. The eyes were mechanical. They opened and closed and occasionally the mouth spoke. *I was murdered*, it would say. Or: *The fates favored my brother*. And now, suddenly, in hollow, mechanical tones: *Hello, Kleopatra*. Followed by ghastly laughter.

She flinched, all but turned back, and the man behind her put his hands on her shoulders and turned her to face him. She wore a chiton: Antonius had provided it for her. ("Don't look remarkable," Antonius had begged her. "Klea, don't—at-

tract him, for godssakes.") Antonius himself was
in tunica and sandals, not the 1970's dress he favored. He was young, the way he had been before
they were married, when he was trim of waist and
his hair was black and thick and curling: he had
been Julius' Master of Horse in those years, before
the extravagance and the dissolution that made
him the darling of the streets took its toll on body
and spirit; before he set himself in Julius' shoes
and failed the measure, disasterously for them both.
She did not think about these things. It was all
long ago. A great many things had changed, Julius
was with her—and they managed, they three, with
their temptations, by Julius' good sense. ("He was
your husband too, Klea. Forever's not a practical
length of time. Do what you have to do, do what
you want to do—")

It was that cold, deliberate judgement that made
Julius what he was, his own experience wide as
the army and three continents and the unexplored
north: Julius had a cold, clear perspective. Even in
bed. She never understood it. Or she did: that
Antonius nor any other lover had any lasting attraction for her. She had loved Caius Julius in his
declining years and discovered him in his thirties,
handsome and gallant and having that cool humor
that so bewildered her and attracted her in a way
no more passionate man could have. With Antonius it was—O Zeus, only ashes, warm ashes. She
was a talisman to him, his lord's wife, she had
sustained him, propped him, tolerated his alcoholism and his wild swings between hubristic plans
and profound dread of his own incompetence—there
was too much of remorse between them to let the
fire light again. He was mostly impotent with her
despite Julius' permission for their rare nights;
and he dreaded that Julius might know that. She
assured him again and again that she would never

tell Julius, that she had never said a word of it.
And being Antonius, he would never be sure that
she had told the truth or that she might not betray
him.

It was what repelled her in Antonius, that lack
of the confidence Julius had in such measure that
it wore at those around him, baffled his enemies,
confounded his lovers and his friends. It was not
magnanimity in Julius; it was deep, unshakeable
belief in himself. Antonius was all fears. Even when
he took her in his strong hands to plead with her.

"Don't do this, Klea. Dammit, let Caius ask his
own damn favors. Tiberius has got the scent of
someone wanting something he has, that's what.
You've set him off—"

"*My name was Drusus,*" the statue intoned. "*Augustus' policies murdered me.*"

"That *thing*—" Kleopatra whispered, shuddering, there in the dim and smoky light. "He's talking through it again. *Antoni,* stay close. Don't leave
me alone with him whatever—whatever he does."

"I can't reason with him."

"*The way from Gaul is rain and mud.*
The way to the throne is death and blood."

"My gods, now it's bad poetry." Her fingers
clenched on his arms. "*Antoni,* can he hear us?"

"No." He was emphatic. But his eyes were terrified, and darted and tried to tell her things. "I told
you, it's a bad time."

"Why do you *stay* in this place?" It was an old
question. It was where hell decided he should be,
and there was torment in the look he gave her
back. It was where hell decided her son should be.
But Caesarion had fled to the enemy. And hell had
allowed that. "*Antoni—*"

"I'm useful here," Antonius said, and reminded
her, as he could do at the worst and blackest of
times, that for all his weaknesses, for all his fool-

ish loyalties and more foolish treasons, he had
moments of extravagant and devastating courage.
He loved them both. He never betrayed Julius,
even knowing (it was the knife that kept his inade-
quacy a bleeding wound) that Julius knew he was
too weak to trust, but brave enough to rely on. Not
quite man enough. But almost. And she loved Antonius, a little, even yet. She let her head down
against his chest, with great tenderness, and hugged
him tight, then clutched his hand in hers and
walked on through that dreadful atrium and down
the hall.

She had paid Antonius with his night; now he
gained her audience with the old madman. And
she had as soon have faced a legion as walk down
that stairs into the deepcut passages where the
Emperor had his safe-rooms and his bedchambers
and his throne room. There were times that Tiberius came up to the light, but this was as Antonius
had said, one of the bad ones: he held no court on
the balcony that overlooked the water, held no
revels (at the memory of which she shuddered),
saw no visitors. In his worst fancies he imagined it
was February, the dead-rites, and he spoke with
his brother, whom he had never found in Hell. He
saw ghosts of his victims everywhere and feared
poisons and daggers. He was haunted by men with
hooks and by jeering mobs, and he waked with
fancies that he was drowning and that the fishes of
the Tiber were nibbling at his dead flesh. All these
things were true in some degree. Rome had held
holiday when this Emperor died.

Julius did not know this place. Julius had never
seen the inside of it. Or, she believed, he would
never have let his Klea come to this terrible hall.

But she wanted her own part in what he did, she
was anxious to handle things for herself and she
would not flinch when he asked, no more than

Antonius would. "Antonius will help me," she had said. And he had let her go.

Murder, murder, murder, the brazen voice pursued them. *A plague on all horses. I'll walk home.*

"Hello, hello?" Octavianus Augustus always distrusted the telephone. Mostly it rang in Julius' offices or in Machiavelli's or Hatshepsut's. The phone in his own study frightened him when it went off, like unexpected explosives, so his voice was sharp enough when he snatched it up. "Who are you?"

"Is this Augustus?"

"Of course I am! Who are you?"

"The Supreme Commander," a faint voice said, "has met with an accident."

"Rameses?" He shouted. Julius had told him a thousand times not to shout. And to hold the receiver near his ear, promising him that it would not electrocute him, but it took an act of courage. The thin, distant voice over the sputter sounded in no wise familiar. "Who is this?"

Silence from the other end.

"Are you finished?" The etiquette of these abysmal devices, this talking to a disembodied voice without visual cues, frayed Augustus' nerves. "Hello, hello?"

"Hadrian," the voice said, "is with the Undertaker."

There was a click. Augustus flinched and held the receiver away from his ear, feeling less safe than he had felt before that voice came whispering in its ugly way, right into his study.

He held the phone and looked at it. And then he had to do something he loathed almost as much. He hung it up (Julius had drilled that procedure into him) and picked it up again to dial the armory.

"This is the Emperor," he shouted at the man

who answered. "Tell Caesar his call came. Do you understand? Hello, hello?"

The steps led down and down, a masonry track through living stone, where the air was cold. They were beyond the lightshafts now. Dim bulbs shone at wide intervals, and showed them an iron door in the shape of an embracing couple.

Chain rattled and the couple slid apart with a metallic thunder. Kleopatra never flinched, but walked through into the golden and orange light and the reek of incense and corruption, with Antonius beside her.

Smoke puffed and belched at her right. Fire shot out in a sudden blast and Antonius snatched her aside. "Damn this!" Kleopatra yelled to the surrounds. "Emperor, Egypt is here!"

"Careful—" Antonius said; as a second erotic gateway parted, on a dim room and a stark throne and a man in a black toga. There was a single brazier for light; the walls round about were painted with cabalistic signs.

It was a man at first glance in his fifties, hard-jawed and rawboned. He sat with his chin on his fist and his brows lowered. But the dryness of a mummy was about his skin, and his eyes when he looked at them burned with furtive and furious anger. "Well," he said, "well, I own Egypt. Do I own you, pretty pet, do I, pet?"

"I'm before your time, Emperor. I—"

"You've corrupted Antonius, have you? Turned him against me. They all turn on me. Do you think I'm a fool? Do you?"

"Would the pharaoh of Egypt call another emperor a fool? Absolutely not. We have our unique interests."

"You have Antonius." A dark and lascivious chuckle. "Damned, useless Antonius. Augustus killed him, you know. Your dear housemate killed him. Do you have unique interests with Augustus, mmmn? That butcher. Married our mother, you know. Unique interests there too. He made her send that doctor. Augustus did. What's he like in bed? You do those things he likes?"

"Sir," Antonius said.

"Shut up. I'm talking to Egypt. What are you like, Egypt, what *do* you like?"

"What I'd like, since you ask—"

"Killed my brother. I walked. Wanted no part of horses. Hundreds of miles back from Gaul. He stank by then. I walked that funeral procession all the way back to that bastard Octavianus Augustus. *That bastard and my mother, do you know that, do they still visit?*"

"Never. Majesty—"

"I am a god." He slammed his fist on the arm of the throne. Spittle flew. *"I am a god."*

"Well, so, dammit to Set, am I!" It flew out. Careful with him, Antonius had said. Humor his fancies. She gulped a mouthful of air, felt Antonius' hand touch her back as she set her feet. "I'm Zeus-Ammon like my predecessor, I'm Osiris under the earth!"

His eyes flew open, burning bright and mad. "God of the dead. God of the dead." He gripped the arms of his throne and looked at her from one wildly-focussed eye, as if he were braced against some terrible wind. "Get away from me!"

"I want your damn Germans!"

The rigid body relaxed, limb by limb, the bracing arm first, quite as if that impalpable wind had quit blowing. "You want my guard? You want the poor bastard Germans?"

There was no reasoning with this man, no negotiating. A chill sweat was on her limbs. Her heart was slamming against her ribs. "Yes," she said. "Give them to me and I'll leave."

"Treason, *treason!*"

"Klea—" Antonius took her by the arm and pulled her backward. "Get out of here, come on, Klea—"

"Treason!"

It *was* time to go. She edged further back, hating to turn her back on this lunatic. Then she whisked about and matched strides with Antonius in haste to leave this place.

"Osiris," the voice rang at her back. "Osiris!"

It was summons. She kept walking a pace and another, and heard the rising note of petulance, dangerous at her back. She glanced over her shoulder, just to see if there was a weapon there.

"Osiris. You want my Germans?"

It seemed a fool's act to stop. But the German Guard was what she had come for, and it was a coward's part to run skittering out the door with this madman perhaps about to send assassins after them, which made it not at all foolish to stop again and face this lunatic.

"Osiris is a woman," Tiberius said, and laughed, giggled, this huge wreck of a grim old soldier. The eyes went quickly grim, the right more focused than its mate. The mouth grinned. "The lord of the dead comes to visit me. Wants my Germans. What will the god pay me? Come sit on my lap, pretty god?"

"Klea." Antonius slipped his hand inside her elbow. "Klea, for the gods' sake get out of here."

It seemed like a good idea. She started to turn away.

"Osiris. My brother's dead."

She walked for the door, carefully, the doorway which was worse on the obverse than on its facing image. Her heart beat and fluttered like something trapped. The very air seemed strangling.

"You want my Germans, Egypt, find my brother!"

She stopped, resisting Antonius' hand. Turned and faced him again.

"Give me my brother," Tiberius said plaintively. His jaw knotted and his chin quivered. "God of the dead, give him back and you can have anything, I'll give you anything if you give him back."

The tears ran down the mummified skin. The lineaments of the face were suddenly, in the dim light, that of the stern old soldier who had lost the gentler part of him. Drusus had died of a fall off a horse. Not even a heroic death. Dead of a fall and nothing more.

And she drove right into the wound. "We might learn something. We might learn where he is. Give us the Guard and we might find him."

"Wonderful, isn't she pretty? Find my brother." Tiberius wiped at his eyes and put his fingers to his lips and gave a piercing and startling whistle, that echoed off the walls.

There was a rattle behind them. Kleopatra whirled about as Antonius did, and froze. A German stood in that disgraceful doorway, blond giant in leather and furs, with braided hair and beard and frosty eyes; and an M-16 in his arms dead-leveled at them.

A rustle from behind them again. "Heh. Doesn't speak anything civilized. It's Perfidy, isn't it? Yes, it's Perfidy." Tiberius' voice was closer, the rustle of his garments and the whisper of his steps on the pavings betraying his movements. "His twin is Murder. Heh. I give you Perfidy and Murder and all their band. Perfidy has a few words of Latin, don't you? Pretty fellow. Cut your throat, wouldn't he? Perfidy!" And a guttural and rapid discourse after, to which the blond giant's eyes flickered, and his face, no less grim, looked as if it had some life in it and some thinking going on behind it.

"Huh," the German said, and lifted up his rifle as Tiberius strolled into their vision, at the side.

"Loyal," Tiberius said. "Die with their chief. All of them do. Get out. *Get out,* go find my brother. Find Drusus. Find Drusus. I want him—"

She delayed for nothing. She darted out the door wiht never a backward look until:

"*I give you Cowardice too!*" the Emperor screamed after them. "I give you Antonius! Take him too, damned traitor, damned, damned, damned *impotent* traitor, let death into my house, find my brother, find him, find him!"

Sobs attended them. And Perfidy's steps, quick as their own.

"Gods," Kleopatra said when that first door had closed itself, when they reached the hallway. She was shaking. She turned and grasped Antonius by the arms. And saw a dreadful look on his face.

"Let's get out of here," Antonius said.

"Don't—don't let—"

But there was no arguing with Antonius. She had been married to him long enough to know that look, that terrible, driven look.

All the while Perfidy stood there staring at them with his rifle in his hands, lost in his own uncomprehending world. As the erotic doors opened on the upward stairs.

3.　　　The Oracle

Due east of New Hell, where the mountains guarded by the Erinys sloped to a pass through which an army could thunder—that was where Alexander had wanted to meet Caesar's forces. Not here, in New Hell by the sea, so far from the country and so completely out of Alexander's element.

But here they were—Maccabee, Diomedes, and he—to meet the man called Julius and his Egyptian whore and his armies of the night: the great physeters which were battle tanks (so much more impressive than Alexander's forty horse), the blond and smelly German guards and the retinue of an entire household (including countless flitting sycophants and a woman in a pink jumpsuit like a second skin who rode up on a litter that put Alexander in mind of Darius and his bathtubs and his familial baggage).

"This is not what I wanted," Alexander said, hating the slap of the parking lot's tarmac against his sandals and wishing that he had a horse under him, to put him eye-to-eye with his taller companions.

"Not?" said Maccabee, who had accompanied

him into Che Guevara's camp to see to the liberation of Hadrian. (And "see" was all they'd done about it—the Devil had sent an emissary, a woman—fittingly enough—who'd killed the Supreme Commander to get him out of the clutches of the rebels and back to the Undertaker's table.)

"Not," Alexander snapped, with the fumes of hot tank in his nostrils and the hellish halogen light hurting his eyes.

Diomedes had come with them to the rebel camp's edge, but no farther. Without explanation, the hero had simply leaned upon his Alexander-sized shield, saying, "I'll wait here."

And he had done that, been right there. But it had ruined the whole adventure for Alexander. The *basileus* wanted his new Friend with him, not waiting in the bushes to guard his back or do whatever Achaeans did. Alexander still thought it might have had something to do with Homer's presence in Che's base camp.

But now was no time to ask. Diomedes was in possession of the "Litton field phone," which the little modern Jew, Zaki, had bestowed on his betters. Into this, Diomedes would sometimes speak, as if to an oracle, asking questions.

And, like an oracle, the box gave answers—cryptic answers, bossy answers, ultimata. Alexander the Great didn't like taking orders from a box, no matter what Sibyl spoke through it.

But it was the will of the oracle named Litton that had brought them here, to meet with Caesar's army in the parking lot of the armory.

Like the Oracle at Siwah, it was not to be denied. Like the Sibyl at Cumae, it spoke in riddles. Like the Pythia, it was treacherous. And it needed no water to drink or bay to chew or leaves to write upon. Nor did it sit upon a tripod over a smoking chasm of the gods. It merely belched or farted out its orders, and even the best of the Achaeans obeyed without question.

Even now, walking toward the glare of light in which men and arms and wagons of death and mighty chariots with rearing horses (who knew as well as the Macedonian that those tanks were frightful beyond flesh's ability to bide), Diomedes spoke into the Litton as if to a lover: his lips to its talisman, its scepter, his fingers stroking its nipples sensuously.

The jealousy which Alexander was beginning to feel toward the Litton oracle was of proportions which presaged violence: either Diomedes must be persuaded to renounce the Oracle, despite the seductiveness of its wisdom, or Alexander would destroy it. Where was Bucephalus when the Macedonian needed a trusty war horse with iron hooves to rend and pound?

At that thought, the *basileus* shook off his black mood—Bucephalus had not come to hell. The very recollection of the steed was one he shied from; he'd not wish it here, but he missed it more than any man. Sometimes he missed it more than life.

"Not," he said again to Maccabee, while with his other ear he listened as Diomedes whispered Zaki's name to the Oracle of Litton and the box hissed back like a brazier. "How is it that we can raise an army in New Hell without raising alarms? If there was no triumphant procession for us—returning heroes from Che's camp—how is it that this Julius can command the very streets of the Devil's lair?"

"You suspect a trap?" The tall Israelite swiped backhanded at his chin, though it wasn't hot enough this ruddy night in New Hell for sweating. Eyes which had withstood a desert and the Roman empire turned to him and held, with gentleness there for a spirit who'd not lived long enough to fail and thus had never learned the lessons which had brought such as Maccabee—and Caesar—here.

"There'll be no trap, Alksandr," the handsome ancient promised. "Not of the sort you mean, at any rate. Holes out of Hell you want, holes we'll find. We've got Germans as auguries. We can split one and read his liver, if you don't believe me. Or ask Diomedes, who's been in touch with Zaki this whole time."

The implication was, of course, that no Jew would ever let Maccabee down, that Jews didn't make the sort of error Alexander half expected. Maccabee, when on the subject of his Jews, was tiresome.

But Maccabee was like an extension of Alexander, like an arm or any other member of his body, as necessary as moonlit nights or wine. . . . Then the *basileus* remembered there was no moonlight here, just the glare of New Hell in the night sky and Paradise glowering down in its phases.

So, to cover his discomfiture as they came up to the chicken-wire fence and two German hulks crossed spears to bar their way, he asked Diomedes, "And what does Litton say, Achaean? Are the omens good? The prognostications pleasing? Where's our little spy?"

"Spying. As your army is arming and your camp followers following and your horses snorting at the wind back at the pass where the trek begins."

"In other words, all things are in their place in heaven and earth—and Hell?" The voice that interjected itself into a private conversation was female.

Alexander looked right and left, before and behind. To the right was the baggage train's refuse, to the left an open street, deserted but for parked chariots-with-no-horses—cars, as Zaki said. Before were still the pair of Germans barring the gate with festooned, long-handled spears or axes. Behind was only the night and the way they'd come.

Yet the woman's voice came again, tinkling with laughter: "Basileus, are you there? Is it really you? And your army—is this the whole of it?"

Then the Oracle of Litton farted and Diomedes snatched its appurtenance from its cradle with a heavenward rolling of eyes. "Who speaks to us? Name yourself, and say why we should hear you."

The box hissed like a cat with its tail underfoot. Diomedes shook the thing he held and swore in Zaki's name and, at the same time, Maccabee's iron grip came down on Alexander's arm, to slow and caution him, with its promise of protection welcome in the city's night.

The Macedonian had stayed away from this hellish haven of the Old Dead who were his juniors, of the New Dead and their weird ways, for many reasons: he sought a new empire to make him its Great King in the hills; he sought elephants and chariots; he thought to placate Zeus and come here, some day, triumphant and a conqueror, entering a city on its knees in a parade of blood and blossoms.

He'd sought none of this—oracles trapped in boxes, women's voices from the air, the New Dead with their madness which Zaki said had destroyed the living world above—until Maccabee had come into his life and made him think there was a way out from here. He'd been, metaphorically, sulking in his tent until Reality came to its senses and petitioned him to come out and lead it to glory once again. Maccabee had convinced him that, in the Devil's world, human nature could not repent, foolishness was rampant, and a man—even a *basileus*—must take the initiative and revenge all slights, eye for eye, tooth for tooth.

Yet he mistrusted his decision to rejoin the struggling masses at that moment, while Diomedes quieted the oracle of Litton and slung it over his shoulder, pointing with his spear to a figure for which all chaos parted, even the giant German guards.

"*Ite! Agite!*" the oncoming woman swore like a general, and the huge Germans backed away. "*Perdi*, Great King, you must forgive these . . . creatures: Perfidy and Murder, this pair, the twins. We've just got them, and they don't have much of any language."

Behind Kleopatra, the Germans closed, crossing their war implements with a *thunk* as final as burial.

Over her shoulder was slung a second Oracle of Litton; around her throat was an intricate piece of Egyptian jewelry which had a serpent that curled up toward her mouth but didn't touch it. She strode right up to Alexander without more than a bob of head as obeisance and put her hand on her hip: "I asked, is this the whole of your army? If so, there's the matter of command. If you're not bringing an equal share . . . ?"

"You!" Klea, as Julius called this creature of wiles, this woman who thought like a man and thought she was in possession of a piece of Alexander's soul, had spoken through the Litton oracle. Oracles, Alexander well knew, could be corrupted into tools of political manipulation. At Siwah, he'd been greeted as a Son of Zeus and the rest of what was said hadn't mattered . . . much. Inside, where the doomsayers had spoken evil, he'd chosen not to believe them. Now, in public, a more forceful statement was necessary. He held out his hand to Diomedes, his eyes never leaving the beautiful, pouting face full of challenge before him. The woman would have to learn her place.

"The box," he demanded.

Diomedes gave it into his hand and its weight was a surprise. It took all the stubbornness which had made Alexander great to keep his arm from dropping with the weight of the Oracle of Litton he now held. He felt muscles burn, and knew that later his arm would be sore to the elbow; but with grace and very slowly, in a very kingly fashion, he raised the box high, still eye-locked with this slut whom, Zaki had told them, slept with not only Julius but also with an underling of his called Antonius.

Then he opened his left hand and the Oracle of Litton crashed to the macadam while, with his right, Alexander drew his sword.

The action caused Diomedes' long and weighty sword to leave its sheath also, and the Achaean's eyes to sweep the shadows for unseen threats. Into Maccabee's big hands came not a sword, but a magical and thunderous slingshot called an Uzi, a souvenir from their trip to Che's camp.

Both companions had misconstrued, however: it wasn't the woman, Kleopatra, or any stalkers-from-shadows that Alexander sought to rend, but the Oracle of Litton.

Three times he drove down, from a full overhead swing, into the heart of the oracle with his ivory-hilted sword.

Light came from the box, sparkling shards that hissed and magic that ran up his sword and bit his fingers the first time. But Alexander was full of rage, the pain a thing to be dealt with later. On the second swing, worms of many colors were revealed within the broken casing; on the third, the oracle was halved and shattered.

But there was no blood. There was, in fact, nothing inside of flesh and blood—no tiny person, as he'd suspected, sitting in a tiny chair over a tiny brazier, no tiny skull mashed to pulp. Just worms of many colors and shattered Roman glass and enameled bosses like pieces of an Egyptian collar.

The woman had given back a pace, but not knelt as had both of Alexander's companions. More disrespect: her head was higher than his. And behind her, all the others were still standing.

Maccabee saw the direction of Alexander's glance and touched his arm: "Ignorance, my lord Basileus. And strange customs, from different lands. Tolerance."

It was a watchword of kingship, one that had helped make him great.

And in that interval the woman had knelt down also. She was close enough that, despite her khakis and her New weapons, he realized for the first time what attribute had made her the single confidant of Caesar on their first meeting: she had magnetism which was like tides in the distant sea.

Alexander felt it and so did both men, on his right and left. With Diomedes' muttered curse, she cocked her head: "Think of me not as a whore, then, but as a brother." She offered a gamin smile. "I am a king, a great king. I am Egypt. Respect the office, hero, and we'll do well enough." As she spoke, her fingers stirred the wreckage. They were long and shapely fingers, gilded on the nails.

Maccabee reached out to imprison her wrist, and stopped his hand at the sound she made. But he said, "Our forces are at a safe place; we'll meet with them soon. Where's your . . . friend, the Roman?"

Her laughter tinkled again, but this time it was as deadly as the shards of sharp glass that were all which remained of the Oracle of Litton. "*Which*

Roman? *Meum Iulium*—Julius? Or Antonius? He's coming along, did you know? Caesar didn't, and he's not pleased. Decius Mus, perhaps? Or Mucius Scaevola? All these Romans have found this little outing to be of interest. As have Machiavelli, and (though let's not tell the others just yet) Hatshepsut. So, are you going to tell me? Or must I guess?"

"Caesar, woman. It's him with whom I treated, king to king."

"It's him and me with whom you treated, king to king to king," she said, did the frail creature, running her fingers through the worms of Litton, her eyes now on Maccabee's Uzi. "Tell your Israelite to put his weapon by."

Alexander nodded and Maccabee did, backing a step in a crablike fashion and excusing himself to "go find Zaki. If she's witched him, or the Romans have, this goes no further."

"And does he speak for you?" said the woman who was beginning to seem like a Pythia, the more because Alexander couldn't seem to stop watching her hand fondling the shards of the oracle.

"Sometimes," Diomedes interjected before Alexander could think of an answer due a woman who thought she was Egypt that would dismiss her—he couldn't be seen chatting with women—without too obvious a slight.

"Then," said Egypt, "perhaps you'll tell me, Hero, the answer to my question: will you tell me, or must I guess, why you destroyed the field phone? They're shielded, I'm told. Your own man Zaki gave this one his blessing."

"If we want oracles, we'll get them at New Cumae," Alexander said without waiting for Diomedes, and without forethought. "As a matter of fact, we'll stop there when we've met up with my forces. The Sybil will speak of holes with less artifice than your Oracle of Litton."

Kleopatra blinked and it seemed that she ordered her face very carefully before she rose up saying, "I see. Well, Great King, if an oracle is what you want, we can definitely do better than the ... ah ... Oracle of Litton, you're correct in that."

Diomedes was rising as Alexander did, his gaze beyond, where Maccabee was on one side of the German guards and Zaki on the other.

When Alexander reached the impasse of Jews and Germans, the two blond giants made some sort of primitive obeisance in his direction, their eyes eloquent where their mouths could not be.

And the man who had formed the Companion cavalry saw, in the big Germans named Perfidy and Murder, loyalty aching to be bestowed on someone worthy, honor covered with grime and starving to be redeemed, and much else of lost time so poignant that Alexander's eyes filled with tears.

Then he gave the two Germans, each nearly twice his size, a look which had won him more hearts and minds and sword arms than any soul in Hell, and they melted before him like water, to fall in behind, their previous gate duties forgotten or given over to others.

Alexander didn't ask, and didn't have enough Latin to tell whether Kleopatra had directed them to follow him or complained when they did.

With the two Germans on his heels, and Diomedes, Maccabee, and Zaki at his side, he strode straight up to a commotion of horseless chariots and dray beasts—if he wanted to confront the Roman Caesar, he had to do it around, not through, Kleopatra.

And he must: as Great King, he had spoken a decree before witnesses that he would visit the Oracle at New Cumae. And visit it the party would, or the venture would end here and now, before it had even begun.

Caesar might be breath and life to his family, every tendril of it like a spider's web, but Alexander had wanted only his tanks, and Germans.

Even though these Germans, if they knew a way out of Hell, could not have told him, they were Germans. And Alexander had long ago learned that Fate was no respecter of Hell: like Diomedes, who had come to him unsolicited and would stay until his word was good, the journey done, and Achilles met on the other side of it, the Germans were fated to be his.

He could just feel it. You didn't become king of the known world without paying more heed to your instinct than to all the "wise counsel" of your advisors, even if one of them was Diomedes who'd fought on the beach at Ilium.

So when he found Caesar in the midst of a chaos of logistics, sitting on what he referred to as a "jeep" with two men he introduced as "Aziru, late prince of Amurru, who'll be coming with us as my driver, and Sargon, Great King of Akkad, who won't," Alexander made his wishes known clearly and concisely.

"Caesar, we need to leave immediately. This party is too big as it is, but we'll manage. I'll cut down on the size of my own retinue to accommodate you."

Caesar ducked his chin magnanimously, his eyes never leaving Alexander's, eyes that were full of fire and brilliance and made Alexander remember that rumor said how Caesar loved him; eyes that drew more words from Alexander's lips than those meant to hide the fact that this army was more than thrice what Alexander the Great could field.

"If, that is, you'll accommodate me, Caesar."

"In any reasonable request, Basileus, you have the power of Rome behind you." The voice was cultured beyond measure, promissory of more than accomodation.

Alexander said, feeling a hot flush creep up his neck, "I want to stop at New Cumae and ask the Sibyl about the ... journey ahead. Unless you've unearthed a German with a map?"

"No map, Basileus, and only what Germans you see here—those of the guard. But we should stop at Cumae. I haven't had an oracle I could stomach in years."

"It's agreed, then? We start within the hour, Caesar?" Behind Alexander, the two Germans who had followed him from the gatepost still stood, at a respectful distance, their eyes on him and the eyes of Maccabee, Zaki, and Diomedes on them for any twitch of betrayal or havoc in the making.

"Within the hour, but only because we are both 'Living' Gods," said the Roman with wry humor, surveying the chaotic comings and goings of well-wishers and sycophants, and spying Machiavelli threading his way through the crowd. "But only on one condition, Basileus."

Alexander stiffened to his full height. "And that is?"

"Call me Julius. All my friends do ... Alexander."

Pulling out of New Hell in convoy during the middle of the night would have made Zaki exceedingly nervous, even if he hadn't been in the midst of Egyptians, Germans, and Romans—all armed to the teeth with everything from war axes to 21st century molecular disruptors.

One little Jew with a couple of crazy Old Dead wouldn't be any match for this crew if things got nasty. But they were all on the same side, at least at the outset.

He'd been given a command jeep and in it he was driving his charges. He thought of them that way, the ancient Israelite Maccabee (whose name meant "the hammerer," or just "the hammer"), in whose honor he was up to his neck in whatever meshugganer venture was just beginning; Alexander of Macedon, who'd slaughtered enough Persians to qualify as a friend; and Diomedes, who was somehow more akin to Zaki than even Maccabee, though there was no reason for it.

If he had a real affinity for anyone in this task force, it was Machiavelli, who was riding in the camouflaged communications truck and would have let Zaki accompany him. If Alexander hadn't got all kinglike about who was sitting where and mixed in, Zaki would have been where he could have done the most good—at the side of history's master spy, the most dangerous man in the party and the one most in need of watching, instead of driving Alexander's jeep.

He'd have to talk to Diomedes about that, because the pecking order, as pecking orders do, had shaken out that way: Zaki went through Diomedes, who did whatever you had to do to get Alexander's attention.

And he and Diomedes had a surprise for the little Macedonian: Bashir Gemayel, and certain other fighters among the New Dead, were going to rendezvous with this bunch at the first designated campsite. Probably while the omen-seekers were at New Cumae, Alexander's forces would swell to equal Caesar's. It really had been an obvious move: you don't go into action without enough of your own troops to get you out, not when you're co-venturing with someone like Julius Caesar and Caesar has ground-effect tanks, not to mention Hatshepsut and Kleopatra.

So Zaki had done what he'd always done—used his connections, his modest networks, and his talent for looking a dozen moves ahead in any man's chess game to make sure that his own butt, and the butts of his teammates, were protected, even though this was the weirdest bunch of "teammates" he'd ever encountered.

Sometimes he thought he was sleeping off some bad Lebanese food in a cheap hotel, somewhere in the Bekaa, and that he'd wake up with a red-alert blaring from his ear-piece and his station chief shaking his shoulder.

Sometimes.

Around the first cookfire, sixteen hours later, three of the Old Dead—Alexander, Maccabee, and Diomedes—were trading tales of oracles they had known.

"Agamemnon asked, at the beginning of the War," said Diomedes, "when it would end, and got this answer: 'Agamemnon will take Ilion when the best of the Achaeans quarrel.' Bitch. But she was right. And before the War, when Menelaos asked, 'How can I punish Alexander?' Delphi told him, 'Bring me the necklace that Aphrodite gave to Helen.' "

Someone stirred; Diomedes glanced away from the fire and saw the look on the Macedonian's face, then said, "*That* Alexander was Paris; no offense meant."

"None taken. But tell me how the Oracle looked, and how she divined, and what Delphi was like in your time," said Alexander.

Diomedes kept seeing, as he looked into the fire-licked gloom behind Alexander's head, black bird wings flapping like hungry shadows. If he could have gotten home even as far as Tiryns, the Argive city in his earthly domain, by lopping the boy-king's head from his shapely shoulders, he would

have done so without hesitation, as he'd killed
when Odysseus had said to him, *Here's our man,
see, Diomedes, and here his horses. Come then, put
forth your great strength. . . .*

On that night hunt, gray-eyed Athene had breathed
strength into him and he began to kill the Thracian
owners of the bright-maned, single-foot horses until he had killed twelve, while Odysseus dragged
away the corpses, one after another by the foot, so
that the horses should not be affrighted stepping
on dead men.

And the vision of the blood-soaked killing ground
and the bright armor and fine chariots of the
Thracians which he and Odysseus, with Athene's
help, had taken, was so much more real than this
about him, or his memories of Delphi, that Diomedes had to struggle to remember any of the
questions put to him by Alexander of Macedon.

Concerning the oracle he, Diomedes, had seen—a
black-winged bird with the head and then the form
of Achilles, who had urged Diomedes on this
venture—he spoke not at all, lest it displease the
gods of Hell.

He let his eyes rove beyond the fire of these
Hellenic Old Dead, to where six tanks and three
jeeps and two lorries were parked around the Roman tents of Caesar's party. It reminded him too
much of the way Achilles had sequestered himself,
of the fighting among the nobles on the beach at
Ilion where the hollow ships were beached, of all
that had been wrong in the War.

But he answered Alexander conversationally,
"The Sibyl of Delphi was also called Daphne,
Artemis, and Manto, as were other seeresses. It is
said she came from Helikon and was raised by the
Muses, but however, she predicted that Helen would
bring war on all Asia and Europe and cause the

fall of Ilion." He shrugged. "Women. I told you at the outset, I wanted nothing to do with a sortie that included them."

Female laughter came tinkling on the smoky breeze full of spices: these Romans traveled with their cooks and servants. Ill would come of it, for they dined on bird this night.

And the black wings beat in Diomedes' inner sight as they had beaten upward into the Italian sky, and down as if from Paradise itself to bring Achilles' shade upon him with orders.

He was restless, too restless to answer Alexander when the youthful king asked, "But what was it *like?* Did the oracle drink the water and writhe in fits, or breathe the smoke, or chew the leaves . . . ?"

"Leaves," Diomedes said, retreating from the fireside so that the two were alone, but for two hulking German guards well back in the shadows who went everywhere Alexander did, now, without a complaint from either Maccabee or the Macedonian, as if the blonds called Murder and Perfidy had always been there.

To Diomedes, picking up companions thusly named was omen enough for any night on the Argive coast in Troizen; in Hell, it screamed upon deaf ears of what was to come.

He saluted Maccabee with his spear as he slipped his shield upon his arm and left the fireside. Wise eyes fogged with affection for Alexander brushed his, wavered, fell away.

Maccabee, Zaki had told Diomedes, had exterminated Hellenizers in his day, and subjected the Seleucid army of occupation to guerrilla warfare of unparalleled ferocity. That Maccabee the Hasmonaean should have taken up with Alexander, from whom the Seleucids had sprung, troubled Zaki. But Diomedes understood it: the two men had shared an epoch in common; among so much strangeness, what was familiar outweighed what was held in dispute.

As the Roman cadre across the camp proved, disputes were themselves precious—all your past concerns validated by grudges held and accommodations made.

The New Dead were more lonely, in their way; perhaps as lonely as the single veteran of Ilion, who sought only the hollow ships or Charon and his boat—a Hell of his beliefs, not this anguishing posset of passion and prejudice.

"Be back by Paradise's rise," Alexander called imperiously after him. "We'll want you for the descent into New Cumae."

It was a cave by a riverside. He'd asked the name of the river and Machiavelli, during the unloading of the com truck, had answered, "Lethe."

Machiavelli had a tongue for foul humor. Zaki said there was a brain behind it, but Achilles had had a brain. He just failed to use it.

The camp was too big for stealth, too raucous to police, too mixed of type and lacking in discipline. Caesar's Germans walked the perimeter—all but the two assigned to Alexander—and Alexander's forty horse had drawn lots to guard their steeds, but that was all.

A night attack could leave them horseless and kill the tanks where they heaved. Machiavelli had spoken of the danger to the physeters from "siphoning." So the tanks had their guards, as well.

And there was nothing right about the encampment, or the night enfolding it, in the Achaean's estimation—like all else he'd seen in Hell, this enterprise was bound to fail by the very hubris and arrogance that had mounted it.

Luckily, he didn't care if they ever found the holes. He walked among the horse lines until he came to a bright-maned steed who pricked its ears at him and lipped his arm with a velvet touch.

Either the horse pressed its long flat head against the hero's chest, or the man embraced the steed's neck to the same result. One way or another, they stood thus, breathing each other's welcome scent until an urgent whisper cut the night.

"Diomed? Over here!" It was Zaki, who shortened all names and knew too many outcomes: Zaki, like a seer in his own right, the newest dead among them, with the least to lose.

He left the comfort of the horse, wondering if he could buy it from its owner, and headed toward the whispering bushes.

In them, eyewhites gleamed, and he hunkered down in the brush before his eyes adjusted enough to realize that Zaki, and two men with him, wore branches about their persons.

Looking farther, he discerned others, dressed in leaves and black and grey and green, looking like shrubbery on the move.

"President Gemayel, this is Diomedes, a great hero from ancient times, who fought the Etruscans—the Trojans. Diomedes, President Gemayel would have been another Alexander, had not he been assassinated by Persians and Philistenes."

The New Dead shook hands; Diomedes had learned how: elbow crooked, a grip with at least half your power.

Gemayel had a sharp face and thick dark hair; his skin seemed dark, under the layers of soot and paint. In English, he said, "May God be with you," and Diomedes answered, "Right. And with you," just before he heard a man come up behind him.

"Aziru," Zaki's whisper held satisfaction, "prince of Amurru, this is Bashir Gemayel, probably a descendent of yours, and Diomedes of . . . Ahhiyawa."

So many ways to say the same thing, Diomedes thought as the slight ancient crowded into the bushes and, among these Semites, the fair Achaean began to feel large and uncomfortable.

Zaki may have sensed it, for he said, "Diomedes doesn't know that I went down under the Administration building with Machiavelli and Dante, or that, if treachery is afoot, telling Authority that Machiavelli masterminded a trek there, and falsified records, will turn all tables. Some of the rest of you may not realize what it means: we've got a handle on Caesar's pack—they don't want to lose all they've built up in New Hell. They're trusted, part of the ruling class, really. We can use that, if we have to."

Gemayel had a lilting accent: "Meaning that we're being followed? There will be violence from the Angels to which we must say this or that?"

"Meaning," the man called Aziru suggested before Zaki could clarify, "that we won't be followed unless Zaki and Niccolo mucked things up. It's sanctioned, this action. Your troubles won't be from tanks. More likely, from the internecine nature of Roman 'politics,' or from yourselves." And he stood amid a rustle of leaves, which increased as he started plucking boughs from his person. "I'll get back, now. Wouldn't do to be missed. Watch out for Klea—she'll seduce your Alexander if she can. And Hatshepsut. Two women—not enough to share, and both of them royal. And for Niccolo, who'll find a way to win, even if everyone else loses all."

Diomedes caught one of the boughs the Amurrite dropped like sacrifices and brushed in the dirt with it, watching Caesar's driver disappear among the dumped supplies into the Roman part of camp.

"How many have you brought, Gemayel?" Alex-

ander's forty horse and his camp followers had
been waiting at Perdition Pass, as requested. There
wasn't need enough, or trek enough, for much more
army than they had now.

"A dozen Maronites—equal to all those Romans,
and probably to the Macedonian horse, by themselves."

Zaki said nothing, but there was a flash of teeth,
ruddy in Paradise's waxing glow.

This grin, Diomedes took to mean that Gemayel
had more men than he admitted. Too complex,
this venture. Too risky. Like leaving Troizen, like
leaving his Argive domain for reasons he'd never
cared about. Like coming home to treachery and
magic and death.

And black wings.

"Diomedes! *Diomedes!*" The call echoed through
the camp, edged with petulance.

"The oracle. I must go."

"We'll saunter in later," Zaki promised, cheek
by jowl with his contemporary.

Diomedes may have heard the Lebanese mutter,
"His master's voice?" under his breath and Zaki
answer, "That's the only way to play the Macedonian."

Or he may have misheard it.

The Achaean was settling his shield on his arm
and using his long spear as a staff and sorting
through the horses for his own, to get his long
cloak and put it upon his shoulders, his horsehair-
crested helmet for his head.

If he was going to confront an oracle, even a
Hellish one, he wasn't taking any chances on being
under-dressed.

Those going to consult the oracle were all present: Caesar, Alexander, Diomedes, Machiavelli, and
herself.

Kleopatra wouldn't have missed this for all of Asia. Hatshepsut had turned up her nose and sniffed, "*I* am an oracle in my own right. When you come out of there confounded, you'll ask of my wisdom. Perhaps, if you are pleasing in my sight, I will grant your petition."

Klea's luck, holding again.

If only Diomedes would fade away, with Niccolo, it would be as the gods intended: Julius, Alexander and she, before whatever oracle resided in New Cumae.

They had brought their own leaves—bay grew wild here. No one had forgotten how King Tarquin had acquired the Sibylline Books, either, so they had money aplenty—and enough spare Germans to make a juicy sacrifice, if one were required.

The Achaean had the most experience with oracles, Alexander said brightly, his fine, blond head held high, excitement in every line of his body. "You go first through the portal, then, Diomedes, and sanctify this venture." The *basileus* handed the Achaean a sprig of bay, an oxtail wrapped in fat, and a pouch of coins.

Diomedes, offerings in hand, in his long cloak, sandals, and a helmet right off a votive rhyton, took her breath away for a moment: he was antiquity, if any of them were.

He made her feel young and he made her feel special—he was the perfect prefect for Alexander the Great.

She'd gotten out of her khakis for this, into a ceremonial robe, diaphanous and sensual (one that Caesar well knew from private "ceremonies" of their own), and that had stopped poor Antonius in his tracks.

But it was Alexander she wanted to stop. And she would. To clarify this matter of souls and pri-

mogeniture, of descendents and spirits, of *ka, ba,*
and *sahu*—of a legend come to life in Hell.

Alexander's mummy—she wondered if he knew
what had become of it, or how they'd treated it, or
what had resulted from that. Or even knew about
Alexandria and the library.

The whole encounter with him made her wonder if she'd been born into the right time, or just
marking time—if this night wasn't the entire purpose of her life, and of her death, and of her rebirth here.

But Niccolo was sliding inkily through the little
procession headed by Fear and Panic, two German
brothers, and ended with Perfidy and Murder. The
mere sight of Machiavelli brought her back to earth,
to herself and her responsibilities. And to the re-
bellious nature that always dwelled in her.

Poor Antonius, poor kit, who'd wanted to be
part of this. Julius had to make things clear—
both to him, and to Hatshepsut, whose addition
to this party had caused some little argument
among them.

But neither of the above were fit to attend a
sybil, whatever sort of sybil this might be.

The cave they headed toward was by a stream;
water gurgled, with Paradise's ruddy reflection rippled in its course.

In they went, the two Germans stepping aside at
the cave's mouth, taking torches and a halogen
flashlight (Machiavelli's) that stopped working as
soon as Diomedes had passed in the portal and
waved the others by him.

Now, silent, the four Germans left behind, they
trekked on: Machiavelli in the lead, then Caesar,
then herself, the Macedonian behind her (where
she wanted him, seeing what she wanted him to
see), and Diomedes guarding their rear.

None spoke; the occasional pebble rattled. The

cave was low-ceilinged and their torches threw
bended shadows. She cast a look behind as sweat
began to run down her neck, thinking to catch the
look on Alexander's face, but what her eyes focused on was the giant shadow of the Achaean, in
his long cloak and helmet, with his spear and
shield, looking so ancient and portentous. Whither,
this one? And what omen did they need, beyond
the presence of the archetype of passion's wages?

The man whose domain had been all Argolis
watched her, expressionless eyes under fair brows.
Greeks hadn't looked like that in her time. Alexander was as slight as a child next to him.

But it was Alexander who reached out to her
with a sure and kingly smile, misunderstanding
why she'd looked back. "Klea, don't worry. We're
here."

Any other time, with any other man, she might
have argued, set arrogant assumptions to rights.
She didn't. He was Alexander. He was, in his way,
her soul.

They went round a bend, and stopped abruptly,
like court fools, walking up one another's heels.

For the oracle was revealed: on a dais hewn
from living rock, under a domed reach of crystal-
line stone, squatted a woman, naked and huge,
with breasts that rested on her knees.

She was flanked on either side by torches; from
up under her buttocks, a tripod's legs protruded;
she had a monkey's tail wrapped around her neck
and the monkey gibbered and pointed, hanging by
one hand from a sconce in the rock which held a
snapping torch.

The sybil wore a mask.

From its open maw, words issued: "Come forth
and lay sacrifice."

Klea's body hair horripilated; despite her experience with priests and omens, seers of every sort,
her mouth went dry.

Machiavelli and Diomedes, without talk between them, went forward, lay their sacrifices—the oxtail and the dead flashlight—on the bottom step of the dais, then retreated.

Their party, by some unspoken agreement or hidden knowledge of protocol, lined up before the oracle as the monkey, chattering, skittered down, grabbed the flashlight, pounded with it on the dais step and screeched.

Then it threw the flashlight toward the shadowy rear of the cave and, oxtail in its mouth, scrambled up the hewn rock until it dangled from some invisible handhold directly above the seeress's head.

Klea thought she smelled sulphur; it might have been a fart—Julius had been eating pigeon eggs—but there was the smoke . . .

The sibyl said, "Questions, petitioners?"

Alexander said, "Will we find what we seek?"

"When the bird is on the wing, and the black shadows fall," said the seeress in a voice that somehow rang now with power, "you will find yourselves."

Klea was aware that Diomedes muttered something and made a sign, but Machiavelli was stepping forward, saying, "Surely, 'ourselves' are not all we seek. We seek an answer for our question."

Overhead, the monkey was hanging by one arm, his other between his legs, gibbering.

No bay leaves, just non sequiturs. Klea had expected little else. Thinking that the game was at an end, she turned to go.

And drops like rain fell upon her, while from the sibyl's mouth she heard a cackle, and, "Answers, is it, Niccolo? It is, we know, Niccolo. Come hither, and have all the answers to all the questions you'll ever ask."

Klea had wheeled on one foot and now realized why Alexander had suddenly stepped behind her, and why Diomedes had drawn his sword, and where the water came from:

The monkey was urinating on their party, shaking its member as it did so.

Despite this yellow rain, Machiavelli had stepped bravely forward and now, one foot upon the dais' lowest step, was receiving something from the sibyl's fat and pasty hand.

It was a ball, a black ball, about the size of a grapefruit.

Hastily, for Alexander's hand was on her arm, pulling her back from the monkey's spray, and Diomedes was already sidling down the corridor, sword drawn, they made their retreat.

For a while, there was just their labored breathing and the slap of sandals on stone in the corridor. Then Diomedes' torch flickered as the wind in the entrance caught it, and Alexander hustled her outside.

Whereupon she looked pointedly at his hand, still tight on her arm, and said, "Sir, if you don't mind . . . ?"

"Madam, it was your welfare I had in my heart," said the Macedonian with just a touch of coquettishness, and let her go.

Diomedes was already holding the torch low over Machiavelli's prize, but Niccolo, mindful of protocol, was offering it to Caesar: "*Cai Iuli*, this is yours, surely."

And Julius didn't disdain it, but took the black ball and turned it slowly in his hands, examining it, while all the others crowded round.

The ball had a single white marking, which Klea took to be the symbol for infinity, but it might well have been the Arabic numeral "8." But for the "8," the ball was possessed of only one break in its smooth black surface: there was a round, windowlike opening, the size of a coin, made of a glasslike substance, through which liquid could be seen sloshing.

"What *is* it?" Alexander demanded querulously, and up through the liquid to the window of the ball came a die of sorts, with the legend written in English there: *Wait and see.*

Diomedes took a half-step backward. Machiavelli barked a short laugh. Caesar said nothing, but turned the ball thoughtfully in his palms, then held it out to Alexander.

"Here, Basileus, my gift to you—mine and Niccolo's. Ask it another question."

And Julius gave it into Alexander's open palms.

Alexander the Great, in his turn, looked into the window of the black ball, muttering, "What hellish trick is this?" and up to the window's surface floated the die again, this time with the legend, in Greek, *Try again.*

Machiavelli pulled on his long nose as Alexander read his answer aloud, then suggested, "Will the *basileus* ask the eight ball if it is to be trusted?"

And before the Macedonian could repeat Niccolo's question, the die dived and resurfaced. The letters on its face spelled: *no.*

Diomedes was edging away from the party, heading toward the riverbank, Klea saw as all other faces turned her way and Julius' gaze rested on her, fond and yet guarded.

It was Alexander, not Caesar, who said to her, "And you, Egypt? Have you a question for the oracle?"

She pursed her lips, thinking of one, when a shout like *Hai!* came from the Lethe's banks.

All heads turned to where Diomedes had gone.

The Achaean was kneeling by the water's edge, and he called over his shoulder: "Alexander. Here is your oracle, a true one!"

The Macedonian hurried thither, the rest of them following close behind, but it wasn't until he reached the artifact beside which Diomedes knelt that Alexander the Great handed the eight ball to Kleopatra like some toy in which a spoilt prince had lost interest.

Then Alexander, too, knelt down, opposite Diomedes in the rushes, beside a shield five feet long and glittering, a shield never broken or crushed.

And, as legends had described it, the shield was a wonder to see, its whole orb ashimmer with enamel and white ivory and electrum, and aglow with shiny gold and zones of cyanus that were as blue as the Aegean.

In its center was the face of Fear, unspeakable with staring, fire-glow eyes and full white teeth, horrible and daunting. And on Fear's brow was worked Strife, pitiless she who dimmed the senses of men. And also on the shield were wrought Pursuit and Flight and Tumult, and Panic and Slaughter, and deadly Fate was holding a wounded man, a man unscathed, and one already dead.

And there was more on the shield: twelve snakes with blue backs and black jaws, and droves of boar and lion glaring and being furious with one another. And there was blood, enameled blood, from man and beast, upon the shield under the glare of golden Ares with his fleet horses and his spear. And he too was limned in blood.

"It is," breathed Alexander. "It could be no other. It *is*, isn't it, Diomedes?"

Machiavelli and Caesar glanced quizzically at Kleopatra, who shrugged one shoulder.

But the eight ball she held offered up its terse

yes at the same time that Diomedes answered, "The shield of Herakles, Alexander? It is that—there could be no other like it."

The Achaean's face was grim in the torchlight as he faced the Macedonian over the shield. "You asked for an omen. This is omen enough for a thousand Hells."

Then, with Diomedes' help, Alexander hefted up the shield of Herakles, which was as tall as he, and strapped it upon his arm, his face radiant and transformed as if a god had touched him, and headed back to camp, the Achaean by his side.

4.   Passage

Decius Mus brought the cycle to a sliding halt
and grimaced at the stench that went up from the
valley downslope. It was one of Hell's own land-
scapes, a cataract of fire sheeting down among the
rocks on his right, a roaring torrent reeking of
naphtha and sulphur as it plunged hundreds of
feet down a narrow chute to meet a river of clear
water near Mouse's vantage. Until this, Lethe had
a kind of dreamy loveliness, a river keenly beautiful in an unreal and difficult way—difficult because try as one would, one could never quite tell
whether one had seen a fish beneath its surface, or
a bird winging above it, or a patch of reeds standing along the shore. Lethe's very aspect seemed to
shift and change like a trick of the eyes and the
mind, so that it was very easy to go astray. But
here was no illusion: it was Phlegethon pouring
down in a great thunder of fire, and the hell-light
off its surface seemed to go through the very rocks;
Mouse was glad of the goggles he wore, and the
mask and the gloves: his knees and one leg and a
forearm, tight against the suit, picked up the heat;
and the very metal of the cycle was heating quickly:
the steam that boiled up where the rivers met

churned the very air into turbulence above the cauldron of the falls, and the water that poured out of that union, sterile and purged of all life, still steaming, flowed out across a broad flat rife with mists and illusions, becoming the fabled waters of the Styx.

It was as he had feared. Phlegethon wandered, and Lethe was a trap always difficult to pin down to a particular location. And where they went, other difficulties attended, not least of which lay beneath this undermined terrain.

Damn the Macedonian anyway. Communications might have been easier, despite the static Phlegethon kicked up, had the man not diced one of their scarce field phones to bits and pieces. It was risk one of the jeeps on recon, or it was do it the oldfashioned way—give or take the motorcycle. And right now, for that and for the reason that the whole area was unstable, he had to make haste back to the column, which was making its own slow pace from the Center—the Center being the most reliable direction in Hell, which had a few too many directions for a sane mind to tolerate.

He revved up the cycle and spun off as quickly as he had come, with the heat of Phlegethon at his back and the wind coming against him, to carry the sulphur stench away from him. But he rode with some care whenever he topped some hillock or skirted a larger hill for a downslope, because Lethe had a way of turning up where you least wanted it and never where you thought you had left it; and Phlegethon, like some fiery serpent, threw its meanders and its sulphurous oxbows wide across the landscape.

The Macedonian wanted a hole. And here, indisputably, was such a hole which led to other parts of Hell, but not such as would tempt many travelers. This one led deep, deep into Hell's strange geography, and where such old lava tubes as this opened up, where Phlegethon had chewed up the land in its strange way and where Lethe had made it unstable, there were often visitants.

The cycle roared and whined through a climb, popped over a hillock and landed on a long sandy stretch full of jolts: Mouse slewed it round another sandy hummock and kept going. It was a good twenty miles back to the column, and rough country where Phlegethon's course changes had chewed and melted the rocks, leaving naphtha ponds and springs, and in places, treacherously thin crust. There was no safe way to the cauldron the first time in, except by aerial reconnaissance they (for several reasons) did not have: one never knew where Phlegethon had gotten to during any given day; and there was only one safe way out after he had found what he was looking for, which was to keep to the tracks he himself had made.

And that held yet *another* hazard, that his course became predictible, which was not a good thing in Hell's wider, wilder reaches.

He shifted and turned, and ran consistently where his eyes had first told him was likeliest the safest ground, and where now his eyes picked out the wheel marks he had made, the engine-sound echoing off the higher rocks that lay jumbled hereabouts, till a narrow chute down a hillside took him onto the firmer earth and scattered grass that marked Lethe's ascendancy over Phlegethon, the boundary where too much change ran into far too little change. The stench of hot stone and sulphur that penetrated the dustmask gave way to the heavy, grass-scented air of the wide meadows, where wild poppies grew and bloomed, and the cycle tires tore bloodred petals and pale green leaves to fragments and showered them behind him.

There was need of such haste. The day was getting on toward afternoon, the cycle motor droned on with its own somnolent consistency, which Mouse punctuated with spurts and deliberate jolts. It sounded distant, like bees in summer sun. It was very easy to let attention wander—

The wheels seemed to have heavier going, as if they were in soft ground, the pitch of the motor changed and deepened. "Haaaiii," Mouse yelled, thin sound in that shift of landscape, and veered off and slewed an S-course down a hill, at the edge of his control. Speed itself was illusory. The earth at his right lifted up in great chunks and there was, if one looked (but he did not) a crawling movement there, a swarming of brown and gray amid the green.

Other figures loomed up on the hillcrest ahead of him. He shook his head and blinked behind the goggles and shook his head again at the ragged shapes, a living wall of them.

He veered, slewed down yet another hillside and saw (another blink and struggle to focus) the rivershore of Lethe, where green meadow ran down to the still waters—Lethe never seemed to move. It only threw its slow coils across the landscape, and turned and twisted in memory.

Mouse shot down that slope and along the shore, up another rise and right through a dozen liches who made a wall of themselves. The cycle bucked and pitched and slewed as the wheels went over a carpet of bodies, the wheel went sideways unexpectedly, and Mouse and the cycle parted company, the heavy machine bound downslope toward the level riverbank, while Mouse entertained a similar trajectory, the cycle tearing up gouts of dirt and spinning as it went, trying its perverse best to entangle its metal bars and projections and its crushing weight with its rider.

They ended together, the cycle coming to a halt as it hit the flat, and Mouse kept traveling a painful extra second, where his body slid up hard against the hollow between the turned front wheel and the engine. The helmet saved his head as the cycle made a vengeful extra bounce and came down dead-stopped, digging a metal pedal into his back. He gasped a dusty mouthful of air through the filtering mask, squirmed and edged up, his legs twisted painfully, his hands finding no leverage that did not hurt—and saw through the goggles a nightmare of ragged bodies gathering themselves up on the hill and starting downward.

The progress was much slower than Alexander would have liked, considering the capabilities of the jeeps, and it was no place for a king, riding deep within the column while the hulking physeters slouched out to the fore of the column virtually obscured in the wind and the dust they kicked up. At rest, they sighed down to earth like expiring pachyderms; in motion they flattened the grass and whirled up a stinging concomitant cloud of twigs and dust and grass and smallish pebbles. It was not just the horses who fled the sight and the sound and the stink of them: no sane man afoot came near one til the roar had stopped and the wind died down. That meant their column was strung out, which he ill-liked. And Zeus! the racket. He could see them now, crawling out to the fore and lumbering up the hills, their long, deadly snouts probing the air ahead of them as if in fact they sniffed and read the air. Behind them came the jeeps, which growled and ground and bucked their way across the pathless land ahead of their respective units—not a road to be had, Julius had complained: even Gaul, Julius had said, had had roads, and good ones.

Gaul (France?) lay (had lain?) northward of the Pillars of Herakles; beyond those Pillars the sea widened and led to new worlds, all of which was of interest: the *basileus* had always found maps of interest. His tutor Aristotle had talked about such lands beyond the mountains of Thrace; tales of the Hyperboreans were in the lore of the dwellers on the Don, who maintained a tenuous contact with Macedon; and most of all in the lore of Epirus, which was his mother Olympias' purview—Olympias of the snakes and the rites in some of which she had initiated him, and the most of which he had gladly evaded: the king-sacrifice was not that far removed among Epirotes, and betimes at night he waked sweating and hearing his mother singing to her snakes and her Goddess. So anything which smacked of Epirote lore touched deep with him, and this land of France (Gallia?) to which Julius compared this landscape seemed a dark and mysterious place—he suspected oak groves like Dodona, whose trees grew since the foundation of the world, and whose deadfalls were sacred and sought after; he suspected obscure rites and kings dancing the fatal circle with Maenads, clawed hands and wild eyes and flashing limbs, bare breasts, the stain of blood—

He blinked hell-sky and grasslands clear again, looked beside him where the inching column of infantry walked beside them, Romans who did not, Maccabee had told him, fight in the phalanx, but in cohorts, quincunx pattern, staggered rows of three ranks—hence the smaller, rectangular, curving shields; efficient, Maccabee said, in terrain where obstacles like trees and rocks might split a shieldwall: each unit of a century under its officer, each three centuries forming a maniple, each three maniples a cohort, of which they had two—of the 10th Legion, which Maccabee called most devoted to Julius. Each maniple and each cohort had its standard and standard-bearer, each century its centurion, and the Firstlance, the seniormost centurion of the entire legion governing the senior centurion of the second cohort and all the subcenturions of the other ten centuries; while the cohorts were both commanded by the Companion Marcus Antonius and the *strategos* Scaevola, who rode in a jeep the other side of the column. Alexander saw these things and studied them, intrigued at the implications of function, intrigued by the implications of a soldiery drilled and trained to function with space between the members of the line, unlike the farmer-trademan soldiers of Greece, who provided the massive bulk of a phalanx, with no more training than to face forward and stay there, holding a section of the long spear that many men held in front of them. This soldiery, trained and drilled to stand separate, was a different matter, came of a different, more constant training, a different breed of state and politics. Republic, the Romans called it, a hybrid of *monarchia* and *demokratia*. Here were no long, group-held spears—just the javelins. Three of them. The shields could interlock, but the swords were useless in that formation, the spears with no more than a single man's strength behind them. Never mind the firearms that some of them carried, rifles slung to their backs along with the shields which they had in leather covers; the small, crestless helmets were slung over shoulders tied by the ring at the top to a similar ring on the top of the band-jointed armor. No greaves, just heavy leather sandals and leather socks laced well up the leg. It was an army suited to traveling long distances. It was an army which walked in step, and which with its precise intervals and precise moves, looked like one monstrous creature snaking along the track the physeters flattened in the grass and the jeeps trampled.

But the concept of so many officers, such independent functions—Alexander watched this strange moving creature with interest, with thoughts flickering behind his eyes, how it would have stood at the Indus against the elephants, how it would have done at Gaugamela against the Persian's serial assaults. He had made innovations in his day. He had had officers to rely on, and he had increased the mobility and the flexibility of the phalanx, using the cavalry. But he had not conceived a thing so precise as this, with its iron regimens that dictated the precise angle at which shields and javelins were disposed at rest stops, in each case in easy reach, but altogether lacking any randomness. It was like the jeep, which had a tendency once in motion, to develop a rhythm to its workings and even to its bounces. It seemed to him that the world, whatever had happened to it, had gotten very strange and full of such rhythms to replace the randomness and the beauty of the horses and the bright armor. There was an attraction in them, like the beat of unheard drums; there was seduction in such power.

But the seat of this machine was not a saddle a man could get used to; the toss and pitch however rhythmical never forecast the jolts that snapped the teeth together. In one part of him he wanted never to have seen this machine at all; in another he saw the speed with which they could move, and their tirelessness, and knew that they were better than horses without *being* better than horses, the way the stinking physeters were better than heavy cavalry, and had their own sinister attraction.

It was a bit more change in a short time than he had ever wanted to deal with, lost as he had been in his hills and sulking in his tents and hoping (O

Zeus) that among so many dead he might find certain dead that he longed for.

Fate gave him none of those. Having been a man who loved his comrades he found all too few of them; and most of the Macedonians with him had been common men, and only faces to him, in all his army. There came the time he would have longed even for feckless Darius to sit with over a cup or two; and even to see his father's limping figure shambling into his camp to curse him for a bastard and a traitor. But none of these things had happened. There was only solitude, and the companionship of one and another heroes who had stayed a while and left him, some by death and some by those affairs which drew souls apart after a long, long time, just of slow disaffection with the tedium of the place. Some he had driven away, when they inflicted too much insanity on him. And that Maccabee would go, someday, he did not doubt. He was even jealous of the little Israeli; and the gun which Maccabee had taken up, secured there by Maccabee's leg, was like a prophecy of future desertion—seduction by the desire for these strange and terrible engines of war.

So he had been right, that Maccabee was drifting from him. And it angered him that he thought enough of Maccabee to leave his hills and to come to this place and to be ignorant in front of these people with their belching and grumbling machines and their strange oracles, but that Maccabee was leaving him by slow degrees—that ached in his soul. He knew beyond a doubt that he could master these things: he could hear his old tutor at his left shoulder (another presence he had never found again, and longed for) telling him of foreign things and arguing with him that the right questions made right answers, and that all humans were rational, at bottom, and moved by predictable tides.

Has then, my old tutor, the whole cosmos such a rhythm as these engines and do these and our hearts and the whole universe have such a beat that we never hear until we listen to these engines? Is there such a thing in all machines, even that cursed gun of Judah's, and in the oracles, and is Judah right and am I wrong who cannot believe in these things?

The Persian was a fool, who played at war by old theories at Gaugamela.

Then I brought him something new. It was not Thermopylae again and it was not Persian against Persian or Persian against barbarian. We did not let him encircle us. Fool that he was, he was thinking lines and I thought in direction of force. A phalanx pushes and turns.

But what are these cohorts but a human cavalry, to strike by squadrons? I invented such things. This is what I begat, this human machine.

I left my empire to the strongest. Was it finally this man Caesar? And who is this fool woman, this little blond Egyptian, who claims to be my heir? And the other, Zeus and Hecate! the blackhaired she-pharaoh. There was no such creature I knew of and I lived long after her day and knew the king-lists of Egypt. But the others know her, and can they know less? Can history have turned inside out and are we all mad?

My mother was such a woman as Hatshepsut. She cost my father an eye, she and her snakes and her rituals. Priestess-queens and year-kings. Beware this one and drink no cups at her hand, who whispers to spirits and listens to them. She is Fate-led and numinous and she dances to the beat of these machines: beware this one and dance no dances with her. She wants something and it is not what others want.

For the rest of these—Antonius has the stench of disaster about him; and this onehanded Scaevola, a boy hardly older than I was at Chaeronea, yet I was

*formidable then and so might this one be: older dead
than I, and armed with a gun—*

*I might demand one of these things. It would
please Judah.*

*But where then are my omens? Can I take to these
oil-smelling things and not lose my omens?*

Ah, Diomedes of the wise counsel— He turned in
the seat and looked behind him, where Diomedes
trudged at the hoplites' pace, a little behind, dog-
gedly bearing his great shield and suffering for it
at the pace these machines set, and these small-
statured legionaries held, in their light armor.
Diomedes shone in the hell-light, all ruddy-bronze
and ruddy gold, the light flashing from shield and
spear: he went in a haze of dust, for the passage of
so many wheels and so many feet behind the
physeters stripped the land down and bared it to
the wind and the tramp of horses and others. And
there seemed monumental tragedy about him and
something forlorn and still greater than the Macedonians beside him. He declined the jeeps. Perhaps he did not believe in them, whereas the
Germans, in their own haze of dust and their own
pale strangeness, walked near him, bearing their
guns and their spears—no such thing would Diomedes touch.

*But are you wise, Diomedes? In this are you sure,
and was I always wrong? I compelled the Pythia to
give me good prophecy. But had she her revenge?*

How trust any prophetess?

*And men who See the future are always unsighted
in this world, like Teiresias, like Oedipus.*

The figure hazed and vanished in a cloud of
dust, reappeared like a vision and vanished again
like a shadow.

"What is it?" Maccabee asked.

Alexander blinked and blinked again, for a moment having seen the shadow of wings in that

dust. And turned about again. "Diomedes," he said.
And saw in that glance that passed by Maccabee—
something of doubt. And perhaps of anger. He did
not glance back, not to catch whatever followed it,
but stared through the dirty glass, and glanced
instead at Zaki, at the little man he trusted only so
far as Maccabee governed him. Zaki would have
wished to be with Machiavelli, but he had forbidden that. The man was Maccabee's, but even that
was marginal. He would be someone else's with
equal zeal. The Great King of all Persia and all
Egypt had not ruled long, but of conspiracy he had
seen all too much. And Zaki reeked of it.

Why have you brought him? he wondered, of
Maccabee. And recalled that he had tossed the
oracle to Kleopatra as a gesture; she kept it like
some trinket, and Julius permitted it, all of which
vexed him: he was not accustomed to unrequited
generosity. Such a gift should have meant a gift in
return. But the Roman let this campfollowing queen
keep it, which perplexed him and distressed him,
and made him know well he would not be twice
generous to ingrates.

*Why have you needed this little spy, Judah? And
why do you keep the gun and prefer it? And where
are you going, Judah, and where are you leading me?
This escaping is not to my taste.*

*How many fours-of-years have you planned this?
And how does a god so weaken, to go into a trap and
know it?*

He did look at Maccabee then, turning his head,
and saw Maccabee looking backward, his arm on
the back of the seat and his hair blowing in the
dusty wind. He almost spoke.

But a small, faint sound came to him, a sharp
report which brought Maccabee's attention around
in the same instant.

"Gunfire," the Israelite said.

"Madness," Alexander said. The sound came from over the hills. The column was strung out farther than he had ever liked to let a column extend, a vulnerable sluggish creature with its physeter-cavalry out probing the way and its long middle of Romans and his own Macedonians, with the horse cavalry; and the noisy trucks and the whole baggage train over the hill to their rear. And the first of the physeters had just dived over a rise in the land so that the fore of their column was also out of contact.

"Is this the way this Julius won his battles?" he wondered, and snapped at Zaki: "Over, over!"— with a motion toward the column. "Curse you, over to the cavalry!"

Zaki veered. Alexander leaped to his feet in the jeep and shouted orders at the horsemen: "Ride to the rear, attack, attack, warn the hindmost, close up the column!"

"We have radio," Zaki objected, and steered onehanded while he jounced and bounced the jeep and meddled with another of those mechanical oracles. He began to speak into it the while he drove, furiously calling on his deity as Alexander snatched at the wheel which directed the jeep. "Ahead!" he cried, and caught himself as the vehicle lurched on one side and tried to throw them out. Zaki dropped the black piece of the radio he was holding and used both hands on the wheel and the stick, sharply veered again and brought the jeep under control.

The soft, far report of the shots continued as the jeep roared and bucked and plunged ahead to the front of the column. Alexander kept his feet: it was no worse than chariots; but Maccabee got up and grabbed onto his arm. "Get down!" Maccabee cried into the wind and the engine noise. "You make too clear a target."

He shook the admonition off, kept his footing with one knee in the seat, and yelled ahead as they came up on the rear of the foremost jeep: "Form up!" he shouted at this self-named heir of his. "What are you doing?"

"Cavalry to the fore," Julius yelled back, with a furious wave of his arm. "Watch our damned rear! And keep your head down!"

That jeep sped off, spitting dust from its wheels, while the little queen ducked her head into a helmet and the driver did things to his jeep which the traitorous Zaki declined to match despite his passenger's evident desire to speak further with this upstart Roman.

Alexander found his mouth open and clamped it shut. *Zeus!* was his only clear thought; the rest a muddle of rage and realization that there were witnesses to this insult; and the sure and infuriating realization that racing after that jeep meant a line further disordered. Julius took the machine-cavalry and left him the infantry and the baggage, this unwieldy, unwanted clutter of men and horses which had done exactly the predicted thing and drawn unwanted attention down on them.

"Back," he yelled at Zaki. And did *not* sit down, even when the jeep executed a sharp turn and headed back along the lines. When he looked back, wind whipping at his hair and half-blinding him with the ends of it, all the great physeters had turned their noses in the same direction and started off as if they had all been part of the same body. The oracle-radio in the jeep was popping and snapping with some voice which Zaki ignored, using both hands as he was. While Maccabee had his rifle in his hands, and the gunfire continued.

There was an endless supply of targets. Unfortunately there was not an endless supply of ammunition, and the liches which poured up out of nowhere were not creatures long on brains. Some of them wore clothing, or bits and pieces of clothing of varied ages; some wore nothing but their own mummified skin, their eyes dark and hollow, the dried flesh drawn back from their teeth, their clawed hands clutching weapons they rarely fired—or perhaps they lacked ammunition. They only poured ahead in a living wave, generally heedless of fire, and Mouse, having extricated himself from the cycle and gotten round behind it, swept the front rank in a fire as rapid as served to confuse them, while occasional bullets spanged off the body of the cycle. The smell of gasoline said the tank was punctured. The tires were blown.

But there was hesitation among the liches, after the first wave. Perhaps they realized after the first several shots the nature of the enemy they faced; perhaps it was blind instinct, that warned them that those Mouse took, were damned to a deeper hell. It was the bargain he had made with the infernal—those he killed, and anyone who might send *him* in his turn to a deeper hell, all of them were bound for the nethermost and most terrible levels of this afterworld.

But unlike his death on earth he had a rifle in his hands, no simple sword and shield that necessitated a rush across the field. He let the enemy come to him, and mowed rank after rank in calm efficiency, regretting—if he were to fall—the company of old friends, the way he regretted his son, lost to the nether hells on similar terms, until the powers in this place should relent. He had infinite patience, had Decius Mus, and hoped, if he hoped for anything in Hell, that if he died here he might find his son somewhere below. Though he had no particular confidence that this would be so in a place so large and many-leveled. Patience ruled every burst of fire. Careful aim. If a man sold his soul he was careful to get correct change, in all the enemies he could possibly take with him and the maximum damage he could do.

Last clip. He reloaded with an economical move and blasted the liches that came pouring toward him at pointblank range, showered with bits and dry pieces of them as the bullets smashed ribs and spines and bony limbs, ricocheting inside a body til they did far more damage than the entry hole. For a moment the oncoming liches flinched, but the press of those behind shoved the ranks forward, and he mowed them down as fast as he could fire until the wings of the advance closed about him from either flank and came at his back. He swept left, trying to prevent this, but bony hands grasped at his sleeves, and grappled with the discharging rifle. A lich's arm went about his neck, others about his arms, his waist, and he laid about him with the rifle butt and the barrel, trying to get room to fire—got off one more burst as they fell with him, and poured over him, bony knees gouging and nails tearing to break his grip on the rifle.

The ground shook and a pressure wave hit his ears. Clods and bits of grass and gods knew what rained down: he was blind at the moment, trying to protect his eyes from their claws as a second and third and fourth explosion hit and rocked the ground.

The liches shrieked, the first sound they had made. And the press of bodies over him thinned, and liches disengaged and scrambled in retreat. He grappled with the last one and got a booted foot into its gut and shoved, trying to get himself clear room and to recover his rifle, which another was stealing. He grabbed the stock and the barrel and kicked out a second time, which spun it free;

and he swept it round and blew the last lich to its destined slot in a nether hell, before equilibrium deserted him and he sprawled on his side by the cycle, his face and arms and shoulders stung by wind and pebbles, his ears full of the sound of the aircushioned tank that was hammering out a steady fire as it came up the rise within a few yards of him.

Prudently then he rolled onto his face and covered his head and made as low a profile as he could. Julius had come after him. So he stayed alive in this hell a while longer. He had no hope then to find his son—yet. But to a man who had forsworn all human contact, all love, all hope for his own soul, in exchange for his comrades and his city, to be loved was infinitely precious; and this rescue very welcome in its own right.

So when the tanks had passed like thunder on the earth, spewing bits of lich from their skirts along with pebbles and wisps of grass and red poppies, he gathered himself up to wait for the jeeps, leaning on his rifle in his exhaustion and somewhat sheepish at the sight he knew he presented, all bloodied and scratched and stinking of dust and tombs, not mentioning the damage to the cycle.

He waited there while Julius' substitute driver whipped the jeep alongside and Julius and Klea looked him up and down.

Then he lifted an arm toward the direction the tanks had taken. "Call them back," he said hoarsely. "The juncture's there."

Aziru did that, using the radio; while Julius clambered out and stood staring at the damaged cycle and the carpet of bodies.

"Sorry," Mouse said. "I ran headon into it."

Julius had one of his thinking-looks. And Klea

got out, holding the black ball of the oracle in her hand. "It says," said Klea, *"Have a nice day."*

It was a camp of Roman pattern, *vallum fossaque*, deep trench round about its perimeters and the dirt from that trench flung up for a rampart behind which they pitched their tents—the Romans dug with a vengeance, asking no questions, the centurions pacing off the measure and the soldiers of the cohorts plying shovels from the baggage vehicle which held their tents, while still another vehicle drove into the perimeters of the square, let down its sides and let the cooks start to their work.

The physeters took up their guard on the perimeters, snouts facing outward, their weight resting on the ground instead of on the wind. They were quiet finally, just a little popping and pinging from the heat, and the inevitable stink of oil.

In the midst of this confusion Alexander ordered his own tent pitched central to the camp; at which the baggage truck had to be unloaded, and the bluff, squarefaced quartermaster turned red and gnawed his lip and finally stalked off to ask a superior.

Alexander stood and fairly shook with outrage at this latter despite. "I'll find Caesar," Maccabee said. "These are Romans. They understand only a chain of command."

"You will not." Alexander rounded on the cluster of Macedonians and the Germans, Perfidy and Murder among them, and swept a gesture toward the baggage truck where the tents were stored. "Take those tents out. Here." Another gesture toward the center of the developing camp, a flat trampled area with legionaries digging on all four sides, a steadily lengthening mound of earth at each corner. "Put my tent there. The largest one. In the center."

The legionary driver opened the door and got out, looking frightened and angry both. And another, his companion, went out the other side and ran for it. "Here," the driver objected as the Macedonians started round the truck. "At least don't throw things about." But he shut up quickly when Perfidy leveled his gun; and stood there by the front wheel of the truck while Macedonians swarmed up into the vehicle and started throwing down bundles of canvas and stakes.

Alexander watched, arms folded, while the heap grew. "That one," he said, as a massive bundle hit the ground among the smaller, common-soldier lumps of canvas. Large poles followed, rattling and ringing as they hit and bounced, while the driver, held with the barrel of Perfidy's rifle against his ribs, watched and glowered.

Then Marcus Antonius came striding up with the redfaced officer, the latter out of breath.

"If the Great King would wait—"

"The Great King is tired of waiting," Maccabee said. "The *basileus* will take precedence in this camp. *His* tent will take centermost place. His troops will occupy the central position in the camp. You will appoint aides to see to his comfort."

Marcus Antonius bit his lip, and looked from Macedonians and Germans to Alexander, and wisely moved carefully when he hooked one thumb in the side of his belt and thought the situation over. "I'll speak to Caesar," Antonius said. "We'll arrange something."

"You will arrange what I say," Alexander declared. "No less."

"It is," Julius said to the small gathering in his own (offcentered) tent, "a problem. Diplomacy."

Marcus Antonius was there, Scaevola and the centurions of the 10th, Hatshepsut and Kleopatra and Mouse, a Mouse all scratched and streaked with merthiolate and in a couple of places having a stitch or two. Mouse was easy. Mouse was always easy. It was Scaevola whose countenance was darkest: his millennia of death had not improved the lad's temper, and Scaevola had lost that hand in defiance of another king—that this one had happened to have claimed the world was of no great moment to Scaevola, who refused to title anyone.

"So where do we go with this Macedonian?" Scaevola asked, old Roman and without courtesies. The first legion ever to cross outside Roman lands had sat down on its collective butt in the highway and demanded its officers explain why and where they thought they were going, and followed only when they were convinced it was necessary. And Scaevola was of that age and older, despite his boyish face. "And why?"

"Because," said Antonius, "this Macedonian king is ambitious. And he means trouble. But he also has sources that threaten the peace. So we go along with his madness. What matter what outrageous things he does? He was a great man. But he has the worst blindness of the Old Dead. Humor him."

"He has courage," Mouse said. "And pride."

"The men know," the *primipilus* Baculus said, from where he stood among the lesser centurions, muscular arms crossed across a considerable chest. He spat a bit of something he was chewing, aside onto the carpets. A wind blew through Julius' tent and fluttered the lamps. "Like the damn Aedui prince, ain't it? Be nice to the locals. We done it before. Ain't no difference."

"He's no barbarian," Julius said, offended in his heart of hearts, at this comparison of Alexander with the barbaric Gaulish prince once their ally. But he remembered the field phone. "He always excelled in his adaptability. But you're right. It's like the Aedui. Except this: he's fit to command. You'll take his orders if he's in your perimeter."

Antonius coughed, shifted his feet. "Not with the legions, Caesar. Respectfully. He's not fit."

"You'll act as his lieutenant. Dammit, *Antoni*, I have the tanks and the damn mobile units, you and Scaevola can damn well put a little interpretation on his orders when they come down the line, you know what you're doing and so do all of you—" with a look at the twelve centurions. "Just translate it. What the hell's the navy do when they have a landsman admiral? Same thing here."

"Damn dangerous," Scaevola said. "He won't take advantage of our mobility. Stand and shove, that's what he'll do. Any phalanx-fighter—And we have those damned Macedonians. Where do we *put* them?"

"We had better put the Germans clear to the flank," Antonius said, "the damned berserkers'll run right under our javelins and right in front of our rifles."

"Macedonians won't run," Kleopatra said. "It's hard enough for them to stand our pace. They'll walk in. Like us. But they won't advance with any coordination if their line starts to straggle."

Scaevola sniffed.

"A single disruptor," Hatshepsut said, "and they're with the Undertaker. Arrange an accident. Then we've only Alexander to deal with. He and his companions know what we want to know. So we take it."

"Tttt," Julius hissed. "Friendly fire? Not in my ranks."

"Scruples, scruples. Let the Undertaker sort 'em out. They're an encumbrance. We ought to be rid of the clutter, then he'll *have* to deal with us and mind his manners." Hatshepsut flung up a hand in disgust—never used to republican forms and staff meetings. But she learned. Like a sponge. "Or let him do what he likes with the damn Macedonians and that ancient Greek. And the Germans. Send them in first, if they want the glory. Damn fools deserve what they get. Then we mop it up with the tanks and the legionaries. And get their king back in one piece if we can. Let him *see* what he's up against, then he'll fall in line."

There was a muttering among the centurions. Approval. Hatshepsut was a known quantity with them, and the legions in Hell had some of them marched there behind a female general or a queen or two, Kleopatra not the least and not the only, and Antonius' Roman wife being another. Not mentioning Agrippina and the marines.

Julius listened to all the advice, paced back and forth a moment and then looked at Antonius. "Do what I said, *Antoni*." Darkly. And there came a silence, because when the commander took that attitude he was thinking; and the commander was better than any of the advice he was getting, and knew more than any of the rest, much of which he never said. Julius knew their attitudes and cultivated his own mystique.

"We let Alexander have his way," Julius said slowly. "What did we learn from him, but how to let subject nations have their ways? What's a little courtesy—so long as it doesn't interfere with our operations. Do what I said. Take your orders from Antonius and Scaevola. The tanks are her majesty's. Depend on them. We don't know what we'll meet tomorrow. Depend on each other. That's all we can do. Beware this Maccabee."

And he thought: *And beware Antonius.* But he

did not say that. There were forces aligned against them and he did not know which.

Beside him, Kleopatra sat in one of the few chairs and turned the eight ball in her small, pale hand, obtaining messages some of which were nonsensical and some of which bespoke some Instrumentality; or worse, some Authority.

It was certain that there was more than coincidence operating lately, that had landed Marcus Brutus in the house and stolen and killed Hadrian and set Rameses II, at least the last that they knew, at the top of the Pentagram. Now Alexander was lured out of his hills, and this mad Old Greek Diomedes came out of Hell's far reaches, and Tiberius turned cooperative, while the omens were confused and the liches rose out of nether hells to harass them in a journey which led (he was certain) nowhere except ambush.

There were agencies at work and whether they were agencies of his own alignment or something utterly different he did not know. It was only certain that certain communications flowed along their route, where Mettius Curtius had disposed certain of the cavalry at intervals, equipped with field phones, which in turn patched right into Hell's phone system. Niccolo was not here tonight. He was with the communications truck, making sure that certain messages got to their destinations, making sure that Augustus was more aware of what happened out here than Augustus wanted to be.

And Augustus would then put the matter to a certain Italian with his computers and his numbers.

It was (if he let himself think on the old days) eerie to think of picking up a phone and calling all the way from the battlefield to home, in view of civilized New Hell with its pavements and its parklands and its suburban neighborhoods. But that was precisely what Niccolo did periodically. And it was more than communications equipment that Niccolo had in that truck.

Mostly Julius regretted his position with Alexander, which was growing more and more tangled, regretted it for its necessary deceptions. Most of all, he felt himself disarmed when he came face to face with Alexander, and knew then what sorcery he worked on others. He dismissed his meeting in profound melancholy, the centurions scattering out to their business, his own household seeking their separate tents.

"Come," Hatshepsut said to Mouse, and took him by the wrist, "they've botched up those scratches. I've got something in my tent."

It was certain that she did. And that Kleopatra would not be there for a while. If Hatshepsut had come round to Mouse, it was a dark cold mood indeed; it was stranger yet that Mouse went with her without demur. But perhaps he had come close enough to the Undertaker today that any bed other than that one was welcome.

Julius looked last at Klea and at Antonius. "Get to the troops," he said to Antonius. And that left him Klea.

She turned the eight ball to him, this bauble that had not left her hands. *"Be careful,"* it said.

"Damn him!" Alexander cried, and hurled the goblet he held. Aziru flinched and turned aside, though it was not himself the Great King aimed at. And Maccabee quickly moved to set his hand on Alexander's shoulder and to wave a surreptitious signal to the Amurrite to clear out. "Damn him!" Alexander said again, his eyes suffused with tears. "This is what they think! Damn them all!"

"Alexander." Maccabee bent down and held tight to the king's trembling arm, while Perfidy and

Murder glowered ominously from their guard position by the tentflap, and held their rifles in the crooks of their arms as they had held them ever since Caesar's substitute driver had come into the tent. There was loyalty, blind and complete. But that was not the Romans' mind. Alexander thrust off Maccabee's grip and flung himself to his feet, staggered there in the haze of the wine.

"Let them follow us," Alexander muttered. "Let them think what they like. Damned *fools!*" With a pass of his hand across his eyes. He had seen too much this day, how the great physeters made a plowed field of a grassy hill, how a single man with a gun had held off an army; and Maccabee had his gun, there, in the corner of the tent. He saw it there, and went and snatched it up.

"Alexander!"

"Show me this." He treated it as a spear, and kept the point averted when he held it in his hands and thrust it out at Maccabee. "Show me this thing!"

Maccabee came carefully and positioned his hands on it, showed him the aiming of it. And thrust a finger behind his on the trigger, at which Alexander jerked the gun and Maccabee contested it. "Alexander. You're drunk. Do you understand me? A shot will bring the Romans. Do you want that?"

"They called my father a barbarian. The Greeks laughed at him." He jerked and this time the gun came free. He staggered again. "I am not my father," he said, and swung wildly as Maccabee made a grab for the gun.

It came to dead center on a startled, small figure in the doorway of the tent, Perfidy and Murder instantly alert in that direction.

"No!" Maccabee cried. And Alexander stared at his self-named heir at gunpoint.

She held out a small black ball in both her hands, this diminutive woman in soldier's khaki and with blond hair immaculately waved. Her large eyes were afraid. None of the rest of her showed it.

"Alexander," she said in her quietest, softest voice, "I've brought it back to you. I thought that was what you meant. See, it tells me *Yes*."

He slowly, slowly lowered the Uzi. And shoved it at Maccabee, who took it. For a long moment no one moved, then he walked over and took up the wine pitcher. He held out his hand. Perfidy understood and put a cup in it; and he filled it and set the pitcher down before he looked at the so-named Egyptian.

"Yes to what?"

"I wouldn't know." She came closer and offered the black ball to his hand. He did not take it. It was Maccabee who rescued it. "Julius wants to talk to you. On a delicate matter."

"Does he?" Alexander drank off half the cup, and swallowed hard after it. There was a haze about all his vision and it had overtones of red and black. "And he sends his queen. How generous. Does he want me to come to his tent?"

"I'll bring him," the little woman said.

"You will not." Alexander used that voice which carried over battlefields, and the little queen backed up instinctively. "You will tell him," Alexander said, "that I will take command of this expedition, and that I have seen stranger things than cohorts. And defeated them."

"That you have," Kleopatra said. And set her hands on hips and walked past Maccabee, and turned and looked at the Germans and again at Maccabee before she glanced at Alexander. "Julius has a part of your soul. You might trust him. But you had rather lean to other counsel."

"Get out of here, woman."

"I would go," Maccabee advised her. "Now."

"That you would," Kleopatra said. *"Kai oida ton tou Kleitou thanaton. Hephaistion to onoma mou."*

"Kakomantis!"

"Curse me as you like. I was Hephaistion."

He drained off the rest of the cup and set it down. "Get out."

"Is that my answer? Kleitos turned his back on you and you killed him. Will you kill me too? After you spent so much to send me to heaven?"

"Out!"

"I have a part of his soul. Patrokles, Kleopatra, and the beloved of the Craftsman-god. *Kai su Achilleos?* We are very old, both. I could tell you such things as Hephaistion could have told you. Did he not always tell you you were too rash?"

"Out of here, witch!" He snatched at the sword which hung from the tent-pole, and caught it up sheathed as it was. "Damn you, go back to your lover and let him dance with you. I've no need of you."

"Alexander." She held out her hands, both, and for a moment his heart went cold and numb. So Hephaistion would do. But the gods could not be so twisted as this.

"Out!" he cried again.

"Trust the centurions," she said. "You're not dealing with a phalanx. Julius loves you. He gives you command, to let you surprise them with your brilliance. He knows what they do not, that you are still what you were. Don't fail him. He risks so much for your sake. And I do. Because of what we are."

She turned and left then, giving him her back. Kleitos had made that mistake. But he stood with the sword in hand, trembling.

"Liar," he muttered to himself. "Liar . . ." And

shoved again as Maccabee laid a light hand on his arm.

"Many times a liar. Caesar is adept at deceptions and this is Ptolmaeus' get, Ptolemaeus the Fluteplayer they called her father, the Fool of Egypt. You had no heirs."

"Where is Diomedes?"

"Out with the men. Shall I call him?"

"I have no need. No need." Alexander stretched out his hand and blinked Maccabee's face into focus again. And walked over to the side of the tent where, tall and venerable and gilt, the shield of Herakles stood. It stood in a haze, the way Diomedes had come like an omen from the river. It was cool beneath his fingertips when he traced its maze of designs, the deeds of gods and men. It sang to him in Homeric accents.

No one in the tent moved. It was the way with the Great King, that no one dared disturb his thinking. Even when he was drunk. The woman had not knelt to him. She was Macedonian, so she claimed, and his Macedonians had taken kneeling very hard in Persia, creating a schism between his army and his subjects.

Hephaistion had done it, laughing. Everything was easy for Hephaistion. In those days he had had his friend and Bucephalus had leapt under him like a colt; and Kleitos had saved him from an axe stroke that had split his helmet—

Kleitos, Kleitos cursing him and his foreign ways, and the anger and the wine muddling him when he rose up to peg the spear close by Kleitos' retreating back, there at the doorway of the banquet. But wine and too many battles confused him, and a soldier's hand was instinctual and, O Zeus, all too accurate against a moving target.

Kai oida ton tou Kleitou thanaton.

I saw Kleitos die.

He plunged his face into his hands and stood there a moment, before the shield of Herakles.

Then he turned and held out one hand to Maccabee, who was not Hephaistion, in this place which was not Persia. "Show me this gun," he said. "And tell me again about the cohorts."

Zaki watched all the coming and going, the quiet tread of the Amurrite on his way back to Caesar's jeep, the approach and then the departure of Kleopatra. And he cast a curious glance at the communications truck, out of which Machiavelli had stirred but once this night, and that briefly.

There was, for instance, Hatshepsut with Caesar's regular driver in tow: Mouse, whose name and reputation were not hard at all to ferret out among Romans. And whatever reputation Hatshepsut enjoyed as a hedonist, she was also no fool: there was—Zaki plucked a forlorn grass-stem and chewed on it, there by the pegs of Alexander's tent—there was certainly a good chance that Hatshepsut intended more than an amorous exchange with the redoubtable Mouse.

There was, admirably, Kleopatra's attempt to breach Alexander's defenses, shifting tactics moment by moment, slippery as quicksilver. It had not worked. One hoped. And one hoped the Great King kept his wits about him in other particulars. It had an unwholesome smell, all this evening, within reach of placks he had heard about and was glad not to have visited. It was evidently Caesar's intention to introduce them to Hell's more uncomfortable precincts. It was possible that it was all an elaborate trap. But it was not a warning that the Great King was going to regard if that was the case. Zaki had warned Maccabee of that much already, but Judah Maccabee was a little mad himself. It rather had the smell of a trap, and one which was designed not to kill, but to get at information.

Hence the elaborate communications set-up, and Machiavelli or some one of his aides constantly in that truck—when there was no tank and no jeep moving, and nothing, theoretically, with which they ought to be in contact—unless it was with the armory back in New Hell; and if that was the case, then there was more to the train than had yet shown itself.

He gathered himself up and ventured into the Great King's tent. And said as much. To which Alexander, flushed with wine and with an unaccustomed gun on his knees:

"What, by runners?"

"Radio." But that was all oracles. Zaki cast a desperate look at Maccabee. "Make him understand. They talk at distance."

"Through such things?" Alexander picked up the eight ball from the small folding-table, on which a wine up and pitcher sat beside him.

"The Oracle of Litton. They have others. With these they talk to the tanks."

"Physeters," Maccabee said. "And the jeeps."

A frown came onto Alexander's face like thundercloud. "Talking?"

Zaki had not thought it would be easy. And he could wish the Great King were a little less hazed than he was, though, drunk, he had seemed to reach a kind of intellectual placidity in which radios and oracles might be not too large a step.

"So they will talk without my hearing."

"We have our own, in the jeep," Zaki reminded him. "But they've insisted to put the jeeps all under a legionary guard at night. I find that disturbing."

"That can be mended," Alexander said.

"Slowly," said Maccabee. "Go slowly. We're

outnumbered here. Best you understand these things first."

"Have I said not?" Alexander gestured Zaki to a space at his feet, and rested his chin on his fist. "Explain."

"So," Hatshepsut said, lazing back on her elbow while her little pair of sycophants (terrified and disoriented creatures whose whispering voices pleaded for release back to familiar territory) saw to Mouse's comfort. "Is that better?"

"Much," Mouse confessed, lying on his face on the airmattress, there on the carpeted floor of Hatshepsut's tent, Hatshepsut beshadowing him from her cot, behind which a hanging lamp. "But I will not answer your questions."

"Ttt. Have I even asked?" She raised herself on her arm, swung her feet off, surveying all of Mouse's rather handsome back. She ran a bare toe down an attractive curve. The scratches had her own medications on them, and the merthiolate had left only a slight orange tint beneath the film the sycophants had spread. She slipped off the couch and set a knee beside him, took up a bottle of oil and poured a little into her hand, smoothing it down that back as she settled astride him. "There. Some of the old ways are comfortable, aren't they? Relax, relax, you're still all tense."

"I should get to my tent."

"Should, should, should." She bent down and whispered softly into his ear: "Do you trust this Macedonian?"

The muscles jumped under her hand. "Of course not. Would you think so?"

"Can Julius trust him? Do you think that he does?"

Harder still. As rock. Mouse turned his head to

her side, so that he looked at her with a roll of one dark eye. "What are you saying?"

"That I want out of this place. That the Macedonian wants something else. Look at what he's done. And Julius—Julius allows this. I'm worried, Mouse. I've never doubted Julius' good sense. He brings Antonius along. With Klea. Osiris and Set! And he takes another driver, one this Macedonian affords him." *(Are you not the least bit jealous, Mouse?)* "Mouse, he set great store by this Macedonian king in life. Is he being a fool, Mouse?"

A long silence. Mouse lay still, then suddenly twisted onto his back. "Am I one, to talk to you?"

"With Klea and Antonius caught up in this, you have small choice, do you? Confide in Niccolo? Not likely. In Scaevola, perhaps. But less likely. The house is at risk when Julius is. And if we aren't to find our way out of this place, we have to think of another thing, don't we?—that Julius has enemies and the shells have fallen all too close lately. I don't say even that this Alexander is plotting against him, though he may be. But all these shafts are aimed at Julius himself, doesn't that seem clear enough? You're always there, Mouse, always in earshot: I'm not asking you to betray him. Just to think who in this camp has his interests at heart, except you and me."

Mouse looked scared. He had not looked that disturbed when they pulled him out from his situation with the liches. She did not move. He did not, for the space of several breaths. "What are *you* after?" he asked finally.

"I've told you. A way out. A way back to the worlds. But failing that, failing that, Mouse, I want things stable, I don't want us killed and scattered, I don't want Julius on the Undertaker's table, where they can assign him to gods know what or where, or send him to the Pit, gods know. Shouldn't I worry? Are you worried?"

Mouse bit his lip. "What do you want me to do?"

"Rely on me. Give me the word and a target and I'll blast it to the bottommost hell." She slid her hands to his shoulders, careful of the scratches, and stared closely into his eyes. "So I rely on your judgment. I'm giving you a weapon. I want to get out of here but I want to do it alive. I want all our people alive. Friends should stick together. Get me out of here with him and with you and Klea and the worlds will shake."

"Uhhhnnn."

So Mouse was not quite immune.

5.   Hellhole

Phlegethon . . . *moved*.

In the communications truck, flanked by two of the New Dead who knew their equipment, Machiavelli was sure of it.

For two days Caesar and the Macedonian, their tanks and cavalry and horse, had been following the rivers' course—Phlegethon the fiery as it intertwined itself with Lethe—looking for a place to cross.

But they'd found none. Or else, under Lethe's influence, they'd forgot.

It was not the penchant of the River of Forgetfulness to disappear from sight that bothered Machiavelli, but Phlegethon's insidious movement.

The river of flame seemed to be curving in on them. Phlegethon's embrace would be fatal. Fiery death was something too painful to contemplate, yet the vision of the army, encamped suddenly on a shrinking island surrounded by the very spurting magma that ran in the Devil's veins, haunted Machiavelli as he stared at the bank of electronics before him and listened to the New Dead talk of "heat signatures" and what Phlegethon was doing below the ground.

"Lava tubes all over. Not the holes they wanted, the Old Crazies. Bet you RHIP for a week that if they try to take those tanks up the riverbank," the New Dead called Nichols tapped the hell-red, circular screen before him, stretching out his muscular arm so that the tattooed *101st* on his biceps wriggled, "they're history."

On Machiavelli's right, the second New Dead, Nichols' superior, said economically, "They're *already* history. But you're on," and flashed his contemporary a grin as if Machiavelli weren't present. "Just make sure we're rear echelon when it happens."

Perdio, the New Dead made Machiavelli's skin crawl. Nichols, the tattooed, compact athlete in a black t-shirt, was from some sort of "special forces," Welch, the other communications specialist, had informed him. Where Nichols was brawny, Welch was brainy, a man who'd been "station chief in Athens until 1975," whatever that connoted. Both men, Niccolo knew, had died by violence: been "greased," as they said.

Both, the dark-souled Nichols who was as much a soldier as any of Caesar's centurions, and the bright-minded Welch, a sleek creature of intellect with a sharp head and eyes like waning moons, had come with the communications trucks: been at the parking lot, just part of the equipment.

Part of the equipment he'd appropriated from Authority; part of the machinery that made Hell run.

They'd asked strange questions (could they "read in?" what was the "go?" the "pecking order?") and then stopped when Machiavelli had said, "Fortune makes blind the minds of men when she wishes them not to oppose her designs."

After that, they'd merely followed orders, routing calls back and forth to Augustus and, on one occasion, to crazy Tiberius.

The incoming call Machiavelli had been expecting, since first he'd stooped to enter this truck full of colored stars and wheels of light, had not yet come. The "com-techs," as they called themselves, were agents in good standing with Authority, this was clear and certain.

Also clear and certain was the truth of a remark Machiavelli had made long ago, while life was earthly: *When important things are going to happen in any city or country, signs and portents generally come before them—or men of foresight do.*

The occurrence of the eight ball (which the Macedonian had ceded to Kleopatra and Klea carried now as her crook-and-flail of office) and the appearance of the shield of Herakles which Diomedes bore for Alexander, were omens of a noose tightening.

Like the two New Dead who looked at him out of eyes unsoftened by honor, morality, or even emotion, these oracles—unlike the Oracle of Litton, though perhaps facilitated by it—these oracles whispered to Machiavelli that the Devil would have his due.

It remained only to see what would be exacted.

Meanwhile, Niccolo was content to send Zaki scurrying among the cattle and to take his reports.

He was doing just that, while the New Dead were hunched at their consoles, deaf in headsets, when the priority call came through.

It blanked screens throughout the communications van and was accompanied by whirrs and beeps that caused the com-techs to swivel in their seats and stare at him, while behind them and beside them every monitor said in great red letters: "SEND A COURIER TO REPORT."

Then again the screens went blank, as Zaki muttered disbelievingly, "Uncoded? Who would do such a thing? Send such a message?"

The two com-techs, more circumspect, turned back to their screens, which were normal once again.

Niccolo, every hair risen on his neck, said to Zaki, "And, you were saying, about Klea and Alexander?"

Zaki shrugged one small, hairy shoulder; shirtless in the heat of the com truck, he looked almost Italian. But he wasn't, Niccolo reminded himself. He was a Jew. Therefore, smart. Therefore, not to be trusted. Therefore, dangerous. And, indubitably, here at just the wrong time.

Then the Jew said, "She'll have the Macedonian yet. She's got the eight ball, that tiny body of hers, and some notion that she's Patroklos. If we could turn up the real Patrokles, that might stop it. Nothing less . . ."

Niccolo shook his head. He'd checked. Patroklos wasn't on the master list of internees.

Zaki sighed theatrically. "Then, we'll have whatever trouble it'll bring—she's Caesar's whore, and Antony's, one assumes. And Alexander's relationship with Maccabee is showing strains as it is. . . ."

Machiavelli couldn't keep his mind on Zaki's report. The report he must make, the communique from the Devil's tower—for that was what it was—had wiped lesser concerns from his mind.

This responsibility couldn't be delegated, ignored, or mishandled. One's own security came first. He'd known it would happen. Now it was just a matter of to whom and when. Consequences of dispatching a courier to the Undertaker's table—and hence to the Devil's claws—would not be minor. But Niccolo had known the risk was there.

He dismissed Zaki, promising to see what he could do about the uneasy relations between Zaki's beloved Israelite and Alexander, promising to do something about "that Egyptian whore," and giving Zaki other tasks: "Infiltrate the Romans."

Zaki gave a short, barking laugh: impossible.

Machiavelli, conscious that the com-techs were privy to too much and probably (given their lack of reaction to the override message) infiltrators from the Pentagram or, perhaps, the Insecurity Service, snapped at Zaki: "Just *do* it. Now go."

And left, himself, on Zaki's heels. Out into the sulphurous night air with its spitting bite; out into the semi-dark, lit brown in the distance as night fell everywhere but where Phlegethon raged.

It was as if the Devil had decreed a fireworks display: spouts and gouts of gold and green and silver lava, water-fine sprays dispersing like sparklers, low rumbles and hisses carrying to them on the winds of night.

The com truck was parked between the Macedonian camp center and the Roman headquarters tents, off center. The cohorts of the 10th Legion were spread out behind their leader, and opposite, on the riverward side, sat the six tanks—the physeters, as everyone called them now: two sighing in readiness, the others still as if in sleep.

Firelight mixed with halogen and spotlight; soft eructations and the coarser sound of Romans vomiting up their evening's dinner could be heard.

Machiavelli always wore arms: the dagger he fingered sought only a proper back. Through the pitched tents he wandered, seeking an omen of his own—that of his mind's devising, as to whom he should dispatch this evening, as he'd been ordered.

Ordered. It rankled. And without even a face-to-face confrontation. But then, the Prince of Darkness didn't need to tell Machiavelli who was ruler here. The Old Dead played their old games, but Hell had only one lord.

His steps took him toward the Macedonian camp, where men wrestled and horses stamped on their lines. It was a matter of the right sacrifice, someone who'd tell the right things to Authority; someone who would know enough, and not too much.

Two Germans (Perfidy and Murder?) passed by, Scaevola the Handless in between, talking gutturals.

Not a German, surely. And not Scaevola, not while he was with them.

Beyond the tents, the sky was ragged art: bands of color split with clouds so full of sulphur and dust that the reds were ruby-brights and the pinks as hot as a woman's innards and the golds brighter than the thrones of Paradise.

There was Mouse—Decius Mus. He was expendable. But it was Mouse who had found the first hole, Mouse who cared for nothing but his lost son, and Mouse who bore a curse which took any who killed him to a deeper, danker hell than this.

Machiavelli's hell-life was ordered, bearable, and quite bad enough. No, not Mouse.

And then, quite unbidden, his mind threw up: "And not me." Niccolo Machiavelli always listened to his own counsel.

If it were wrong, the blame then lay with self, where he was content to have it. If *he* should fail, or misconstrue, or act askew, it was more bearable than if some other failed him.

His fingers on the dagger hilt relaxed. Some pawn, then, to do the deed.

He drifted back, unmindful of direction, lost in thought, toward what the New Dead called the "motor pool."

The right man for the job would be one who had no allegiance among these factions, one duplicitous by nature. What was it Welch had said to him about his own "type?"

Ah, Machiavelli remembered the words, because Welch had called them "our heritage from you, old timer: Machiavellian—that's the job description now."

For agents, Welch had meant. Agents of governments, which Machiavelli was not ... unless his unspoken arrangement with the Devil superceded, as it did tonight, all lesser causes. One's own security.

And, still strolling, now among the jeeps, Niccolo Machiavelli ran into Aziru, pirate prince of Amurru, dark of eye and heart, the man who'd lied to Thebes and Amarna and to the Hittites as well, and picked and chosen, moment by moment, a prudent course for a ferret to tread among pachyderms.

"Hold, my lord prince," said Machiavelli softly to the Amurrite, just lifting a wineskin out of the back of one of the jeeps.

The Amurrite, a field phone slung at his hip, squinted over his shoulder at Machiavelli, backlit by Phlegethon's fierce display.

"So, my lord trickster, what would you with me?" The Amurrite, like most of the Legion these nights, was drunk.

And the omen was the question, and the answer. "What do you think, Aziru, Kleopatra would make of you, or Hatshepsut, or Caesar who has your trust, if they knew what sort of lies went from your mouth, down into Egypt and up into Naharin? If Hatshepsut knew that it was as much the doings of your country, in league with the Hittite, that toppled Egypt from her glory during the reign of the Akhnenaten, the Heretic? A fall from which the Sphinx never recovered? Kleopatra still mourns the end of that golden age—Egypt in her glory would never have fallen, not to the Meriotes, not to Rome. Caesar, of course, hates Falls. And traitors. Where would you ride out this campaign, with three enemies of such magnitude?"

Aziru straightened up slowly, the flicker of Phlegethon's fireworks playing havoc with the emotions on his face. He rubbed the back of his neck and said slowly, in modern English, "What is it you want me to do? Fetch someone a cup of Lethe's water?"

Maccabee was with Alexander, in the Macedonian's tent, arguing.

The arguing, these days with Alexander too drunk and too full of remembrance, was painful, if low key.

"And if something ill befell me? What would you say, when they came to tell you? 'Alexander who?' "

Maccabee got up, head bowed, careful of the tent luffing, his stomach knotting. Alexander saw betrayal everywhere, lately. Whatever Maccabee did—or anyone did—could be misconstrued. Tonight, it had been Jews that bothered the Macedonian.

And Maccabee, in his turn, was bothered by Egyptians—one Egyptian in particular: Kleopatra, who had the eight ball and, it seemed to him, dark designs on the *basileus*. She was confusing Alexander, but Maccabee had been wrong to mention it.

And Diomedes had been right, at the outset, when he predicted ill would come from these women on the journey. Egyptian bitches in heat. "Notching their bedposts," Zaki had said earlier, when the two Semites had discussed the problem.

"Basileus, I love you better than any of these." Maccabee waved his hand to encompass the 10th Legion, the Macedonian Horse, and the Germans outside the tent—Perfidy and Murder, or Chance and Slaughter, for all he knew—all these Germans looked alike.

And then came the response, thoughtlessly invited, that Maccabee had not wanted to hear.

"Prove it," said the Macedonian hoarsely.

But Maccabee could not, would not. It was not

his way to go beyond the prohibitions of Talmudic law. He could give manly affection, comfort, even embraces, to Alexander the Great. But the Hellenes took it farther, and Alexander did, as well.

So, in this moment of supreme importance, he would be bested by a woman, who could do what he would not, and do it with no conscience.

"The way that Egyptian slut will, if you'll let her? We're better than that. My loyalty must be enough," Maccabee managed through gritted teeth as he bent nearly double to hurry through the tent's flap and he heard, behind him, in a forlorn and thickened voice, Alexander reply: "But it's not."

Maccabee half-expected a blade to come whizzing after him.

He walked blindly among the tentpoles, wrestling with his conscience. He'd known it would come to this—not the argument, such as one might have with a wife, but the demand.

He'd known that Alexander needed—expected—more from him. He'd thought he'd find a way around it. Between them, he'd told himself, it didn't have to be this way.

Heading for the horse lines, he was hoping to find Diomedes, who'd fallen in love with another man's horse and spent long hours with the beast.

Diomedes gave wise counsel, and Maccabee could use some. Was it worth it to betray himself, to prove a point and stymie the Egyptian bitch? Or would he lose more? Would he then deserve to be here? He couldn't do anything that would make him believe he belonged in Hell. Otherwise, this trek and everything else would become futile. He couldn't lose himself. Not even for the love of Alexander.

All this time, he'd lived with the assumptions that men made and never said a word. He didn't care what others thought, only what *he* thought. And, true, what Alexander thought.

And what the Macedonian wanted was not a sin among his own kind. Nor among Romans. Nor among many cultures. What God wanted—did it matter here?

For Maccabee, the answer was yes. God was within, and thus wherever Maccabee was; God had not deserted him, was only testing him. And even for the sake of a friend, he would not desert God, nor himself.

Unless Diomedes could find a way to make it right, or make Alexander understand, Maccabee could do no more. And it was a betrayal of all good in man to leave Alexander, alone and confused, on this downhill slide to a deeper hell. The Macedonian had been happy in his hills, away from all the New Dead and the intricacies of the city-dwelling Old Dead.

Alexander hadn't wanted this trek. It was Maccabee's doing.

And thus, responsibility for the Macedonian was also his.

He thought he saw Diomedes among the horses, and veered to intercept.

Earlier that evening, Kleopatra had come to Alexander's tent spouting nonsense about their shared souls and asking the eight ball if Alexander and she should "become one" and the damned thing had answered "yes" like a parrot. He shouldn't have been nasty to her.

But he wasn't used to such women. He wasn't prepared for—

The pain came abruptly, lancing down along his spine, glancing off, and striking deep into his kidneys.

It blinded him, turning everything white transiently. Then his knees hit the ground and they, like jelly, wouldn't hold him.

He reached back, to where it hurt, while the ground came up to meet him and he felt his teeth crack against a rock, and his fingers met wetness, and a blade's hilt was there, sticking from his lower back.

He was sliced open like a haunch of meat.

He was going to yell, but his body seemed unresponsive: everything hurt and muscles weren't obeying his commands.

He thought of Alexander, alone now and friendless, with no one to protect him from his enemies and himself. And that he'd never finish what he started—not this time.

And then he was remembering another death, with more left behind and more to lose, with too many sacrificed to an idea and an ideal and a God who sometimes didn't seem to care.

And, forgetful that Hell was forever and death no hiding place, he tried once again to cry out for all the Israelites dying in that other place, suicide commandos because he'd wished it, demanded it, enforced it. And in the end, it was the idea he clung to, as it had always been and would always be, that freedom was worth any price.

As if death was freedom.

Klea had still been outside the Macedonian's tent, loitering in the shadows, when the Israelite left.

She was ultimately safe, with the Germans a whisper away, but the emergence of Hatshepsut from darkness still startled her.

"Ready to pounce, kitten?" The Great King had her blaster strapped to her thigh, and her thigh encased in the outlandish post-modern jumpsuits she affected: this one was as purple as the trails the naphtha left when it fell back to Phlegethon from the sky.

"Pounce?" Klea repeated innocently. "Whatever do you mean, *kit?*"

"Mean? Antony's heart, Caesar's pride, and all you can think of is what it'll be like to fuck yourself? That's who you think he is, if I'm not mistaken—yourself."

"Your language is appalling," Klea said, rising from the rock she'd been sitting on now that Maccabee had disappeared from sight, one wary eye on Hatshepsut's weapon.

They were all too nervous. Tempers were getting short. Quarters were too close. "If you want Antonius, kit, be my guest." Pursing her lips, Klea made a kissing noise that caused one of the Germans to turn his head. And laughed. "For my part, I have business elsewhere." She sidled past Hatshepsut.

The taller woman had her dark hair loose tonight; it fell thick to her shoulders and swung against her neck as she turned her head to follow Klea's movements. "You and your eight ball? Befuddling that poor sot in there?" She flicked her chin toward Alexander's tent. "You need him? To legitimize yourself in some way? Any true pharaoh needs only *hu*—commanding utterance—and *sia*—transcendent perception. Not some silly ball."

With that double entendre, before Klea could reply, Hatshepsut turned on her booted heel and stalked off into the night, among the tents where ancient songs were beginning to be sung as men got drunker.

Field actions should have meant field rations of wine, but not in the Macedonian section of camp.

Are we all doomed to repeat our mistakes eternally? she wondered as she slipped past the Germans, who nodded and averted their eyes from her, and into Alexander's tent.

The *basileus* was sulky tonight, stretched out on a rug, staring into his wine, his fine small body glistening in an oil lamp's light.

Klea felt desire stirring: he was her dream, after all. If anyone's, he should be hers.

He didn't look up before he said, "Back, are you?"

He thought she was someone else, but she answered, "Indeed, Basileus." And held out both hands, empty, as if she were his long lost love.

Diomedes sent up no cry when he found Maccabee. The weapon that had butchered the Israelite was gone. Not only had he been sliced, but the back of his head was caved in as if from a boot or staff.

It was murder and murder demanded something more than a fatalistic shrug.

He crouched for some time over the corpse, to which snorting horses had alerted him, wondering what the repercussions would be and whom to tell.

One of the inner circle would soon be on the Undertaker's table. Already the body was beginning to smoke.

Diomedes thought he heard the beat of wings and wondered if there was some way to anchor the corpse—or, failing that, bathe it in Lethe water and perhaps it would forget what it knew.

He let out a yell and a sentry came running.

It was one of the 10th. "Murder! Send someone for Caesar, tell Caesar to come alone. And go yourself to the Lethe and fetch a horse-bucket of water to douse the corpse. Now. Fast."

The Roman sentry put a hand on his girdled hips and inquired as to who Diomedes thought he was.

"Your master's counsellor," he said without thought. "Now move, or you'll regret it."

The man moved sullenly off.

Which left Diomedes with the corpse and his memories. Trying to foil the Devil was like trying to cheat the gods. If Athene would appear to him and tell him what to do, he might have had a chance at it. He considered that if he'd had the shield of Herakles on his arm and could have laid the body on the shield, the corpse might be constrained to stay.

But he'd left it in his tent and, before his eyes, Maccabee was beginning to glow like coals afire.

He got up, disquieted, backed three paces, and hunkered down again to watch. It was like the old days, when no events could be counted on to be purely natural.

Too much was going up in flames with this man: all their secrets, back to New Hell; what camaraderie was left in camp; and more.

Murder was an evil omen, wherever. A dead minority in a camp such as this, especially when the dead was Alexander's favorite: the consequences were endless, and none good.

Diomedes wanted, more than anything else, Caesar to see the body before it disappeared.

By the time the Roman arrived—alone, as requested, but with his bodyguard hanging back and others behind them—Maccabee was already in flames and the sentry hadn't returned with the Lethe water.

Caesar seemed to pale in the yellow light of burning flesh, a consequence of more than the foul smelling smoke.

He'd been murdered too, Diomedes had heard.

Julius Caesar made a face and came to stand beside him. "You're sure it was murder, Diomedes?"

"Certain. Men don't slice their own kidneys or flay their bladders."

Caesar took a deep breath. "A weapon?"

"Dagger, perhaps, but none I saw. And staff or boot—he was silenced by a blow to the head. Afterward, one assumes."

"You'll tell the Macedonian?"

"Why not? You'll have to call a search for the killer—he'll demand it. And fit punishment, once he's found."

"*He?* How can you be certain it's 'he'?"

Diomedes flashed a sidelong look at the charismatic profile that had misjudged close friends, and said softly, "A figure of speech only, Caesar. Though the head blow would have needed power behind it, perhaps too much for a woman."

"We'll see where the women were," mused the Roman, and waved a hand dismissively.

Diomedes was not used to being dismissed offhandedly. He bristled, thought a moment, then said, "There's a horse that belongs to one of your men. I'd like to borrow it."

"Take it," said Caesar absently. "My gift to you."

So, with the bright-maned steed under him, Diomedes rode through the camp, trusting Caesar to keep matters contained, and to understand about the Lethe water when the sentry arrived—to sprinkle Maccabee's remains, just in case. Already, as Diomedes left the corpse, it had been burning low.

By now it must be embers, a banked blaze barely enough to warm your hands. The conflagration that murder in the ranks might start—it would burn longer.

And overhead, Diomedes felt the beat of wings against the evil sky.

Kleopatra was tiny, hot in his arms, both man and woman, boy and girl, all and everything Alexander needed.

If only he could have consummated the act, the night would have been perfect, almost perfect enough to make him forget that Maccabee was betraying him for Jews.

When Judah found out that he'd driven Alexander into the embrace of an Egyptian woman, the Hasmonaean would see the error of his ways.

Or not. The woman was magic, full of wiles, part of him (she said) and more than he'd ever dreamed a wench could be when he'd had the Sogdian witch to deal with.

The eight ball was by their heads and Klea was on top, stretched full-length, her toes entwined with his, when a commotion began outside his tied tentflaps.

Since one voice was Diomedes', repeating *"Agite!"* and the other two were those of his German guards, Alexander rolled sideways, gently.

One did not unceremoniously unhorse a queen.

And she'd heard it too; her fine brow was knitted as she groped for her clothes.

He saw, slipping into his chiton, the eight ball between two pillows, and the oracle it gave was, *You won't like the answer.*

A shiver coursed him. The oracle was capricious, true to type.

He was already striding over to untie the flaps when he saw the gun—the Uzi—Maccabee had been training him to use and picked it up, a gesture prompted by instinct.

There'd been one lich attack. . . .

The face revealed when he opened the tent flaps was Diomedes', all right.

And it was full of tragedy.

Klea was nearly as quick, still buttoning her shirt, and reached his side as he said, "So? What is it?"

And the Argive answered: "Basileus. Alexander, come walk with me. Alone."

Alexander felt the woman stiffen as his own gut went cold.

He slung the Uzi over his shoulder and left Kleopatra without a word, falling in alongside the tall and golden Diomedes, whose sidelong look was compassionate and, by that, terrifying.

But it wouldn't do to demand answers, to act like a fearful child.

They strode toward the riverbank, where the tanks were, in silence.

On the way, Antonius passed them at a trot, and raised a fist.

The handsign was unfamiliar but the attitude was hostile.

"Klea, that's all he meant," Diomedes said, not looking after the son of Caesar. "Not what I wanted to talk to you about."

"Then what?" Alexander expelled breath and words together, so that they came out on a sigh.

They were near the rivers now, where you could edge your way down into marsh grass bathed in Lethe's water, cool and quiet here yet: Phlegethon had writhed back from shore during the day, leaving behind a lava bar like an island, beyond which hot water spewed mist and fire began to flow.

Alexander knew, now, that something was very wrong. He would not ask again. He hunkered down in the marsh grass as soon as mud seeped in between his sandals' straps and waited.

Diomedes looked out over the infernal join of waters and said, "Maccabee was murdered while you were with the Egyptian. Out by the horse lines. There's no corpse to see, don't get up. No weapon found, no signs left. Caesar's people are handling the search."

His knees might not have held him in any case, if he'd tried to rise. He said, "No corpse—you mean it burned."

"A fiery pyre of its own devising. There was no way to stop it. No way I know, at least. I told them to pour Lethe water on it, but there's no way to tell if he'll forget.... We'll need to hear what you've told him, what you think he'll tell Authority. When you can. As soon as you can."

Diomedes was trying gently to remind him that death was not death here, merely separation. But it was loss. It hit Alexander in the solar plexus and took his breath away.

He steadied himself in the reeds, the physical pain a wave against which he closed his eyes. When it was gone, Diomedes was still standing there, just gazing out toward the place where the rivers joined.

"You brought me here so that I could drink away my memories of him, is that it? If I wasn't strong enough?" Alexander's voice came out hard. He pushed himself upright, brushed mud and decomposing reeds from his knees. "We argued, you know, tonight. I—" He couldn't talk about it with Diomedes, a hero. "I am ready to come with you. We'll sit with Caesar and devise a capture and punishment fit to the crime. And revise our plans. Authority will not thwart us."

So he went with the Achaean, thinking that he should never have talked to Judah as he had and wishing he'd done so many things he hadn't. As with Hephaistion. It hurt too much to love. If his soul could just remember that, he'd be better off.

But then, he wouldn't have been what he was. And, walking back with Diomedes, he came to terms with his punishment, sent from Zeus who could reach him even here—punishment for lying in with the Egyptian and betraying one he loved.

And even though the quest had been begun for Maccabee, to make him smile and give him hope, Alexander determined to keep on with it at any cost—it wasn't golden prows in Babylon, but it was the best that he could do.

Zaki hadn't been invited to the staff meeting, but Machiavelli was. With Niccolo in there, they weren't going to solve anything, Zaki knew.

But it meant a break for the New Dead, and the three who had the answers but not the rank to be asked the questions, strolled down to the water's edge to watch the naphtha and the magma and each other.

The com truck would keep without them, Zaki had proposed to his two contemporaries, and Nichols and Welch were glad enough to take a break, and gladder of the wine Zaki had filched from the 10th's stores.

The two Americans drank and the Israeli watched the direction in which the small talk went, wondering only when the subject in need of discussion would be broached.

When Zaki waded into the Lethe far enough to fill a hip flask, Nichols called out, "Hey, watch out, or you'll forget stuff . . . won't you?"

"You have to drink it," Welch corrected. "If I remember my history. Right, Zaki?"

"This is so," Zaki agreed, and came up on the bank—a farther walk than he'd taken to wade to his knees. "It's moving again . . . the shore, I mean."

Welch wiped his lips with the back of his hand and squinted at the sky, shades of blood-red and purple that tended toward black. Dawn—or Paradise rising—was still hours away. "Damned lucky it's not moving *under* you—whole thing could cave. You saw the scopes. Meters never lie."

"What I don't understand," said Nichols, and

belched loudly, lying back on his elbows, "is how we can be sure we're just not misremembering where it's been all along." Nichols wasn't stupid, Zaki knew, just a field man, slow in contrast to Welch.

Zaki related to Welch as what he was—a station chief—and to Nichols as he might to a loaded weapon. There was a comfort in being alone with these New Dead. They'd all been to the same school, played by the same rules. Even here, where Authority ruled, things were familiar when in the company of two of his kind: even in life, there'd been no friendliness among his American contemporaries in the intelligence services; there had been, however, mutuality of interest.

He'd never ask if these two were penetrations from the Pentagram or Higher Authority itself. He didn't have to. It didn't matter, wouldn't until somebody moved.

Then, if these players asked him, Zaki would do what he had always done: his best. He'd had allegiance only to Maccabee, never Machiavelli. Now he had an enemy.

Welch said, "What's the water for?"

Nichols, as Zaki stretched out beside him, added, "Yeah, Zaki . . . somebody going to get amnesia?"

"A precaution." Zaki turned to face Welch, whose supremely American profile was lit intermittently by the gouts and spurts of Phlegethon. "Amnesia is what we're all pretending. We all saw the orders— sent in clear, uncoded. Then the murder. . . ."

Welch seemed to stop breathing. Nichols, behind Zaki's turned back, drank loudly from the wineskin.

Zaki pressed: "What of Machiavelli's part in this?"

"Know who he used? He was with us, so . . ."

No attempt at an assumption of innocence, just

the circumstantial data. And fishing for more. So Zaki said, "No, I don't know who. But I know why." And felt the danger of his unprotected back, offered to Welch's human weapon. And the difficult game of chess he played with a man he unconsciously deferred to as he would to any case officer. He was asking for confirmation of the game plan, that his part in it be recognized. Not pushing, but needing to be recognized. Americans thought in certain ways. If you were not with them, you were against them. Even here, it would hold true.

"You think you know why. Maybe you know more than we do. Let Machiavelli run, Zaki," said Welch, a suggestion that was like a scalpel: painless, cutting deep, unequivocal and final. "Unless they trip to him."

"Unless Diomedes does," Nichols said in a voice like a targeting array locking on. They knew who was who, here. Understood what they wanted.

Something in Zaki relaxed: there was a game, a plan, a method. It wasn't just chaos. Even the Devil's game was preferable to anarchic bumbling. Or to Caesar's gambits, or Machiavelli's self-interest. And they'd let him in, now. With Nichols' comment, on the heels of Welch's "suggestion," came Zaki's admission to the club.

Once more a professional among professionals, it didn't matter that he might be working for the Fallen Angel himself, if not the Insecurity Service or any of the myriad other tentacles of Authority. Zaki was officially in a double game—doing what he knew how to do, comfortable. He felt almost at home.

There remained only to make it clear: "Maccabee was the best friend I had here. It's a score that needs settling."

Nichols chuckled, "An eye for an eye. I hear that."

"Maybe more," Welch said. "Stay on Machiavelli. Zero the perpetrator."

Zaki, feeling better than he had since arriving in Hell, lay back on the grass without a word.

It was Nichols who said, "If Diomedes doesn't beat our time," while Phlegethon writhed a half mile away and Zaki remembered what it was like to be torn between conflicting loyalties.

Diomedes, whatever else he was, was not a Jew. Maccabee must be avenged, if possible by another Jew. Those rules obtained even here.

And then it was Welch's turn to roll over, prop his head on a crooked arm, and stare at Zaki appraisingly. "What think, Zaki? Can you do something about that—keep tabs on Diomedes for us?"

Zaki shrugged at the vault of Hell above. "I can try."

The staff meeting was raucous and angry, full of too much wine and too much passion and too many Romans, all of whom gave their opinions freely.

In fact, the Egyptian women, Machiavelli, and Alexander were the only non-Romans present.

Diomedes was off somewhere, making friends with his new horse. It was a small desertion, but Alexander was drunk and angry, and it rankled.

But then, the Romans might not have invited the Achaean: this was, the way Caesar told it, a Roman matter, to be dealt with under Roman law.

The penalties bandied about were too Roman, the tactics too obvious: rewards, proclamations to be made in cohortese, Scaevola's one-handed table-pounding. All of it left Alexander increasingly cold.

And Kleopatra kept meeting his eyes across the smokey confines of the tent, and licking her lips slowly with her tongue.

Among these iron-and-leather soldiers with their

convoluted ranks and their nervous smell, the Macedonian felt supremely alone.

"Bring us your wisdom, Basileus," Caesar said finally into a pause. "It was your man, slain. How would you have it?"

But before Alexander could answer, Antony leaned forward, elbow on the low map table, his head thrust out like a bull's and his eyes bright: "*His* wisdom? *He'll* tell us to sit in our tents and throw tantrums until the men find the culprit for us. That's the boy-king tactic, isn't it? Make the ranks fear you'll stop loving them?"

Alexander clamped his jaws together in a long pause and considered storming out without a word.

Before he could do so, a centurion Alexander couldn't place said, "So what's your suggestion, Antonius, Master of Horse—turn tail and run, like Actium? Similar, isn't it? Here, too, your lady love's deserted you—"

Caesar's head jerked and hand raised and the speaker subsided.

The drunken Antony—Antonius, as the Romans called him—spat a curse and stood up shakily, his face full of wine's confusion and pain—and a struggle for control.

Someone whooped, from shadows, that "He's too afraid of being poisoned to try her again," and then a scuffle broke out, which Caesar seemed content to let rage.

On his feet, edging toward the clean night and open air, Alexander at first didn't understand why Caesar had hesitated to quell the disruption.

Then he saw Julius' eyes, fixed on his Master of Horse, whose face was flaming red and who stared back at him as if stares could kill.

Antony strode out, through the open tent-flaps and Caesar took a step, as if to follow.

The step brought him to Klea's side and his arm

came down on hers and Alexander heard, "Let him go. Let him think. This had to happen. There's too much he won't remember. We can't keep him from it forever."

And the wild look Klea threw Julius made Alexander know that he didn't belong there, watching some personal battle—and that Klea had other, powerful lovers.

Alexander sidled out, alone, his Germans falling in behind him. As he'd never questioned their loyalty or trustworthiness, despite their provenance—never feared they'd knife him or strangle him—he'd never given a thought to Klea's other lovers.

Until now. Now, when he needed love and she would, except for Julius' intervention, have chased after a Roman field commander who concertedly tried to ignore most of what deeds, in life, had brought him here.

When that red and besotted face loomed up at Alexander out of darkness and Antony said, "Fight you for her. Come on, kingy, let's settle it man to ... whatever you are," the Germans looked at Alexander inquiringly. Did he want them to intervene, escort the drunken Roman back to his legion?

Alexander shook his head and the Germans gave back.

But Antony misconstrued. Waving a half-empty wineskin of Macedonian manufacture, he trumpeted, "A race, then? For her favor—Klea's? And the loser to keep hands off? Come on, Alex—surely you're *man* enough for that!"

In Alexander, a fury began to grow—not just at the innuendo and accusation, but an affronted wrath that, in this hour of his loss, with Maccabee's ashes still warm, a Roman would dare to quibble with him over a slut whom, he should have known, slept around.

Of course, there could be no real fidelity in Hell—

not among the weak-willed, lascivious and hedonistic Romans, at any rate. Not when eternity was the span in question.

Though, if she'd really *been* Patroklos, or Hephaistion, Alexander's love would never have wavered, his eyes never strayed, his hands never touched another, not in thousands of thousands of years. . . .

If she was who she said she was . . .

"A race," he said coldly. "And when I win, you'll keep your eyes, your hands, even your mind, from sullying her. Eternally." It wasn't Kleopatra, he told himself. It was that, in the tents about and the shadows they threw, too many of the ranks had heard the slight and the challenge.

"Fine. Horses? Chariots, old man? You can't handle machinery, I've heard, don't know the first thing about modern—"

"Physeters," Alexander decreed. "To that end of camp and back." He pointed, his finger describing a course from the motor pool to the other end of the encampment.

The Roman whooped and threw him the wineskin. A German intercepted it and, when Alexander looked again, the drunken Antony was loping toward the tanks parked down by the river.

He'd chosen the tanks without thought. He'd only once been inside them—that first encounter with Klea and Julius, in the parking lot.

But he remembered, he told himself, enough. He couldn't bear being called ignorant of the New weaponry.

His genius would guide him. Aristotle had convinced him that all things were discernable by logic. The physeters were made by men; men's minds hadn't changed much over the centuries, only their fingers—those had grown cleverer.

Germans in tow, he made his way to the motor

pool, thinking that Maccabee would know, some-where, that funerary games were being held in his honor.

It had a point, then, beyond Antony's.

For Maccabee, he would win the physeter race. And the prize would not be Kleopatra, but Alexander's honor.

He swigged repeatedly from the wineskin as he walked.

And thus, getting drunker, angrier, and more lonely, Alexander put out his arms to Diomedes when the horseman rode up.

"Come, Diomedes, to Maccabee's funeral games!" His eyes were shining, his cheeks flushed.

"Games?" A frown came and went on Diomedes' high brow. "I've enough games of my own, to-night. But luck to you, Basileus. May you triumph."

And man and horse moved off among the tents.

Beyond, Alexander could see through a thicken-ing fog of wine that Antony was already scram-bling aboard one of the two breathing physeters.

Choice of weapons, then. Or of mounts. Only one other physeter was sighing on a cushion of air—the others all slept.

But by the time he reached it, and his Germans gave him a leg up as if he were mounting a horse, Alexander had drunk the wineskin dry and only the race was in his mind.

Maccabee's funerary games: he would win them; he was Alexander. He would master the mysteries of the physeter as he had mastered the world.

By Zeus, he would do it.

Alexander scrambled up, over the metal flanks of the physeter, over the main gun, and looked into the open hatch under it.

There was one man in the tank's close confines, reading something in his seat. All around were

colored lights and buttons; before the man, between his legs, was a wheel.

Alexander, sandaled feet hooked around a sec-
ondary turret's extension, leaned in: "Soldier, do
you know me?"

The man looked up, said, "Yessir, King Alexander, sir. What can I do you for?"

Alexander jacknifed down into the tank, whose
lesser thrones were empty, and stood beside the
seated man.

"Quickly, show me how to ride this beast, how
to make it go as fast as it can, and then get out. I
race an enemy, and the prize is to the glory of a
slain comrade."

Alexander's English made the soldier screw up
his face for a moment—or the meaning of the words
did.

Their eyes met and locked.

Then the driver said, "Yes, sir," methodically
marked his place and put away his book, and
showed Alexander the brakes, beneath his feet, the
override manual brake on the chair's right arm,
and how pulling forward and back on the wheel,
or up and down, or side to side, guided the physeter
through her paces.

A female it was, for the soldier called it so.

Then the driver said, "Sure you don't want me
with you, sir? I . . . I'm not supposed to leave her.
Should check with—"

From outside, a whoosh and low roar and beeping sound came from the other tank: Antony was
backing up his physeter.

"No time," Alexander said, and the soldier took
his leave, hardly protesting.

Alone in the tank, Alexander touched the wheel
gingerly, sat in the seat, then stood: he was just
tall enough, with one knee on the seat, to be able
to stick his head out the hatch under the main gun.

He stretched his arm up, waving to the other physeter imperiously, and to the man who had just instructed him and dismounted his.

Several of the New Dead were coming near, now.

Alexander pulled on the wheel and spun it and the physeter rose, lurched and—thanks be to Zeus—backed awkwardly toward Antony's vehicle, the same beeping noise coming from it as it warned the world it was in reverse.

The man whose tank this had been yelled something, but the physeter's breathing was too loud: Alexander could hear only his own heartbeat in his ears.

And then Antony popped his head out of his tank's hatch, and waved, and lurched forward: the race had begun.

Klea watched, Julius at her side, helplessly as the tanks tore breakneck along the riverward edge of camp.

There was no use in recriminations; Julius' jaw was set. All their folly was there before them, two drunken men careening toward their honor in tons of metal.

Horses screamed and jerked back along the horse lines; tents went flat from the force of their passage; refuse and dirt blew.

One couldn't even shout over the din and be heard.

So when Diomedes came up, ponying two extra horses behind his sweating sorrel, it was handsigns that got them mounted.

Then a second, and as deadly, race began: the horses wanted nothing to do with the great growling tanks.

But the three of them followed, as best they could, and Klea's horsemanship was sorely tested, her arms pulled and her knees aching, nearly numb, as she clung to her shivering beast.

Damned tanks: turn one on, and it went. A fool could drive one.

Two fools were driving a pair of them to chaos.

And Paradise was just beginning to rise.

Diomedes' face was grim, and Julius' stoic—except for once, when she caught him glancing at her with sad amusement in his eyes as one of the tanks reared up like a horse and almost overturned.

If it had done, the driver would have been crushed.

In the beginning glow of morning, Klea could see, once as she raced her wall-eyed horse close, a head sticking out of one open hatch.

Alexander. He was famous for never keeping his head down.

So the nearer tank was the *basileus'*, the farther, Antonius'.

Gods, what men were like still eluded her after all these years. How they thought and what they'd do for honor still escaped her understanding. She'd seduced Alexander for Caesar, as much as for herself. Antonius refused to remember what she could never forget.

She'd gone to Alexander never thinking what it might mean to Antonius, poor man. A race for her honor?

She didn't want it. Funerary games for Maccabee, the Germans thought he'd said. Or that was the best that could be drawn from them in their limited vocabulary.

Maccabee wouldn't give a fig for all the physeters in the Great Green, let alone these metal ones.

The horse under her shied and skidded to a halt as Antonius' physeter came down with a crash on its belly, teetered as if it would roll down the embankment, and then seemed to right itself.

At that instant, Alexander's passed it.

But Antonius' tank didn't lunge forward to catch

it. It seemed to wallow. It sighed deeply, and then it squealed.

Underneath Antonius' craft, the ground suddenly seemed to heave up.

Julius saw it, and clapped his knees against his horse so that beast leaped forward, neighing shrilly.

And Caesar had understood better than she what they'd both seen: the ground under the tank heaved up, true, but also fell away, revealing a hellhole full of flame.

The tank teetered over nothingness, as if in slow motion, and tilted, tipped toward the hole and, before Julius' horse could reach it, toppled sideways into a widening chasm.

Klea realized her horse wasn't moving: Diomedes had grabbed it by the bridle and was shaking his head, one hand outstretched to her to stop, more eloquent than words would have been if there was any use in screaming when the earth itself had begun to howl.

Steam and foul humors were issuing out of the breach in the earth into which Antonius and his tank had tipped. Its near gun and half its turret were still visible when another crack opened in the earth, closer by, and Julius' horse came to a screeching halt, refusing to jump it and almost throwing Julius into the naphtha and magma suddenly spouting up: Phlegethon was taking the land for its domain.

Julius' horse backed up, its rider holding to its neck.

The river, Klea realized, had tunneled under the land and now was eating it up from beneath.

When she looked again toward the place where Antonius' tank had been, all that could be seen was steam and buckled chunks of the earth's surface.

Tears streamed down her face and she brushed at them angrily. Damned sulphurous smoke.

She stared out at the new riverbank, where Julius' horse snorted and reared, and then remembered Alexander.

Alexander's physeter had forged ahead, into the lead.

Now it was gone somewhere, into the shadows of the dawn and the mists of Phlegethon, or veered round the camp. She couldn't tell.

She couldn't have seen it, if it had been there, through the tears in her eyes. She could barely see Diomedes, who let go her horse's bridle to extend a comforting hand.

Aziru was with the Maronites when the river got hungry and angry and started spouting naphtha and eating up the land.

Gemayel was almost swallowed; the rising of Paradise was dim compared to the lurid firelight.

Killing the Israelite had been of no moment—death was nothing here, his own affiliations as yet unmade. Aziru didn't understand why the gods were angry.

But the Maronites came down from trees and out of tents and everywhere they went, the ground was opening up and swallowing them.

Up from those fiery pools, in which nothing could have lived, were coming beings—liches, Gemayel told him, shoving Aziru to cover, to safer ground and the guerrilla chieftain's tent, as if Aziru were a child.

He didn't understand any of this, but he knew that angry elementals must be placated.

And the liches were like the demons in Babylon—except there, they'd been content to remain stone guardians of tiled gates.

Here, they rose up and grabbed men and bit out their throats and hefted fighters over their shoulders like sacks of spelt.

The guerrillas had their automatic rifles, though, and for every lich that got through, many died, so that the ground was littered with their corpses and only Phlegethon's voracious progress made it seem that few had died.

The river swallowed up everything—man and lich and horse and tent—in its path and cast a stinking pall about it so that one could hardly see.

Through this hellish mist, Aziru bolted, the safety—if such it was—of the tent forsaken.

He knew what he must do. A sacrifice was needed, something to make the river happy, fill its maw.

If mere bodies would have done it, it would now be done: there were liches and men aplenty roasting in the flames.

He ran through the Roman part of camp and saw Scaevola, with a century of the 10th, falling back to guard their center, and big Germans laying about them with abandon, liches falling like wheat before their blades.

He saw Scaevola fall, swung about by his stump and flung away, into the flaming, hungry river, by a lich—a great one twice their kind's normal size—that, in its own turn, was cleaved into two by a German with blind hatred in his eyes.

The 10th was looking for something—Caesar, Aziru realized as Mettius Curtius sped by in a jeep, a communications truck wheeling precariously behind it over ground that cracked and smoked and threatened to give way.

Aziru ran on, past an empty horse line: the Macedonian cavalry was mounted, it too on the move.

Men fought everywhere, except where Aziru was bound: to Kleopatra's tent, to find the eight ball and give it to the lord of the fiery underworld.

This, obviously, was what the demons wanted.

And the eight ball was there, when he'd stolen

inside to find it, among her silks and pillows, saying to him as he picked it up, *Are you sure?*

But he was sure. It was in his heart that only the eight ball could save him. If not this artifact of wisdom, then he himself was what the river hungered for.

Outside, when he crawled under the tent and along between the rows, smoke billowed so thickly he could hardly tell where he was.

Men screamed and liches burbled (the only sound they made while dying) and soon, despite the smoke that was thicker if he stood than if he crawled, Aziru gained his feet. Crawling over corpses was just too fearful.

Then he ran with all his stealth and all his skill, back toward the Maronite fringes, with death all around him, in blinding smoke and mist and fog.

So thick was that miasma, when his foot came down on nothing and he tumbled downward, losing his grip on the eight ball and then his grip on consciousness, that he didn't even see the eight ball float away on the river of fire.

6.   Iron Lady Down

"They're what?" Hatshepsut cried, to the whispering of a sycophant, and headed out of the meeting tent, eeling past a confused centurion and streaking out into the night-turned-day in time to see two behemoths career along the edge of the wall and trench, ride up and over and go off down the rivershore like a pair of landfaring, sporting porpoises against Phlegethon's fires. "Set and Typhon!" she howled in utter disbelief, and ran for the jeeps, holding the disruptor in its holster and trying in between the jolts of her strides, to get clear transmission out of her jewelry. "Niccolo, *Niccolo!* dammit!" But it was all static. She came pelting up to the motorpool, out of which two legionaries came running and a third sentry stood gawking helplessly after the escapees.

"Here," that one yelled at her when she ran past, and swung a rifle round.

"You damned fool!" Hatshepsut yelled at him, fist clenched and the other hand empty, she was so beside herself. In that moment she could have gone for the sentry bodily and barehanded: and in that moment the legionary's jaw dropped and the gun went down. "Who let them? What thrice-damned-to-Set fool let them?"

"Dunno," the sentry said, "they just come in here, we got no—"

"*Fool!*" She spun on her foot and ran for the nearest jeep, with the guard running after and yelling now at her to stop.

Now the sentry got interested in authorizations.

She got the motor started, grabbed for her gun as a man in khaki came running up to the jeep. It was Mouse, his face still showing scratches in the light. He was coming aboard. Julius' driver. "Move over!" he yelled at her, and Hatshepsut who yielded place to no one, shoved it into neutral and dived for the next seat, gearshift be damned, as Mouse climbed in and took over, sending the jeep into motion before she had even gotten straightway about again. She shook the hair out of her eyes and clutched at a handhold as the jeep swerved wildly to miss a knot of running men.

"Catch them!" she yelled at Mouse, not to the point of wondering yet what they were going to do to stop two drunken fools in tanks.

Maccabee opened his eyes and flinched at bright light and white walls and cold all around him. He was stark naked and on his back on something cold as hell and all at once he knew what that something was and where he had come, because he had come in this way, and he panicked.

He panicked in that way of nightmares because his body absolutely would not move, and there was someone moving behind his head, an aged face loomed over his upside down against the glaring lights, foul breath enveloped him, and the oldest man he had ever seen grimaced in what might be a two-toothed smile and patted him on the shoulders with age-soft hands. "There, there," the old man said, "I'll fix you, poor boy."

Maccabee tried shutting it out, simply closing his eyes again and refusing to pay any attention to the old man, but metal crashed and clashed, and a lot of little objects rattled and tinkled onto something else metal. "Damn, damn," the old man said, out of sight, and came up again with a little knife he had dropped. He laid it on a tray beside other little instruments and pushed the whole affair toward Maccabee's side.

Maccabee rolled his eyes in that direction. The old man picked up another little knife and that hand shook with palsy. "There, there, there. Mustn't worry, *nassty* headwound you've got, yes, poor boy. Shall I tell you a story? There, yes—I get them all the time, heads missing, bits and pieces—oh, I tell you, bombs make the worst messes, tchch, *nassty* messes—Now don't take on, nice boy, there, yes—I was working on this dear fellow's eye—I think that's a fracture of the orbital bone there, isn't it? Oh, dear, they did do you a mess, didn't they, blood just everywhere. Dear! I'm sorry. The hands just aren't what they were. There was this fellow last week ... did I already tell you about poor Hadrian? Oh. Does that hurt?"

He could not move his jaw either. Neither to protest nor to scream.

The jeep swerved out the gate and right, hard over again, through a rolling orange cloud; and Hatshepsut cursed and yelled, as they swung dangerously close to unstable ground. Mouse spun the wheel violently in the other direction, bouncing the jeep atilt over a ridge and around the corner the ditch took around the camp.

"There!" Hatshepsut cried, spying riders through the rolling murk, figures sometimes black and some-

times having color. "Set and the Unnameable!
That's Julius up there! *Go, Mouse!*"

Mouse gunned it; and the jeep left the safe track,
lurched over a soft spot, spewed mud and went
after the horses and the tanks, a long, long jolting
run as Mouse shifted and veered and kept them
going toward the riders, if not the tanks, which
were out of sight over the roll of the land. Smoke
rolled between them and the horsemen, cleared
again.

They topped the rise into hellglare, looking down
at Phlegethon in its course, Phlegethon's cratered
landscape under the light of rising Paradise and
the river like the offspilling of a foundry at the
edges, the heart of it impossible to look at. Lines of
magnetic flux came off it, gouted up and came
down again like solar prominences. In the face of
this thing the two tanks hurtled along side by side,
lurching and righting themselves in the craters
and gouges.

"It's moved again!" Mouse yelled, and the wind
carried a cloud of heated air rolling out over the
tanks, like a firestorm. *"Prodi,* it's shifting—"

Hatshepsut grabbed for stability with both hands,
trying to keep clear of Mouse as the jeep avoided a
crater. She shook hair from her eyes and blinked
again as one of the tanks foundered, tilted, with
the ground cracking and showing a bright seam of
fire. "O my *gods!*"—as it went down and the seam
of light grew wider, the riders all but one stopped,
then the last, as the tank tilted further and slipped
down in a showering of sparks and a rolling of
fiery haze. The other tank had vanished into that
haze, that much she saw as Mouse sent them
downslope full out.

"How is he doing?" someone asked, and Maccabee
could not see who that someone was. It was not

darkness. It was no color at all, was blindness. Hearing was all he had, and of a sudden he knew that the old man was going to take that away too, and leave him conscious inside a body which only felt, which had neither sight nor sound nor smell nor any sense of where it was. Just the pain. And himself alone inside. He wanted that voice. He wanted very badly for someone to notice that he was still alive after the old man's palsied bungling. He wanted his mouth to work and his hearing to go on and his sight to come back: *I'm still in here, I'm still inside, don't leave me with this old man, don't go away and leave me like this.*

Hell was forever. If someone had made a mistake, if the Undertaker had botched him, and taken everything away, then he was not coming back, he was going to be put away somewhere.

"I don't know," the old man said. All but toothless, he talked with a liquid sound, a little spitting. That voice was hatefully distinct. "They carved him up, I don't know what they expect me to do—Here, he's still hearing, let me fix this. . . ."

No!

"Behind us!" Hatshepsut cried as the jeep jounced its way downslope; and as the riders were coming up it in haste. Of a sudden fire had broken out from the direction of the camp; and hard after it the mechanical hammering of another and then another of the tanks.

"The damned liches," Mouse said, and swung the jeep about as Julius and the other riders labored up the slope to them. *"Dictator! Mitte istud animal perdidum! Veni!"*

Julius tied off the reins and dismounted on the upslope, yelled at Klea and jerked the bridle off her horse as she slid down and ran, fire gouting closer and closer.

"Greek!" Hatshepsut shouted. "Come on! *Speude!*"
As the horses ran off in panic, hooffalls drowned in
Phlegethon's roar and the shellfire, and Julius and
Klea clambered into the jeep. But the damnfool
Hellene stayed aboard the shying horse and headed
on up the hill.

They passed him a moment later, Julius shouting orders at Mouse and Klea yelling at Diomedes,
as the jeep left him behind.

"Niccolo!" Hatshepsut shouted into her electronics, and winced at the static that roared out of
Phlegethon. "Niccolo!"

A garbled voice came back to her. She tried the
radio in the jeep, trying to hang on and shout at
once, as they came up over the rise and into full
view of the camp. A seam of fire opened beside
them.

"Mouse! Look out!"

He veered over, as it ran like jagged lightning
and part of the hill tumbled away. In utter madness, tanks had faced inward on the camp and
rampaged right through the tents, firing as they
went. The enemy was inside. In the dawning there
was a gleam of metal, a kind of order trying to
happen over toward the lefthand corner of the
camp as the cohorts tried to rally and form their
battle line near a tank position. She could *see* the
communications truck from here and still had nothing but static and sputter; and something ghastly
loomed up in the face of the jeep, something that
might—once—have been an animal. Or a man.
Mouse clipped it with the left fender and swerved
left again, Julius yelling in profane Latin and a
squeal from the earpiece nearly deafening her.
"Aiii!" she yelled in rage, and: *"Ai!"* in stark shock
as the ground cracked near them and a thing came
clambering up out of it, a rack of mouldering bones
that had decidedly been an elephant. With rider.

"Damn!" She grabbed the disruptor and forgot the radio, firing indiscriminately at whatever targets Mouse's driving provided her ahead, while Klea cut loose from the other side of the jeep and Julius got the ones that came up at their other flank.

"He's coming around again ..." the voice said, coming into and out of focus.

Maccabee held to it, clung desperately to that thread of sound. They were not gone. He was not abandoned. *Please*, he tried to say, instinctive attempt at speech. But his lungs would not even draw breath enough for life, let alone to speak. He was frozen in that colorless place, neither warm nor cold, neither seeing nor in dark, and there was that sound, faint as the fall of a leaf.

"It's very irregular."

I'm alive, dammit, I'm alive, don't listen to that doddering fool, O God, I'm alive in here, down here, out here—

"Really, you don't have to wait here." The voice grew louder. There was pressure on Maccabee's shoulder. "There's been a little mistake."

O my God. My God.

"Computer just wiped your records. I'm afraid you've got an enemy somewhere."

Help me.

"You wouldn't have any idea who that might be."

I don't know. I don't know. I don't understand what you're talking about. O God, get me out.

The voice went away again, into distance.

" .... I think he is hearing...."

" .... do something...."

The pressure came back to his shoulder. A warm breath stirred against his cheek. "Listen. This is Reassignments, do you understand me?"

Yes. I hear you. I hear you. Don't go away again.

". . . . It's not insurmountable. If we could just get a little data from you we could put you back where you belong. What's your name?"

Judah. Judah Maccabee. I'm Judah Maccabee. I want to go home.

"We can't find that anywhere. Your record's broken into a thousand pieces, we know it's in the computer, you understand, it's not irretrievable, but we just have to locate a few of those pieces and put them back together again. Where were you last? What were you doing?"

There was void where that answer was. Panic rolled over him like a tide. Memory of somewhere dark. Memory of shapes, hunched in rows.

"Name a friend."

Alexander. Alexander. ". . . xander. . . ."

"That helps. Where did you leave him?"

River of fire. River of. . . . Void again. "Alexander!"

"What is Alexander doing?"

"Caesar—Machiavelli—"

"What were you doing?"

Void.

"You know you have to help us. Or we can't find you again."

Warning. Treachery. "Murdered. Murdered. Murdered."

"We know that. But you'd really like to go back to your own place, wouldn't you? I just need a few more details. Who authorized it?"

Void.

"Where were you going?"

Void.

"Who sent you?"

"Hell—Hell—"

"Not where. Who?" The pressure at his shoulder became pain. "You know we don't have all day at this. You can be a little more cooperative. We can just put you back in storage. Can't we?"

"Maccabee. My name is Maccabee."

"We don't have anyone by that name. You want to try again?"

"I was with Alexander, on the river—river—Send me back to him!"

It was chaos. Smoke rolled and fire gouted up, but the battered ranks of the cohorts held under another assault, and Hatshepsut saved her shots: the disruptor had gone red-light and the powerpack was fading. She worked with the radio and tried to hear what Niccolo was saying, something about attack coming—"Dammit, *where?*" she yelled at Niccolo. "Say again!"

As the jeep tilted in sudden instability and a soldier near them yelled and vanished, right under the ground, as others suffered the same fate and a roaring came up on their backs.

Shells hammered the ground beyond them. It was one of the tanks coming in to join the others that waltzed about the lines of the undead like pachydermic dancers. The wind buffeted them, rocked the tilted jeep, and bits and pieces of lich went flying as the skirts of the tank went right over the outbreak. Romans went down and covered themselves with their shields as the monster kept coming, and Hatshepsut ducked down behind the windshield as a rock hit it.

There was less noise then. The tank had passed. The jeep tilted no further. She put her head up as the rest of the occupants of the jeep crawled up from their own cover, looked through the impact-starred windshield at a quartet of huge tanks grouped out across a black and smoking field; and a fifth, the tank that had come from their backs, from the turret of which a recognizable head and shoulders were visible.

"Alexander," Mouse muttered. As across the field liches began to smoke and to moulder at an unnatural rate, as legionaries picked themselves up from under their shields, and Niccolo came through loud and clear:

"Cesare, do you read?"

Julius grabbed the mike out of her hand and blistered the air with soldier's Latin.

While Hatshepsut climbed on shaking legs out of the jeep and landed in soft ground, caught herself on the fender and shoved herself away, walked and staggered and finally walked over smoking remnants of lich on her way until she had the Macedonian in shouting distance.

"Get out of my tank, you damned lunatic!" With the disruptor in her fist and an awareness of Mouse and Julius running behind her. "Get your butt down here right now, *right now*, hear me?"

The tank rested level. At least it seemed to, though Antonius, crawling up against the seat in the dark where he had fallen, could not be certain of up and down in his own case, let alone that of the machine.

He was cold sober. And dazed. Somehow the tank had escaped the river. He was sure of that. It had gone unstable and the gyros had felt that and sealed the hatch, which was why he was stifling and the sweat was pouring down his face and the exposed metal of the tank's interior burned his hands and stank as it did.

He reached over and powered the hatch open. Hot air came in, bringing a sulphur stench with it. He got himself to his feet and put his head out.

There was pitch blackness all about him. The tank pinged and stank, and he was totally blind, the dark so complete something might be right in front of his face and he could not tell.

Something. Liches. Gods knew. He fumbled after the front floods, ducking down in an agony of panic til the lights cut on and he looked up.

At a stone ceiling, not far above the turret. He stood up again and saw stone on either side of him, chewed and ridged and smoothed by fire and melting. Ahead and back, behind the hinged turret cover—was nothing but black and the meanders of the tunnel walls.

"Prodi," he mumbled, and clenched his hand on the rim of the turret opening til it burned him and he let it go stupidly, in pain. He climbed up, burning his bare knee—he had worn the chiton, nothing more. Had no gun, no—

—radio.

He scrambled down again and turned it on. "Red One, this is Titan Three, do you read?"

Static came back. For long minutes of trying, there was nothing but spitting static.

He tried the engine. The fans whined and whirred and the turret hatch scraped against the ceiling with a shower of rock as the sound became deafening. He shut down. The tank settled.

"Damn. Oh, damn!"

He wanted a drink. He wanted it badly. He found the wineskin he had dropped, and uncapped it and drank the small bit that was left.

He was steadier then. And braver. He climbed up, careful of his hands and his knees on the rim, and balanced there, squatting, the hobnails of his legionary's sandals finding precarious purchase on the metal of the tank; and the soles of his feet were heating; the heat was coming up at him from the tank surface. And the batteries were going to die and leave him in the dark, alone.

Rock chinked and rattled. A foot disturbed something. He grabbed onto the hot metal, ready to duck down again, when he saw a man stagger into the focus of the lights in front of him, a man—

"O gods." It was Julius' driver. The foreigner, staggering his way up the passage, battered and burned. Another living soul down here in this cavern. *"Salve!"* Antonius hailed the Amurrite. *"Heus!* Hey!"

"Antonius!" Aziru cried, staggering forward. His clothes were cinders and rags. His skin showed red with burns and his hair and beard were singed. He fell to his knees, and Antonius leaped down to the body of the tank, slipped and staggered and managed, despite burns, to get down the hand and foot-holds till he could drop down to the stone floor of this hole. The Amurrite had fallen on his face a distance away and tried to get up again.

Antonius reached him and squatted down, risked a burned knee on the stony floor, as Aziru grabbed at his arms and held onto him as if he were a longlost brother.

It was mutual. He was shaking too. "Do you know where we are?" Antonius asked of him, and Aziru shook his head, fighting for breath. "Fire," Aziru said. "Fire."

And recoiled as if a snake had turned up beside him. A small black ball had come rolling down the slight incline after him.

It stopped. Antonius put out his hand gingerly and picked it up. *A decision is pending*, it said.

"Where are we?" he cried. He did not even *believe* in the damned oracle, was a Roman of the eighth century A.U.C., and civilized. Educated in philosophy and rhetoric. And he was shaking and his voice trembling when he screamed at the thing. "Where are we?"

Down the tubes, it said.

*   *   *

They had gotten the Macedonian down off the tank. Mouse had gotten his arms around Hatshepsut and hauled her backward, disruptor and all, talking to her urgently, while Julius in all the chaos, had gotten up close to the tank and set his hands on his hips and called up to the King of Macedon and half the known world: "Good job you came in when you did!" (Flatter the man. Give him his out. It was like arguing with a mirror-image. He *knew* the young hothead standing up there on that tank, weaponless and embarrassed as hell and by now cold sober. It was himself before Gaul, about the time of Asia.) "Come down off there, we have a problem!"

It had been that easy. In the start of things. But Klea was still crying her eyes out, the camp was a shambles, and the damned liches had dragged down men of his gods knew where. He had one advantage over Alexander: he had lived to more than sixty, despite his present dark and abundant hair, his apparent mid-thirties physique: he had lived to more than sixty and had an old man's self-control when he wanted to use it. Which was a good idea, with the Macedonians and the Germans coming their way as they were doing, a straggle of men afoot—gods knew who could get a horse across that field. "What officers have we got left?" he yelled, if nothing else to confuse them and the Romans, who were also moving in, in no fine mood either. "Count 'em off!" And to Alexander: "We've lost Antonius. He went into the river."

"I saw." The *basileus* was remote, his head up, his expression hostile and guarded. He offered no excuses and no reasons. *So what will you do about it?* the attitude said.

"We've lost officers. We don't know what's coming in on us next. We've got to get this thing in order. Fast."

If anything Alexander was relieved. A little of the guardedness went away and left a worried man, an anxious man. He turned away of a sudden and started shouting orders in Macedonian Greek. Alexander was missing an essential man too. One had to remember that. He was not as sure where that man was or what his fate was or what had happened to him.

Baculus was there, the square-jawed centurion making his way across the field from a knot where the maniple standards had grouped. That fast, the Roman army took stock of itself, on its own. "Sir." The head centurion was disarrayed and his armor buckled askew, his helmet dented. And his face when he saluted promised no cheerful news. "We're missing Antonius, Scaevola, Gracchus, Paulus, and thirty-seven of the line, sir. Scaevola went under, we got Gracchus' body, Antonius and Paulus we ain't accounted for. Thirty-seven's what the centurions got names on, we got a guy doing up the lists."

Two senior officers, two centurions and thirty-seven men.

Fifteen Macedonians and gods knew how many horses, when that count came in. And two of the Germans, Famine and Grief, had either made their valhalla or gone back to Tiberius. The Germans were determined on appropriate rites, and went off to themselves, where they piled up debris and weapons and insisted on making a fire despite the fact the bodies were doing what bodies did, burning on their own; which outraged the surviving Maronites. (Gods knew what Gemayel's casualties were, since the Maronites refused to admit to any.)

Meanwhile it was time to sort it out: the exhausted soldiers of the 10th had cleared a space on the field beyond the battlezone, tramped the grass flat, got canvas over it, at least an awning, and set up seats of any kind they could patch together. All this while the Macedonians were still reporting to Alexander. And a furtive man from Gemayel showed up to say the peripheries were secure.

And while Mouse and finally Klea reasoned Hatshepsut out of sending *all* the Macedonians *and* their king back to the Undertaker, forthwith: Hatshepsut came over to propose that in person.

"Julius! Quietly and quickly. We have an excellent excuse. The troops will understand it, plain and simple—Osiris and Set! we just face those lads about and we open fire, nice and neat, and no recriminations. They got Maccabee, for godssakes, they got Scaevola and Antonius and who knows how many of the troops! What more can they learn?"

"Patiently, *patiently*, Egypt. It's not so easy as that." He was still in diplomat mode. With difficulty. He had not wanted Hatshepsut in this venture, foreseeing this. There were altogether an excess of Great Kings in this expedition, and Hatshepsut, while she managed well enough shepherding the tanks and their drivers, was an Old Dead and a god-king and, if she had had Egyptian troops under her command instead of Roman armored personnel, gods knew it would have taken more than Mouse and Klea to stop a bloodbath. "We're out here to *learn*, hear me? We're out here because something damned peculiar is going on in Administration and elsewhere, and someone's set up a trap, do you understand that?"

Hatshepsut drew in a large breath and blinked; and shut her mouth, with a flicker of those kohl-rimmed (and dust-spattered) eyes that was astonishingly sane.

She put her hands on her hips, pressed her lips to a thin line, and spat dirt in the next second, a small aversion of her head. "Paugh. I was wondering whether you had that figured."

It was his turn to collect himself. Romans were blunt-spoken. They were generally out of the habit of talking to him that way. "You asked for this, you wormed your way in, now, dammit, you take orders. I've got *one* damned problem to deal with, I don't need two. That's why I didn't want you here."

"You'd be back on that damn slope and they'd have chewed your men to bits!"

"Mouse would have gotten there. Without you."

"Without this—" She slapped the gun at her thigh. "You wouldn't have gotten *up* that slope. Without *that*—" She pointed toward the Macedonians in the distance. "We wouldn't be out here cut all to bits and with half our damn equipment missing. Leave me off the list and take Antonius, do you?"

"*Shut it up* and use your head! You weren't the only one who forced his way in. *Think* about it, Egypt. And shut your mouth and make your throw with the rest of us or hike home, right now."

A second time the Pharaoh closed her mouth. Not angry. There was thinking going on behind those wide kohl-dark eyes. "With," she said, and slapped her chest, an Old Dead gesture. "With, or no damn deal. Foulups you've got, I can't do worse."

"I'm not sure they were accidents."

That told a smart woman something too. The eyes flickered again. "All right, all right," she said. "Deal. You. Me. The Macedonian if we have to have him."

"You think that damn toy of yours puts you equal to a couple of cohorts? You're not playing Hounds, woman, and we're not talking about the council table! Field's another thing than book theory!"

"Damn well saved your ass, *dictator*. Give me my tanks and give me autonomy. And watch."

"All right, all right, houseguest. But you follow my signals. Prove you can do *that* and I'll give you the whole damn motorpool! Mouse has got his hands full and I'm going to have to fill holes with whatever I've got."

He wished he had not said quite that thing. Freudian, the New Dead called it. Back in Rome they called it ominous.

And he watched her walk away, with an unpharaonic sway of shapely hips, and counted to himself the number of add-ons who had somehow gotten wind of what was toward and invited themselves along: too damned many. Some of them might be his Luck operating.

Some of them were just plain operators.

He was sure of that.

It was unfortunate, Niccolo concluded, watching from the shadow of the com truck. Very unfortunate, and disturbing.

A message demanded a courier. And attack exploded around them within the hour on the act of two drunken men, which was a wholesale way of accomplishing the same thing.

Coincidence was one of several explanations that occurred to a man in his trade. It was not, of course, to be discounted. But one worried. One worried considerably.

He rubbed at his nose and watched the gathering over by the tent. He stood at distance, uninvited, because Julius for various reasons kept him low-profile—as far from the Romans and their day as they were from Hatshepsut on her end and as far as Nichols and Welch and Zaki were on theirs. It was not that they were Old Dead over there and exclusive. It was that the whole mix was volatile and Julius had not wanted Hatshepsut in, for that reason. The Macedonian, King of Kings, was unstable enough. Brilliant, and dangerous, the way a man was dangerous who had never discovered limits.

Niccolo cherished the meeting. And took notes, not alone for his own theses. He had a microphone over there—Hatshepsut; if she deigned to oblige. The Great King was touchy herself at the moment and he delayed a little before going into the truck to whisper endearments into her ear and ask that she keep that little array of hers live and useful.

Julius of course expected as much when he let her into the expedition. He had never asked her to turn it off, never betrayed its existence to those who did not know that where Hatshepsut walked, other ears listened. So Julius (Niccolo thought habitually in loops and circles, many of which interlocked) either thought that she would not do his bidding in that regard; or that she was loyal; or that she was in someone's employ and that he could not trust her, except to feed her disinformation.

Disinformation. He loved that word. The world had invented such precisions to describe what had always existed.

He was after all, an artist, if a frequently abused one. And a wise man, in his own estimation, since there was no one else with whom to share his estimates. He trod a very careful path, and kept a certain integrity, as best a man could who saw as many possibilities as he.

Hatshepsut's proposition to blow the Macedonian to the next hell he had indeed heard; and it had a certain merit. There was a random element loose in this, and while he cherished such diversions in his long existence, there was a touch too much randomness involving far too high a wager to let him enjoy it.

The list of missing was not least of the things troubling him.

". . . Enough," the voice said. "I don't think he's lying."

Maccabee attempted to talk. They were fading away again and his faculty of speech had gone. *Don't leave! I've told you what I can.*

And with that, deeper buried, where the terror was: *But not everything. I can't remember everything.*

And I don't trust you. I don't trust you. Even if your computer has lost who I am.

O God, don't go away and leave me like this. What are you going to do? Where am I going to be? What are you going to send me to?

Who are you?

"Easy, easy." Having found another living soul in this place, Antonius was desperately careful with him, supported the burned and bloody Amurrite on the ascent to the turret of the tank and, getting inside first, helped him on descent into the safe if overheated interior. Aziru smelled of scorch; and let down to the seat in the cramped interior, hung his head and moaned.

"Here." Such was the measure of Antonius' concern he unstopped the wineskin and tilted Aziru's chin back, measured a bit of the last out. Aziru swallowed and gasped.

"Not—the best vintage. But good enough."

Antonius took a bit himself. "It'll do til we've got more." He had the shakes, not from the wine. Dead, he would go back to Tiberius. Tiberius would have questions. And Tigellinus was in Tiberius' employ, master of Tiberius' security since Nero had gone—away. But terrible as that prospect was, there was growing in him the suspicion that they had transgressed some law, if law there was in this place, and offended some Power, and that might lead to change, and take away all certainties. Even of the chance to die and go home. Even of finding Tiberius again or anything, however dark or insane, that was Roman or familiar.

He was grateful, nevertheless, that the Amurrite bore things as he did. He could not have endured hysteria or recriminations—for with sobriety in his predicament came a reckoning how he had gotten there, and how he had failed Julius and Klea, how wretchedly he had failed.

"Where are we?" Aziru wondered.

"In one of Phlegethon's old courses," Antonius said. "We found one of the damned holes."

"Some god hates us."

It sent a shiver up Antonius' back. For all that he was an 8th century Roman and educated. It sent two shivers. And he pulled the eight ball from inside his tunic where he had put it for the climb into the tank.

"Who is our enemy?" he asked it, and the writing floated up to the surface of the black sphere, there in the dim and unnatural light of the tank's controls: *Not apparent at this time.*

"Ask it where is the way out," Aziru said.

Antonius turned it. Again the writing surfaced. *Proceed with caution.*

"How?" Antonius cried, shaking the thing.

Use your own resources.

"What? What have we got?"

Look around you.

Antonius took in his breath. Shook it again. *Yes,* it said. And: *Seize the initiative.*

"Damn. It's *connected.* The damned thing's *connected.*"

"Where?" Aziru asked, blinking swollen eyes and reaching out to touch the thing.

"It's no damned accident. Move over. Move *over.*"

He shoved at the Amurrite, got the seat cleared, and sealed the hatch. It whined down and shut firmly. He activated the engines, and the roar was deafening as the tank lifted up to the height of its skirts.

Aziru yelled something at him he could not hear. He set the tank into gingerly motion—it grated past stone, shocked against another projection and proceeded by noisy if infinitesimal ricochets off the walls.

Bang—scrape—bang—BANG-SCRAPE—scrape— scrape—top and sides, this way and that, til it stuck fast and the fans roared to no avail.

Reverse, then. Slow scrape. Antonius angled the small guns of the turret and imagined the obstacle from the location of the bangs. And cut loose a barrage while Aziru held his afflicted ears and screamed at him without a word audible. Sweat ran on him. The air reeked of burning and of dust, coming in through the vents.

Forward again, by tiny degrees. *Bang—scrape.* And silence except for the fans for about five heart-beats. Then: *BANG* into another projection of the walls.

Back off and fire. Advance. Back and fire. Advance again, with the roar of the fans and the unnatural behavior of the groundeffect tank in this narrow tube. Back and try again, while the sound scrambled the brain and pierced the ears and the shock of confined fire and ricocheting stone rack-eted and banged in a different tone against the uncompromising alloy of the tank. Aziru subsided into a knot with his hands over his ears. Antonius gritted his teeth and blinked sweat and kept it up while his ears rang and ached and ached the more, and the whole of existence seemed reduced to that inching progress.

Then the whole world gave way, the tank nosed

over and began to slide with increasing angle and heartstopping and frictionless acceleration.

"Haiiii!" Antonius yelled, hand frozen on the control that could cut the engines, stop their slide but leave them without cushion, on gods knew what surface.

"Stop!" Aziru cried. "Stop this creature!"

He threw it in reverse. Panicked.

And went airborne as the tank slammed into bottom. His head hit metal and he came down right back against the seat, neck all but snapped, slewed as the tank skewed round and the fans thundered in a great open space of some kind. Humidity came through the vents. Stench of rotting things. And he was blinded, moisture pouring down his face and into his eyes.

"Stop us!"

"Not here!" Antonius cried, fending off Aziru's grab at his sleeve. "Off, dammit! I've got to see where we are!" He wiped his eyes with the back of his hand and toggled the hatch open, got up on one knee and got a faceful of swamp-flavored mist that blinded him anew. He blinked it clear, made out some black and ungainly shape through the gray-white haze, a tree with limbs outstretched and dead. He made for it, and the tank lumbered up through black reeds, onto something like solid ground.

With trepidation he cut the fans. The silence as they died away was total, so that he feared his ears were damaged. Then he heard the faint creaking and croaking of frogs.

Aziru got his slight body up beside him. And for a long time neither of them spoke.

"Where are we now?" Aziru asked.

"Where's our oracle?" Antonius asked in turn; and wiped again at his face. His hand came away covered in blood and he felt sick.

But the Amurrite disappeared below and came up with the eightball in his hand.

Cocytus, it said.

"The river of sand," Antonius murmured.

"What such river? Do you know this place?"

"Oh, I know it, we know it, beyond a doubt, up above we never leave it far, our fates bring us back again to this district, the villas, this wilderness— Have you a hell, king of the Amurrites? We do. It's here." His teeth chattered. He was not outstandingly brave. He proved this always in crises. When he was sober he knew his faults. When he was drunk he was immune to them. Events would try him. And there was not enough wine left. There was not enough in all the world to make him equal to this. "You've involved yourself with us, and here we both are."

Not back to Tiberius and the open skies near the city. Not a death, easy or hard, and a quick transfer back to a despair he known for centuries. Nothing so predictable as Tigellinus or any enemy he knew.

"What does one find in this place?" Aziru asked in a subdued voice. "What does one expect?"

"One's own dead. One's ghosts." Water dripped and the frogs kept up a manic chirping, while the tank pinged and gurgled. "The issue of one's mistakes. Is there a worse thing?"

He realized then that he had asked a question, and that the ball was in view: he did not want to look, but his eyes slid in that direction in helpless attraction.

Wait and see, it said.

Alexander showed at the meeting with the shield of Herakles, a pair of sullen Macedonians and one German. Perfidy, Julius thought, though he could not tell Perfidy from Murder. Whichever one it was, was inebriate: the air about him was damned near flammable. Alexander, thank the gods, was still sober.

They were very few in this conference, with legionaries and Macedonians standing guard in equal suspicion, with hallooing and shouting in the distance, where the quartermaster and the motorpool and anyone they could dragoon trying to sort the whole equipment from the damaged and the useless.

Himself; Alexander; Klea, whose face was pale and composed now—how brittle that composure was, Julius well knew; Hatshepsut standing near Klea; and Mouse not accidentally standing very near the pharaoh.

There was a disturbance. Legionaries reacted as someone started through, but Julius signed a letpass. Gemayel had shown up, darkhaired and dark all over his face, his fatigues dark camouflage. And he folded his arms and stopped on the edges, not a word said.

Likewise Alexander, third point of a triangle, in the same attitude. Julius found his own arms folded, became selfconscious of his independence, and dropped them, staring from bright-haired Macedonian, past Egypts early and late, Rome, and lastly and latest, Lebanon.

"It was stupidity," Alexander said forthwith, "to burden ourselves with all this train. Now we have paid for it."

Auspicious beginning. Julius clamped his jaw tight, got control of his temper, and lifted that jaw ominously toward Hatshepsut, whose look betokened war and carrion.

"This clutter of women and cooktrains and such," Alexander said, "I never asked for. You think I misunderstand your cohorts and your guns. Perfidy!"

The German walked precariously forward, and

Alexander held out his hand, demanding. And the German suddenly shoved his rifle forward crosswise as he held it, as Klea and Hatshepsut came out of their chairs and Alexander snatched up the rifle and aimed it skyward.

The burst of fire was abrupt, economical; guns and assorted weapons tumbled and lifted to dead aim all around their circle, the whole camp would be reacting and grabbing after weapons; and Alexander shoved the rifle back into the German's hands and stood there like a statue Phidias had conceived.

Julius' heart lurched. Not alone for the move and the instincts it triggered. But for the sight of the hero of his boyhood dreams, suddenly all of a piece, like a mosaic not making sense until one saw it in perspectives. The barbarian, intrigued by modern weapons; the sullen, self-centered prince, sulking in his tent and surrounded by equally destructive types, each with motives; the hubris of the lunatic standing on the tank, in fire and wreckage of his own making; now this clear-eyed, defiant man who all of a sudden loomed as tall as his legends and seemed clearer than the daylight. None of these things were Alexander. All of them were, taken together. The dangerous brilliance. The genius disciplined only by its own decision.

"We will not turn back," Alexander said.

Had said that at the Indus. Had meant to march to the sea. To the ends of the earth. To bring it all into the limits of civilization, under one law, one assemblage of diversity, one king who would reign forever, because such a mind as this planned for no mortality and no successors.

"We will not turn back," Julius said. As if he had no independence in the matter. Or as if there were only one of them, and that one was speaking through several mouths. As if he stood again looking out toward Britain and thinking that in this life, this latter age, he might indeed pass beyond the bounds of known lands and find the ends of the earth. "But all things come round again, Basileus. Except in Hell, where I would not guarantee the geography. We have enemies. That much is clear. Whether they're mine or yours or whether that matters—they've taken men of yours and mine."

"Then we will march after them. With the physeters, which care nothing for the ground. With your machines until they founder. Without them, afterward."

"At what enemy?" Gemayel asked. "Where? How far?"

"They will show themselves," Alexander said. "For the other—as far as we can; and make the omens favor us. Where is our oracle?"

Silence, then.

"Where is the thing?" Julius asked, while the mood chilled and things went in doubt. "Klea?"

"I looked," she said in a small voice.

"Well?"

No answer at all. No move at all. From anyone.

"There's the shield," Klea said, pointing where two Macedonians held the great thing between them. "Our luck is still with us."

Eyes turned that way. And that only said that Diomedes was not with them. The silence grew heavier still.

"Osiris and Horus," Hatshepsut said suddenly, "Isis and Hathor, Amon-Ra and Thoth, Anubis, Opener of the Way—"

Gemayel stepped back. Mouse did. Hatshepsut's hands lifted, her kohl-rimmed eyes rolled back til they showed whites, and her voice took on cadence, deep and hollow.

"Sekhmet and Bast, Maat and Ptah, Anubis, Opener of the Way—

"Set and Typhon, Geb and Nut, Anubis, Opener of the Way—

"Shu and Tefnut, Ra Beautiful in Rising, *Anubis, Opener of the Way*—

"Below the earth, below the river, the shadow of wings,

"The shadow of shadows, aiiiii! Anubis, Opener of the Way!—"

The hands clenched to fists, arms crossed, head bowed and in the same slow sequence, lifted, eyes centered and sane. Hands fell, eyes blinked rapidly. And all about, watchers drew a unified breath.

Mummery, Julius thought; and felt a twinge of that divine sickness that for a moment had disconnected him from the others. There still seemed some sort of insulation between himself and the men around him. Alexander stood still, frozen in place. *Out-theatered, by the gods. What in hell is the woman trying?*

Being Julius Caesar, god-on-earth, he was not generally impressed by the competition. Certainly not an Egyptian witch who feigned sudden weakness and subsided into the chair Kleopatra had vacated in her alarm at the fit. Hatshepsut possessed the chair, disposed her arms on it and drew a larger breath, looking for all the world like a Pharaoh.

Anubis. Jackal-god. Guide of the dead. Damned appropriate, houseguest.

Patron of thieves, as I recall.

"Does the oracle," Julius asked in measured tones, "have a specific direction in mind?"

Hatshepsut looked at him, hands still and curled over the chair-arms. Her admirable breasts were still heaving, her nostrils flaring. "Antonius has not died."

"Hello, hello!" the Emperor cried, holding the

phone receiver prudently out from his ear. "Say this again! What, what?"

The fact that the call was emanating from a jeep miles distant was still incredible to him. He was wary of interceptions and deceptions and found difficulty equating the thin voice at the other end with the clear sane voice of Curtius.

"Saturn has devoured his children. Send us supplies. It will be necessary for us to remain here longer than we wished. We need authorizations, do you copy? Repeat:—"

"There is no need!" Augustus was sweating, and mopped at his face with a large handkerchief, still fearful of spontaneous electrocutions. Saturn had taken in his children. Germans or Antonius himself had perished, possibly to return into Tiberius' household. Something dire had happened. And he could not ask further. "Hello, hello, are you finished?"

Static leaped at him. He snatched the phone back from his ear and resolutely persisted. "Hello, hello!"

But Mettius Curtius had gone.

The rest of the message was code too. A request for investigation into the Pentagram.

The Emperor set the receiver carefully into the cradle and gathered himself up from his desk in haste, showering papers off the edge. No sycophant materialized to catch them and they scattered onto the floor under his departing feet. No sycophant dared this place, though they chittered distressedly in his wake as he went personally down the hall to find the Italian.

He was sure it was Antonius. He *knew* the man. Antonius was disaster on two feet. Ill omen and calamity.

And Tiberius was always there, spiderlike in his nest and apt for corruption by any agency and every power in Hell that could pay him in the coin he wanted.

The tank roared along, suspended over Cocytus' sandbars and sloughs, and spewed a cloud of water from all sides which absolutely confounded vision. For that reason Antonius went slowly, and stopped periodically to reorient. His head was throbbing, and he was soaked to the skin from mist which had hit his face and run down his body. So was Aziru sodden.

"It says we must go on," Aziru said, from somewhere about his waist, where Aziru huddled reading their oracle by the tank's panel lights. "No! No! Left!"

Antonius turned, ducked down to try to clear his eyes and thrust his head up again into the enveloping mist. He believed the oracle enough to steer by it, but not that the thing might warn them of obstacles; and such loomed out of the haze at times.

"Left!"

"I did left!"

"It still says left! No, straight, straight!"

"Straight?"

"Right! No! No! Fool!"

A tree loomed up, more solid than other trees they had seen. He swerved again, and brush appeared through the mist. He was seeing again. The mist was no longer absolute.

"We're on land!" he yelled at Aziru, and slowed to full stop, trembling and shaking and chilled about the face and upper body. The tank sighed down on its supports and he poised his hand ready to send them flying again if the ground proved too soft for the weight. It felt solid. He caught a gulp of thick, reeking air, and shut down entirely, gasp-

ing and trembling as if he had been walking a
narrow beam all the way from their beginnings.

Objects were clear in the fog. Like a large tree. A
reedy patch which surely betokened a bog. Mostly
it had as well be France as where they were. Or
the outskirts of Rome before they drained the
marshes.

"Where are we now?" Aziru asked, thrusting
himself up to see.

"I don't know," Antonius snapped. "How in hell
am I supposed to always know where we are?
We're here! Is it better than there or over yonder?"

"Over there is water and over here is land,"
Aziru snarled back, "and I want my feet on land!"

"Stay in here! Dammit, you go poking about out
there you'll go in up to your neck! I won't get you
out, damned if I will!"

"This is your fault! It's you Romans who made
this absymal place! Let me out of here!"

"Stay put!" He grabbed the Amurrite by the
shoulder and shoved, and felt a sharp point against
his gut.

"Don't lay hands on me," Aziru said.

When had Aziru gotten a knife? *Where* had he
gotten it? "Lunatic," he said, not moving. "All
right, all right, get past me, go out there, see if I
come after you." *Show that knife again and I'll put
it in your gut, Easterner.*

The sharp edge left him. Aziru wormed past him
as he ducked down, and crawled out onto the tank
surface, scrambled out there and just sat down on
the tank's shelving front—as Antonius poked his
head up again. The man had just sat down, hands
laced over the back of his neck, head bowed.

Antonius climbed up after, sat on the rim, drawing large breaths of air that smelled almost as bad
as that inside. Frogs chirped. The silence was incredible after the roar and noise that still had his

ears ringing and his body convinced there was nowhere any still surface.

He swung his legs around and out of the hole and stopped as the move brought him face about toward a bank of mist and a human shadow between the shadow of two trees. "Aziru. Aziru!" As he scrambled to put himself back inside, and Aziru clambered to his feet.

More and more shadows were about them. He looked back as he was sliding inside, his head still out and Aziru fighting him to get past him.

A figure became clear to him, a figure like some old Greek drama, shining dimly with gold about the brow and over all his armor.

"I am Agamemnon," it said in sepulchral tones. And his muscles froze, holding him still while Aziru fought his way past him into the refuge of the tank. "King of Kings."

O gods, Antonius thought, *O gods. Another damn king. A walking myth. I'm going mad.*

This whole place is.

7.   Shadow of Wings, Shadow of Shadows

At Issus, Alexander had had a second line of mercenaries and Greek allied infantry behind the phalanx, as well as light infantry, flank-guards, and skirmishers on the left.

But always he'd put his best in the front line, with his medium-heavy infantry behind it.

Riding down into Hell's lower reaches through a gaping hole so new its sides still glowed with heat, Roman-column style, he was uneasy.

Perhaps in close quarters such as these lava tubes, Caesar was right. But Caesar's army listened only to him, and did what it had been taught by rote, and liches were as mindless as Persians and as careless of their own survival.

Yet nothing he'd been willing to say could have convinced the Roman, who'd looked at him so oddly under the canvas spread over a battlefield on which Roman tactics had been the loser. Caesar saw more in Alexander, the *basileus* knew, than was there.

And less.

He'd refused to give up his tank—"she" was a part of him now, this metal mount, broken to his

186

hand. And they'd acceded to his demands—Caesar and his Egyptian bitches and their trained dogs—as if he were a wayward youth or a doddering oldster.

Now he sat it grimly, his head showered with grit as it scraped the tunnel roof overhead, wending his way into hell as an ancillary to Caesar's command structure.

Why wouldn't the man see what even Gemayel saw? See that two men who'd sought the ends of the earth and the limits of civilization in life could do no less than see the ends and limits of hell. And their missing men.

And so go in glory, with honor and joy. Reclaim their men. Flush their enemies within and without. But do so not with handwringing and fault-finding and laden looks, but proudly. As was their right and duty.

Gemayel, a New Dead from a different school, a swarthy guerrilla warlord from an uncertain age, had asked the only relevant tactical questions, questions that echoed now in Alexander's head precisely because the Romans had failed to consider them before giving answer.

Gemayel had wanted to know *What enemy? And where? How far?*

But Rome had tramped to victory without caring for such answers as had kept men like Gemayel alive.

So Gemayel had come to Alexander later, in his tent, and asked again.

And Alexander had not been able to give a leader's answer, only assurances that he, too, was concerned. "We have lost the Oracle of Eight Ball, we have lost men. But we have the Shield of Herakles still." He'd motioned to it, over in the corner, and wished he had Diomedes here instead. Wise counsel was sorely lacking for the sortie coming.

Gemayel had looked at him from Asiatic eyes,

long and shadowed, that had looked before upon impenetrable men of greater power whose concerns were not his own, and who might spend his little force in a moment for great and nebulous reasons of their own.

Then Gemayel had said, "We're Christians, you know. We tend to die at the hands of men whose concern is for earthly kingdoms."

And paused, waiting for a response.

Alexander felt an uneasy stirring. Diomedes and Maccabee had both known Gemayel to be an ally worth having and told Alexander so. But they'd said nothing about what it meant to be a Christian. He motioned the New Dead with his hawk-nose and his peregrine's eyes to sit.

The man folded into a squat as Alexander said, "Or hellish ones? No one argues that this mission is practical. Are Christians practical?"

A smile flashed, one subdued by the corners of a mouth which did not like the words forming in it. Then Gemayel said, "My family fought for a land you'd consider inconsequential. I died for it. My father died for it. I might have held it, but my enemies knew that. When I was assassinated, it was left to my brother, who had more in common with Antonius than with commanders such as yourself. But we learned things, fighting street to street and house to house, taking territory and losing it and retaking it, about treachery and what the loyalties of men can mean to a battle. . . ."

"The traitors concern you? Ours, I mean?"

"Dragging the entire army—legion, whatever it is—down those holes tomorrow morning concerns me. A fleet little strike force, good intelligence, men we can trust to be playing for our side . . . that's what we need. Yes, traitors concern me. We need Zaki's input, and I can't find him. And we need to control at least the com truck, the field phones, and to find out who it is Hatshepsut talks to with that jewelry of hers. . . . Women are treacherous, by nature."

"The Oracles of Litton, yes—they're a problem. As is the convenient loss of the eight ball. As for Zaki . . . come with me."

And he'd taken the New Dead who was mindful of the lives of his contemporaries out the back of his tent, so that Murder and Perfidy wouldn't know he was gone.

Zaki had secreted himself in the com truck and not come out since before the meeting, when Alexander had seen him pop up from nowhere as he'd driven back from the debacle on the riverbank. Zaki, who was Alexander's last link with Maccabee. . . .

The affection Alexander felt now for the little Jew whom Maccabee had brought to him was no more out of proportion than the funerary race he'd won in Maccabee's honor. The casualty list had included fifteen Macedonians, better than forty Romans of various ranks, and however many Maronites Gemayel would not admit to having.

Now, less than a dozen Maronites were in evidence as men strode through the tubes toward no-one-knew-what in a light composed of tanks' floods, jeeps' halogens, and the glowing of yet-hot rock.

Last night, as Alexander had guided Gemayel to the com truck, the number had been the same: twelve Maronites, no more—the same number to which Gemayel had owned when first he'd joined the foray.

Alexander equated Gemayel with the mercenaries he'd used long ago: given his choice, he'd have put the Maronites behind him. He had that much respect and that much faith—no less, no more.

But Christians—he learned in a weird discussion

with Zaki, Gemayel, and two New Dead that Zaki called Americans and both Alexander and Gemayel recognized as assassins (at best) and agents of Authority (at worst)—had faith. Faith in their god and his ghost and his son.

Which had made Alexander stiffen, living-god that he was, until he met Zaki's eyes that said, "Tolerance, Basileus. For Maccabee's sake."

If Maccabee had been the one who'd fallen down a hole into some deeper hell, this foolishness would have been easier to bear.

If Diomedes had come and said to him, "Alexander, fear not, for there is nothing to fear but death and that, my friend, is something you've already conquered," the heart of the Macedonian would have been at ease.

But Diomedes was nowhere about, or at least so swore Zaki and the Americans, Welch and Nichols, who touched the bright gems of their paneled fortress and promised him, "Even Maccabee back, sir, if it turns out you want him. Once we get where we're going."

And then the one named Welch had raked the close confines of the truck with a stare that made men naked before he rested it on Alexander and added: "*If* you want him. Then. Meanwhile, if there's anything you want done, King, anything at all . . . ask us. Or Zaki. Or Gemayel. Not Machiavelli. Okay, sir?"

And his companion, a man with the veil of death about him, as Alexander's mother would have said, crossed one leg over the other and murmured, "For your own good."

Alexander, hackles risen, had left the New Dead together, sensing a gulf greater than he had even when, under the canvas during the after-battle meeting with Caesar, Gemayel had made the third point of a triangle of men with crossed arms.

Aristotle had known things about triangles, their magic, their deeper meanings. Aristotelian metaphysics had helped inspire the phalanx. . . .

But now, in his tank with the shield of Herakles beside him, driving point because he'd insisted on it, Alexander was beginning to wonder if it had been wise, putting the New Dead together in their wagon of power.

But Zaki had been recommended to him by Maccabee.

And not even Kleopatra could obscure the meaning of that. Hell offered out certain lessons, if men would but learn them. Helplessness and hopelessness need not be wedded; there was no defeat to be feared but that of the soul.

He would find Maccabee again. And even if Diomedes' prescription of Lethe water had made his friend forgetful of all they'd shared, Alexander would build love anew.

It was the only thing which lived forever, he told himself, touching the shield of Herakles and remembering all the promises it represented.

Diomedes had sought him out, come to him and promised companionship and more; this desertion was just a trick of Fate.

Fate, on the shield, was fearsome and hungry. In Hell, all pain made sense.

So when the Macedonian's groaning, muttering tank spun on its aircushion and seemed to sink, plunging into a miasma of mist and then out with a sound like breaking glass, and beyond was a river and a landscape which made his blood run cold, Alexander didn't try to warn the troops behind.

He was, after all, here for a purpose. And even though his educated eye knew Cocytus, the river of sand where one met one's own ghosts, when he saw it, he didn't falter.

With as steady a hand on the wheel of his tank as he'd had on his reins at Gaugamela, he headed her snout for the land on the farther shore.

He saw a great tree, bereft of leaves, looming out of the mist, and on its boughs, unborn dead with tortured faces wrapped in hideous cocoons that swung as if in a wind though the air was dead still and stinking—Hell's orchard.

He saw the Mourning Fields and knew them for what they were, even in the gray and softly wailing mist that tried to caress him as his physeter, shuddering, ground inexorably toward the forest of suicides, where souls forever lost in its mazes softly cried.

And he saw, far to his left, a greater ghost, the ghost of ancient Greece herself, a landscape of dome-tombs and crooked, Cyclopean-stoned citadels on hilltops.

But he didn't slow the tank, or entertain a second thought, or even quaver. He was Alexander. He was in Hell.

And yet he was blessed, for his genius had brought him here, where the missing surely would be found.

If he'd a doubt, somewhere hiding in the back of his mind, the shadow-shape rising out of the mist which swirled around his vehicle dispelled it: it was a second battle-tank, resting on her iridium skirts, the one they'd lost above.

On it, sitting with hand upraised, was a specter: Agamemnon in his golden mask.

While above his head the sky itself beat against him as if cut by giant wings, Alexander guided his tank up close, and caused it to settle to rest: If Agamemnon was here, then Diomedes' promise was half-kept and eight balls and Egypt be damned with their ominous mouthings.

Given this hero, masked in gold, who confronted him, could Achilles be far?

No farther, he knew with the surety that had accompanied him until Siwah, that the Roman legion pouring out of the hole and into Cocytus with shouts and curses and the demands for caution of their kind.

Tiberius sat overlooking the Bay, staring down the cliff and listening to the mechanical Drusus who was his best gate-guard scare the little Italian he'd summoned half to death.

When Dante arrived past the gauntlet, Tiberius had forgotten what he was supposed to do with the little man.

All little men, all of them. *"I was murdered,"* the Drusus-statue told someone else.

Dante was introducing himself when the second visitor shouldered past creaking gates of iron.

Augustus looked through the eye-stinging gloom of incense and aged stink and fish, at Tiberius, throwing carp down the cliff-side.

And at Dante, who reeked of terror. *Almost* too late never counted. Augustus began, "Tiberius—"

"What? You dare address me without . . ." The crazed Tiberius turned, his manic attention fixed on Augustus, who said sotto voce to Dante, "Go. Get out. To the Pentagram; work your computers; they need Maccabee back at the front."

Meanwhile, Tiberius tiraded about assassins and Augustus' policies and wondered what fit punishment should be, now that Augustus had "come to throw yourself at my feet—for punishment, since forgiveness is impossible."

As Dante scuttled backwards, Augustus said softly, "Didn't you invite me to sup with you?" Tiberius hadn't, but probably wouldn't remember. "Aren't we reconciled? Didn't we need to discuss Brutus' education?"

On Tiberius's face, confusion replaced madness, uncertainy beat back hostility.

Not even an Emperor wanted to be mad.

And the Emperor Augustus, currently playing the most dangerous game in town, had to get Maccabee out of the Undertaker's hands, back to the front, before the Israelite remembered too much and the threads of complicity and guilt and plot and misuse of authority all led to Augustus' door.

Damn Julius for being so competent. Damn Augustus, himself, for caring so much. Damn Tiberius, for being Authority's pawn.

And damn the scuttling little Italian who understood not only Hell's computers, but Hell itself.

Dante, squeezing past him, muttered, *"Perdio,* what's the use? They'll find nothing but a deeper hell. I *wrote* it all down, I just can't get the glitch out of the program. . . ."

And then the Italian was past him, through the doors to safety, and Augustus was wondering whether, if he dared push the "panic" button installed in his belt buckle by one of the clever New Dead in his pay, help could come quick enough to save him from Tiberius, now that he'd come blithely into the spider's web of his own accord.

But he wasn't counting on the button—nothing like "panic" could be admitted.

He was Emperor, too. And Tiberius would be exchanged for Maccabee on the Undertaker's table, if the instructions Augustus had left, to be executed if he didn't emerge from this horrid warren by Paradise's rise, must be carried out.

One way or another, in this enterprise, he and his would not fail Julius.

Aziru didn't understand the significance of being met by the man with the golden mask, although Antony whispered to him that "Agamemnon was hacked up in his bathtub by his wife, Clytemnaestra. Sacred labrys-axe, ritual murder, so the story goes."

It was the warning tone that went with the aside which Aziru hadn't understood.

Agamemnon had offered them hospitality, baths and food and shelter and ungents for Aziru's wounds.

The fortress in which the Great King lived (*another* king, like the old days—caught between Egypt and Hatti and all the kinglets squeezed against the Mediterranean) reminded Aziru of the Hittite palace in Hattusas: giant stones, double gates, and full of magic. And also of Alashiya—especially on the lower floors, and below the quarters where a maiden tended him, where dungeons were ... must be, from the moans that issued up through grates and cracks in stones.

There were stables under, too. Aziru could hear the stamping and squealing of an angry stallion, he thought.

But here, in the room where he was being bathed and fed and where blue velvet hung the walls and Achaean women fussed over him, their golden tresses oiled, all seemed peaceful, serene.

"Here," said the wench with a tray of fruit. "Try the figs. And the wine."

Aziru took the wine, wondering if Antony's wounds were being as well tended, and thinking that his host, albeit strange and masked, was truly a king, when the pounding from below grew louder, and became tumult, and from outside the door he heard the slap of sandaled feet and the creak and jingle of armed men moving in a passage.

He would have gone to see, in fact rose on his elbows to try it, but the serving girl with her great blue eyes, so bright, pushed him back with one finger on his chest.

It was then that Aziru realized he was in the

clutches of a witch, or worse. He was weak, drugged, or delirious.

He must be, because how else could the woman have thrust him with one finger back upon the cushions and brought to him a bronze mirror in which he could see, as clear as day, Scaevola the One-Handed fighting his way through dungeons against ghostly adversaries with at least two score of Romans by his side?

Agamemnon wanted to show them his "fine stables and the hospitality due Great Kings."

Machiavelli wanted none of it. The com truck's driver was easier to convince—Alexander merely sent Zaki to him.

It was for Caesar to deal with Caesar's, and Machiavelli was indubitably Caesar's.

Klea sidled over to him as Alexander was wrestling the shield of Herakles from the tank's hatch, saying, "Basileus, we should confer."

The Macedonian snapped at her: "Confer with whom? Or *what?* Your living oracle, Egypt? I've had enough of tranced women. I'm going. We're here to get our men back, aren't we? Agamemnon," the wonder that tinged his words was something Alexander didn't try to hide, "has promised me that, if I partake of his hospitality, our missing will be returned to us."

They were still on the riverbank. The stragglers were just coming out of the hole. Alexander had pulled his tank up next to the one on which Agamemnon had been sitting.

One was expected to wait for Caesar. While waiting, he'd asked Agamemnon of Antony and been told, "Within, within. Where you will soon be," the words coming muffled through the golden mask, heavy with ancient dialect and accent.

He'd told Klea, who'd asked him, what Agamemnon had said. Because Agamemnon wouldn't look at or acknowledge her in any way. He acted as if she didn't exist.

And Klea was pretending not to notice.

But she had. Now she went running back to Caesar and Alexander hefted the shield of Herakles, feeling better when he'd strapped it to his arm and, as an afterthought, slung the Uzi over his shoulder.

The fortress on the hilltop looked uninviting, askew and mist-ridden, as if afflicted by shades. His Macedonians, coming up around him, were glancing at it askance, their remaining horses spooked and dancing.

What had the horses nervous, he told them in a ringing voice (they were his, he knew what they needed to hear) was not the fortress, the citadel on the hill, but the orchard of suicides and the tree of unborn dead, over to their right, steeped in bog and mist.

What had him nervous was the way Agamemnon wouldn't take off his mask, and ignored the two Egyptian women so concertedly.

But his new allies, Gemayel and Zaki, had brought the truck up, at last: "Can't be any worse than that," Gemayel said, his face pale, jerking his chin toward the moaning of the Mourning Fields. "Let's just quit this place before dark."

And so Alexander, looking back once to see Caesar's head bent in conference with what was left of his officers and his Egyptian women, led his Macedonians, his Maronites, and the New Dead (except for Machiavelli, who scurried to Caesar's standard like a cockroach), up to Agamemnon's citadel in the masked king's wake.

Zaki slipped out the rear door of the com truck and headed through the milling army on the beach, unnoticed by any but Hatshepsut, and approached her, as the miniature transmitter curled snakelike around her ear had said he would.

When he reached her, the little Jew petitioned her as so many Jews had in former times, "Pharaoh, we need your help, your wisdom and your judgment, in the matter of a traitor in your midst."

This, too, the voice which spoke in her ear had told her. She'd never met the man who spoke to her from the com truck, who was her link to Augustus' villa in New Hell and to such information as only the Devil had, but she trusted the technology he represented. More than men. More than even the army and its command structure, rife with factions—more than Caesar, tonight.

The jewelry she wore and the Litton phone she had slung over her jumpsuit had never failed her. And if this Jew came with such a recommendation, then he too was trustworthy. For the nonce.

She looked at him closely in the long pause, while around them the cohorts shouted orders, making camp. He had soft brown eyes of the sort behind which warriors of the intellect hid, warriors who fought wars of wits back unto ancient times.

In her day, she'd made use of Jews, who wanted only to survive, who could smell plots with their long noses and who could think twelve moves down the board-game of life.

She had never known a Jew to go against his own best interest. She had never known the soft, clipped voice that came out of her jewelry to lie. And the voice had said, "Listen to Zaki. Help him, or we'll never get out of here. Over."

And perhaps because she'd so recently invoked powers she didn't understand and prophesied truly in her aspect as Amon, she wanted now to stop the disembodied voice from becoming a self-fulfilling prophecy of the sorest kind.

. . . or we'll never get out of here. Over.

Not *over*. Not here, with no Opening of the Mouth and no barge to carry her to a better place. Not yet.

So she said to the velvet-eyed little man who reminded her so much of some emissary from Naharin, whose sharp nose was good for smelling plots and whose dark skin whispered of Nile-side assignations and eucalyptus rustling in the night, "Fear not, Zaki. Say the truth to me."

Little Zaki looked to his right, to his left at the Romans about their camp-making, and said, "We have a traitor among us, this you know. Macabee's murder. . . . And now so many others returned to the Undertaker's table, where all they know can be learned by Authority. . . ."

As he spoke of what a child should understand, Hatshepsut's back stiffened: did he think her unobservant, or merely dense, a woman occupied with matters of kohl and phallus? She was about to tell him to get to the point when Zaki did.

"It's Machiavelli, you see. We can prove it. We have eyewitnesses to a message he received in the truck. Circumstantial, of course, until we retrieve Aziru, but enough. . . ."

The little Israeli trailed off, overtly assessing her reaction.

She showed none, saying, "Niccolo? And you're surprised? Or think I am? Is there a reason for your revelation?"

Zaki took a deep breath as, behind, someone breathed life into a physeter to bring it in line with the others along the riverbank. "Pharaoh. . . ." He grimaced, some personal thought flitting over his face which made it gray and cold. "We wish to reveal him to Caesar. Neuter him by defining him.

If possible, to turn the screw again and make him
ours. Do you understand?"

"Understand?" she bristled at an unintentional
slight. Niccolo, of course, could not be trusted. She
was not in the habit of assuming trust—not even
of this descendent of her slaves. But the voice in
the com truck had never lied, and allies on a foreign shore were few. "You mean, do I agree. Of
course. Now listen and hear what we will do. . . ."

When Diomedes caught up with army, strung
out along the shore of Cocytus, the sight took his
breath away and made his hackles rise.

For a moment he wished it was he, and not the
bright-maned horses he led on a long tether, who
had his eyes and nose and ears bound and stuffed
with clean linen, so as not to be affrighted by what
might be seen, or heard, or smelled.

He'd caught the fleeing horses, haters of fire,
and calmed them and tied them together, all in a
line, and led them with assurances through the
steaming holes of hell to rejoin them with the men
who rode them. As he'd promised the steed that
Caesar had given him, none had come to harm.

But he had never thought he was leading them
into such a Hell as this.

With his skin crawling, he moved down the horse-
line he'd improvised, freeing liquid eyes to see,
nostrils to flare and snort, and ears to twitch and
lay back flat.

Diomedes had thought, when first the horses
bolted, mad with fear of Phlegethon's embrace, to
round them up and return them to those who
loved them. He hadn't thought he'd wind up looking down on a twisted version of his past.

Along Cocytus' bank, the tanks were strung at
intervals like hollow ships beached at Ilion. Cocytus

was an allegory: Diomedes knew exactly what he saw.

He squatted down beside the lead horse, a hand on its foreleg, and watched tiny men move from tent to pitched tent, while above and beyond, lights in the citadel presaged the coming of the night.

Troy, again?

He couldn't bear it. But the men were there, and the citadel was there, and over to the right was every omen he needed to understand what it was he saw: the Mourning Fields, the tree of unborn dead, and the domed tombs of home.

Was one of them his own?

He'd searched long for something Achaean, something familiar. He'd wanted only to feel at home. But here, where soft wailing tickled his ears and Fate chuckled that men seldom like their wishes when they get them, he wished he'd never wished.

Never trekked with Alexander because a bird had flown down and told him so. Never listened to a specter with great pinions and the head of a foolish man. Was Achilles in some domed tomb, thence, sleeping? Menelaos? Agamemnon?

All his ghosts crowded in on him and he nearly called their names. Before his eyes tanks shivered and took on the likeness of hollow ships in the tricky gloom of dusk.

He palmed his eyes and his new mount nuzzled his hair.

When he looked again, it was merely Romans and iridium tanks from unborn ages.

But he could not misread the message. It was Troy again, Hell's version of it, and he was coming home . . .

He started down the slope of scree and cold lava and the horses followed. *Home* was an encampment on a foreign shore, as then, with war and treachery in the offing.

He held tight to sanity on that downward trek, reminding himself that reason mattered more than similarities of dooms or suicides crying in their endless night.

He'd started this, all of it, brought the 10th and its officers here as surely as Agamemnon, son of Atreus, chief of the Achaeans, had begun it last time.

And the oracle had told Agamemnon that he'd take Ilion only when the best of the Achaeans quarreled.

So long ago, so near at hand—Achilles in his beached ship, fighting over wenches that went on and on. Odysseus and the night hunt. . . .

Athene had loved him then; he'd never faltered. But, to do it all *again?* Some hellish version, like a horrid dream that wouldn't end?

All that he saw, down on the flat as he led the snorting horses past the tree whose fruit was tortured souls, was achingly familiar. It made him sweat like a slave and made his belly churn and his mouth dry up.

He'd wanted to find this place, when he thought he never would—some familiar Hell, a balm for all the strangeness up above.

And now he had. He must accept it. Deal with it.

As men acknowledged him—first, Roman sentries, then German ones—he searched in vain for Alexander's tent.

Not finding it, he found instead Decius Mus, to take the horses. No surrogate for all the missing Macedonians, but a clear-eyed soldier, none the less.

So he said to Mus, "Alexander's tank is here. And Antony's. But I see no Macedonian tents . . . ?"

"Gone—the Greeks, that is. Up there." Mus pointed to the citadel on the closest hill, glowering out over the beach with eyes of fire. "Antony, I've heard, is up there too. Your man went to get him out, up to Agamemnon's—"

"*What?*" Agamemnon. Diomedes took a step back, his hand pressed against his brow. Like Ilion, then. It was already started. A hostage, Antony, to begin it.

He looked wildly around. "And the Maronites? The Americans—the *com truck?*" His voice quavered, his words were thick with an accent that, in better times, he could suppress.

" 'Scuse?" said Mus, his face carefully composed. Decius Mus was being gentle, an old soldier who recognized the reaction that he saw. "The truck went up with Alexander—a precaution, I think. But Zaki's skulking around somewhere. . . ."

Diomedes was already saying, "So the gift-horse is in the citadel. Too late to stop it now," and backing away, wanting only solitude to sort out memory from memory, to bed old emotions risen like fearful shades.

He couldn't bear to think of going through all that again, camped on this beach for ten years. The quarreling. The covert ventures. The battles of wits against his own, as well as the other, side. The uselessness of it all.

And yet, if he had to, he would. And if Alexander was in there, he had to.

Had to do something. So he went as close to Caesar's tent as he could get, still sweating and grateful for the cloak of night to hide it, and asked to see the Romans' Emperor.

The guard he met sent another running, and soon two figures came back through the torchlit dark.

One was a woman, Hatshepsut by her blaster and her jumpsuit.

He'd had little contact with the Roman elite. And less with the Egyptian women.

By choice.

Now, he met eyes glittering with paint and full of laughter he didn't understand.

He stared. He couldn't pour out his heart, his fears, to one of these.

The guards backed up. She put her hands upon her hips; he crossed his arms.

She said impatiently, "Diomedes, isn't it? Well, what is it you want with Caesar?"

"Caesar."

"Yes, I know. But what's the message?"

"I want to see him, not you."

"I'll have to do, for now. And, when you speak to me, use some dignity or other: Great King, Pharaoh, or even Ma'am. It's not fitting for discipline," she added, stepping close and saying also, under her breath. "Zaki's here too. We were expecting you ..." She touched her bejeweled neck, and then her ear.

Diomedes leaned upon his spear, his cheek against its bronze and pointed flare. Zaki was here. "I'll wait for Zaki ... down by the river, at Alexander's tank."

"It'll be a while," said Pharaoh, nodding as she spoke. "We're dealing with a little problem of our own. Give me a message for Julius, if it's urgent enough that you're still talking to me." A feline smile rippled across the features of the woman who was a king.

"Tell him," Diomedes said, faltered, and began again. "Tell him it's Ilion all over again, and I'm available, if he wants to talk about it."

"With 'wise counsel'?" she shot back.

"Too late for that. With last resorts, unless you want to spend eternity learning what Hell can really be, from experts."

Before she could respond, Diomedes turned on

his heel and stalked away into the dark full of Romans and the moans of the dead and his ghosts.

Maccabee still couldn't see anything, but he heard voices as he was being moved.

He shouted wordlessly: *Want to go back to the river.*

A voice answered, with a heavy Italian accent. "To Alexander. Yes, we know. Keep shut. Don't think about it."

And then there was rapidfire Italian he couldn't follow, and he thought he felt wind against his skin.

If they sent him back like this. . . .

He groaned and he shuddered at the sound.

The sound?

He'd heard his own voice. Heard it. That was something.

He tried to move but still he couldn't.

He tried to speak but he couldn't move his jaw, not this time.

But he'd heard himself groan. And he felt a bumping, as if he were in a mild earthquake.

He felt. He'd heard. He began to thank God. Favors of this sort were not small.

But then he heard a roaring noise, as if he were close to the very furnaces of Hell, and his body was buffeted by a great wind, and vertigo overtook him, as if he were tilted and shunted, as if he were moving.

And then there was shouting and he tried to add to it. *Please. I've got to get back to Alexander. I'm Maccabee. I've got to get back. I won't say—*

A voice loud and like a roar cut him off, "Can't you shut this guy up?"

And something stung his arm, as if a bee were stabbing at the inside of his elbow.

He'd felt it. He'd felt it. As his soul slid down a

pink whirlpool into an abyss in which he was no longer Maccabee, no longer anyone at all, he held that thought: he'd felt it.

And then there was nothing but the greatest roar he'd ever hear, which never stopped, but pulsed like blood beating in the Devil's veins.

In the citadel, Alexander was preparing to have dinner with his host.

One of the Americans was quartered in the next room, and had slit a latching thong to make the rooms adjoin.

"Precaution," Nichols had said with that tiger's stare.

Welch had refused to leave the com truck, squinting up at Alexander and retorting to a direct order, "King or not, I can't do that, sir. Somebody's got to be here to coordinate. With base camp. Take this. Nobody'll know I'm here if you don't tell."

"This" was a well-wrought brooch and an earring.

Alexander had fingered the earring distastefully. He'd known them in Persia.

He'd slipped it through his ear, hoping no one would misconstrue, and left Welch in his hiding place.

So they had already betrayed the hospitality of their host, Agamemnon the hero, king of the Mykenaioi.

And they hadn't seen Aziru or Antony yet.

Nichols, acting proprietary, came in, tugging his chiton down and demanding that Alexander hurry.

Then there was a woman at the door and, in the hallway, another of the weird sounds drifting up from somewhere below—sounds that made Nichols frown and Alexander mutter aloud that they were emissaries and expected to be treated as such.

The woman was silent with eyes like rainforest pools.

She led them down ancient stairs, handhewn by giants from boulders, stairs so old they'd settled askew, one upon the other.

She led them under sconces and through a maze of corridors that made Nichols mutter under his breath as if memorizing lines of verse, "Two rights, three lefts, one right, one left, big headless statue, one right . . ."

And then there was the great hall, hung with tapestries that echoed the themes on the shield of Herakles, back in Alexander's room.

He'd hesitated about that, but one didn't go to dinner armed, even with Agamemnon.

Then, seeing the king at the end of the great hall, Alexander forgot about the shield.

This was a king of legend, in a hall fit for Homer's praise.

The dais he reclined on was old, so old, and his golden mask glittered in the torchlight.

On his right was Antony, arms on the table, and before them was a great pig, roasted whole, two-pronged forks stuck in its eyes and ears.

And there was fruit there, and every manner of delicacy from the world entire.

Agamemnon saw them, and waved, and called out: "Basileus, *wanax*. Come take this seat beside me."

As he did, Nichols in tow, Alexander realized that in the shadow of the great hall were many statues, man-sized, of warriors, beautifully hewn in ancient style.

He saw, too, newer figures with Boeotian helmets, and some with modern weaponry, all from the same gray stone that was veined with red.

And Nichols whispered into the medallion around his neck, "Take a fix, Welch? Position? Possible extraction, nil without force of arms," as the great doors closed behind them and human sentries were revealed, along with musicians and serving wenches—a dozen in all.

"Take your seat, Alexander," demanded the king impatiently.

Alexander did, sitting on the right of the masked king in his embroidered linen and motioning Nichols to do likewise.

But the American demurred, taking up a position behind Alexander's chair as if it were customary.

The golden mask of Agamemnon turned to stare, or glare, at the man behind the chair and then fixed on Alexander.

"So, you fear treachery." A hollow laugh sounded and a great, scarred hand raised to sweep from right to left. "So do I, boy, so do I."

And it was then that Alexander noticed that, in all this time, Antony had not looked up, or met his eye, or even scratched a flea. The Roman had not moved a muscle, but just sat staring at his laden dinner plate, one hand upon his two-pronged fork, the other on a black ball.

"Antony? An*toni*us?" Alexander said, restraining an impulse to reach out and shake the other man, wondering what he'd do if Antony didn't respond, here where Agamemnon's guard was so attentive and even Nichols was unarmed.

But Antony raised his head at the sound of his name and said, with a half-drunk, vacant smile, "Try the figs. Or the wine."

At which moment the musicians began to play and a chorus to sing and, it seemed to Alexander for just an instant, the nearer statues to the dining table shifted on their plinths.

Zaki had not been satisfied with Caesar's decision regarding Machiavelli, though it *was* Caesar's decision.

Zaki knew, however, that revenge for Maccabee was what he wanted, and Caesar wished another thing.

Making Machiavelli an agent of Roman interest above all other interests might, should the ploy work, be more valuable in the long run.

In the near term, Zaki had other interests of his own to pursue. He was in communication with Welch, inside the citadel, and was trying to talk Diomedes through something like delayed-stress syndrome, brought on when the Argive had glimpsed this very Achaean Hell and then learned, on top of it, that Alexander's party had gone up there.

The big Achaean was readying his horse, his shield oiled and his spear filed to a killing point.

Zaki couldn't tell if the ancient was listening to him, but he kept talking: "In Israel, friend, more evil used to happen in a week than in the rest of the world in a year. We became used to it. We endured it. How much more, in Hell, must a man take? Alexander went there of his own will."

"And Caesar stayed behind, of his. Alexander knows only legends. Agamemnon fought the Trojans with me at his side. A long war. He'll listen to me. You don't understand."

"Old war buddies? I understand. I simply do not agree that you, a single man, should prepare an assault on a citadel."

"Your gift-horse is in there, your mechanical horse with its many ears." Diomedes buckled his horse's bridle, took a handful of mane, and vaulted aboard.

He meant the com truck, Zaki knew. "That's right. And Scaevola, we think, is down underneath it, somewhere—at least somebody's unit is. There's fighting, we can pick up the signatures of men and metal. . . ." Diomedes looked at him askance and Zaki stopped before he had to explain the unexplainable.

Zaki didn't have satisfactory answers on the matter of Welch and Nichols, himself. What part they saw for themselves in this, where everyone took someone's part and allegiances shifted like desert sands.

"Diomedes, I am avenging Maccabee," Zaki said in desperation, as if one more untruth might win the day, "and I need your help."

"The murderer is found?" queried the big man, hesitating, his horse shivering under him.

Zaki craned his neck to stare up at the mounted Argive, this creature from myth with his fearsome helmet and physique, and told the truth: "The culprit here is not the man forced to the deed, but the one who planned and implemented it. Machiavelli."

"And his punishment?" the Argive demanded.

"To serve Caesar's interests truly, to be distrusted and known for what he is. Eternally. It is enough. Now, we need your wise—"

"Bull's dung. I promised Alexander to see him to Achilles, if he distinguished himself. I must do it. He must do it. I must go to him."

The Old Dead were impossibly literal, Zaki had long known.

"If Alexander's in trouble, he'll need more than one man to—"

"You have your army, you and the Romans. If I cannot come back with the *basileus*, then you can still storm the citadel. Use the com truck. Use the tanks to break down the gates." Diomedes shrugged and kneed his horse. "What I do," he said as the beast danced sideways, "I do for myself." He flicked his chin to the east of camp, where a bog wailed like tortured souls. "And for them, all the Mourning Ones."

Zaki almost grabbed for the big horse's bridle, wondering if a Roman order would have done what he could not do, and stopped this foolishness, when a sound Zaki hadn't heard for years split the night.

The horse reared. The Achaean cursed in his ancient tongue.

Zaki was already prone on the ground, speaking urgently into the mike on his lapel. "Welch, what is this? Some trick of yours and I'll let Hatshepsut put your phallus in a jar!"

Crackle. Sputter. Snap. Then Welch's voice came from the transceiver: "Hughes chopper, definitely. Don't ask me who, or how he got it, despite the prohibition. Every time I ask for an ID that hot dog tells me he's Achilles with a Medevac bird. That's all I know. Over."

"Say again?" Zaki demanded, but Welch didn't respond.

And Diomedes was sliding from his horse, grabbing the beast's head and pulling it to his chest, stroking its ears and crooning to it not to be afraid.

But the horse, like every other in camp, was terrified of the chopper, and the waves of air and dirt and debris it threw made Zaki slit his eyes.

He'd explain it to Diomedes when he understood it himself. A chopper, here?

The helicopter shone its landing lights, brighter than anything seen in this part of Hell, and began to settle between the tanks and the camp.

By then, Zaki could see the crowd it drew: even Caesar was out of his tent, arms akimbo, his satellites running to and fro like frightened ants.

The look on Diomedes' face most concerned Zaki: wide-eyed and full of something more like resignation than fear.

... most concerned him until Hatshepsut came

running toward them, blaster drawn and guards pacing her, with Mettius Curtius in her wake.

Although Zaki scrambled to his feet to intercept, it was Diomedes, mounted once more, who reached her first, and grabbed Pharaoh unceremoniously from her feet, slinging her across his horse's withers like a captive and wrestling the blaster from her hand.

As he did so, there was a sudden, aching silence more deafening than the noise had been, as the chopper pilot cut his engines.

In it, Zaki heard Diomedes' yell: "Do harm to the bird of my vision, woman, and I'll drag you by your heels round Agamemnon's fortress!"

Zaki whirled on his heel to face the pair just in time to see Diomedes dump the Great King over the off-side of his horse and Curtius and her guards draw a bead on him with everything from assault rifles to crossbows.

The horseman and the fallen pharaoh were encircled by angry Romans who wanted nothing more than an enemy they could bring to ground.

But Caesar was coming, striding through the press, and Zaki heard the sound of the chopper's doors opening.

And a voice from that direction hallooing: "Hey! I've got somebody named Maccabee on board. Supposed to deliver him here! Who's in charge?"

A man in a helmet and medevac fatigues jumped down from the chopper, clearly limned in its lights, and when he took off his helmet to look at his clipboard, Diomedes let out a blood-curdling cry and raced his horse through the circle of men around it.

"Achilles!" Zaki was almost sure he heard the Argive scream as the bright-maned horse went thundering past, down to the chopper parked half-way to the beach.

*   *   *

The "bird" had brought Achilles. The bird had brought Maccabee, dazed and weak, but unscathed.

The bird had more uses than that, Achilles told Diomedes with that sour, superior quirk to his mouth that Diomedes well remembered.

"Cannon. Machine guns. Mm thirties. . . . Never mind, Diomedes. You'll see. Maccabee here's been filling me in, haven't you, Mac?"

It was disconcerting to be listening to a fellow veteran of Ilion speak American English.

Achilles was sorely changed, more like the Americans than the man Diomedes remembered.

But the bird had come, the wings beating down from the air had been real. The bird was black, night-camouflaged as Achilles said, and the signs Diomedes had been receiving over these last few weeks were all justified, honest portents.

If Fate was not bringing together all the veterans of the war against the Luwians on this ancient beach full of ghosts for Her own purposes, Diomedes would have been triumphant.

Despite this, and the fact that Alexander, Antony, and the com truck languished behind the citadel's walls, Diomedes couldn't help feeling relieved.

Almost redeemed.

Transiently. Until Achilles' selfish, divisive nature reared its ugly head: he was ready for that.

Men who had fought together of old would do so again, this was clear.

Even clear to Achilles, who said, when he heard that Alexander wanted to meet with him but was up at Agamemnon's, "Well, we'd better get him out. The Atreidês never were well-wrapped, any of them, and Agamemnon's had lots of time to brood about being hacked up by his wifey."

Maccabee looked between them, concern for his Macedonian friend putting strength into his pallid face. "Alexander?" the Israelite leaning weakly against the chopper repeated. "In trouble? My memory is vague . . . I must go to him. . . ."

"Soon," Diomedes promised Maccabee, looking at Achilles. "Soon. We must confer with the Romans, they're a part of this."

"Same old shit, Diomedes? Bat the ball around until it's too late? You don't understand what *this* baby," he stroked the black bird as if it were alive, "can do. But then, you wouldn't. You're probably feeling right at home in this spook-ridden refuge for the irredeemable. I, for one, want to get out of here. I'll save your friend, Maccabee, as long as it doesn't take too long." White teeth flashed.

"Impetuous as ever," Diomedes spat, one hand hooking in his belt. "We'll see how soon you leave here. Fate's at the helm of this ship, not you, whatever you may think."

And when a runner came, summoning them all to Caesar's tent, Diomedes' counsel was proved to be true.

Alexander was drunk, drunk as a lord, drunk as Lord Agamemnon. So drunk, in fact, that he was beginning to have visions.

In his visions, two statues of red-veined gray stone came down from their plinths and helped Antony up onto an empty plinth between them and Antony didn't seem to mind.

Meanwhile, the chorus of men dressed as women sang in their sweet voices and women who seemed really to be women wrestled Nichols to the ground.

He could hear Nichols yelling through the singing of the chorus, yelling in American English until he was hoarse, until the yelling faded.

Over and over: *"Welch. Get us out of here! Alex! The Uzi! In our room!"*

But it was only a part of the vision, because Agamemnon wasn't aware of anything untoward.

The Great King was leaning on one prodigious elbow, gold-masked chin cupped in a massive fist, explaining to Alexander what it had been like to fight at Ilion and how, for services rendered and because Justice must be served here in Hell, Agamemnon reigned from this fortress, no longer a soldier on the beach: "No longer an aggressor, but a defender. With the occasional hostage, of course. Until the Achaeans gather to the man and history is ready to repeat. It's my curse, you see, to know my fate." Agamemnon's voice was gravelly, his words slurred from wine. "I've my own oracle, you see."

He hefted the black ball and, even drunk as Alexander was, the Macedonian knew he'd seen it somewhere before.

"Oracle?" Alexander repeated. "Delphic?" He strove for clarity, kingliness. He hadn't drunk enough to be this besotted. And yet he was. Dignity was worth a struggle. "Mantic? I've seen a ball like that . . ."

"Yes, yes, I'm sure you have," said the masked king with a snort and a slight inclination of his head.

Alexander looked over his shoulder, in the direction that the golden mask had dipped.

And there was nothing there. He'd had a companion here, not come alone. He struggled to remember. All he could come up with was: ". . . take Ilion when the best of the Achaeans quarrel."

The mask snapped back and black-hole eyes glowered at him: "What did you say?" Agamemnon's voice echoed off the statues on their plinths, off the rafters, off the musicians' instruments in ugly overtones.

"I said," Alexander enunciated clearly, "that my

friend has gone to bed, and so should I." He'd come here with someone; there was an empty plate across from him that proved it. "A surfeit of hospitality." He stood up, both hands flat upon the table, and for once thanked the gods that he was short in stature.

And, standing, saw the statue opposite him, that looked so much like Antony, pretty and vapid and posed as if frozen between steps.

"Bed. Yes." Agamemnon rose too, and snapped his fingers, so that servants appeared and crowded round, a bevy like sycophants, flitting, confusing Alexander even more, so that he asked, "My own manservant? Where . . . ?"

"In your apartments," a woman crooned. "Dead to the world. Still as stone." Tugging on his arm, with others around to help her, she shepherded him up the stairs.

On the way, still in the throes of his visions, Alexander thought he saw men he'd known among the statues of the great hall. Aziru's likeness was there. And Phidian creations.

He told himself as peril gnawed at drink's curtain and his brain desperately struggled to clear itself, that all these Achaean statues were the natural companion of a lonely, exiled ruler.

There were female statues also, one exceptional in beauty, one with a great labrys-axe. Both were naked, and graffiti was written on their chests, and their nipples and all their hair was painted red.

As red as the veins in the stone, he thought dreamily, falling back toward stupor as hands helped him up the stairs.

In his room was no manservant that he could see, but slaveboys and eunuchs and a bath for him, already drawn.

He recoiled from it: it was hot and the tub reminded him of Darius'. His temper flared and wits cleared in fury's wake: "Out! All of you! Out! I want only my man."

He struggled for the name, and got instead a mental vision of a New Dead in a black t-shirt. And then Alexander remembered that he was in Hell, and pushed the soothing hands of a eunuch from his thighs, a eunuch who, along with a boy and a girl, was trying to strip him and push him toward the bath despite his protests.

They hung on him like leeches, and suddenly he was afraid.

Nichols. Where was the man, sent to guard him? Where? "Nichols?" he bellowed, throwing himself forward so that the eunuch fell to its knees and the boy and girl began to weep.

A voice in his ear answered, with a growl and a popping sound, as if someone had belched in his face: *"Alexander? Welch here. What the fuck's happening up there? Nichols was yelling, now he's snoring his head off. Over."*

The voice was gone, but all the servants in the room were staring at him.

And Alexander was nearly sober with rage. "Out! I command you!" he snarled, and strode to the bedside where he'd left the shield of Herakles, kicking at the bodies trying to trip him and grab him, too many to count and probably all part of this nasty vision which had him in its thrall.

The voice in his ear squawked: *"Alexander. Nichols? Come in?"* as Alexander reached his bedside and picked up the shield of Herakles, meaning to take the Uzi hidden under it and clear the room with slingshotted metal, if threats would not do the job.

But as he raised the shield, the hands on him fell away, the eunuch hissed like a snake, and the boy and girl broke and fled, screaming in weird, twittering tones.

He held the shield out, wondering if it would
work again, and by its aegis, pointing it like a
lance or a phalanx at his enemies who wanted to
force him into that tub, he vanquished each and
all and chased them out the portal.

When he closed the heavy door and leaned against
it, panting with the effort, he was alone.

But for the voice in his ear which was whispering madness about Achilles and Maccabee. Poor
lost Maccabee. He should never have argued with
Maccabee.

Achilles was a dream and Maccabee had been
the best friend Alexander had in Hell.

He sank down, his back against the door, the
shield of Herakles covering him like a blanket,
near to tears.

But the voice in his ear wouldn't stop. Now it
tortured him by speaking Diomedes' name. Diomedes had deserted Alexander, disappeared during the battle with Phlegethon's liches. Diomedes
had left him alone.

*"Nichols! Goddamn it, wake up! ETA three min-
utes! Want your Tac Air, or not?"*

And then Alexander remembered the latching
thong Nichols had cut, between their two apartments. And staggered to his feet, leaning on the
shield of Herakles for balance.

Then, using it as a crutch, he hobbled to that
door and pushed on it.

As it gave inward, revealing Nichols snoring in a
bathtub while his flesh turned gray in blood-red
water and creatures labored over him with sponges,
a hellish noise and bright light came in the open
windows of the tower, and amidst the noise and
light a great shadow fell, a shadow of wings such
as that Diomedes had predicted.

"Nichols? Nichols!" Alexander shouted, and stumbled forward, brandishing the shield of Herakles

with its fearsome hungry Erinys and its unspeakable face of Fear, and with Ares and his fleet-
footed horses and all the Gorgons and the fighting
men thereon.

The light coming in the window from the mighty
bird was caught up by the shield and reflected
onto Nichols in his bath.

And the man woke, and vaulted up, and grabbed
his clothes and spoke into the medallion he held in
one hand, and then to Alexander: "Thanks, King.
Let's get our asses out of here."

"Out? But Antony, and Aziru . . ."

"Out, downstairs. We've been designated the welcoming party for Achilles and his chopper." The
gray tinge was still upon the American, but his
eyes were clearing.

As Alexander leaned upon the shield and the
American hurriedly dressed in his long pants and
black shirt, Alexander thought he could hear,
through the beat of mighty wings, screaming and
crying and once again, up through the floor, the
sound of a battle down below.

Achilles put the chopper down in the citadel's
forecourt and he, Diomedes, and Maccabee jumped
out.

Diomedes held up his hand: wait. Spears and
bows were trained on them from ramparts. The
battle plan, however, was clear and decided.

He glanced at Maccabee, still weak from his trip
back from the Undertaker's table, and thought,
*Thus, for all of us, in the end. It's a way out and no
way out: if we take it, the Devil wins.*

But he said aloud only, "As we agreed, then.
Leave to Caesar what is Caesar's."

Maccabee promised, in the name of his nameless
god.

Achilles only grunted, looking like one of the

New Dead in his camouflage and boots with armaments slung over his chest and a helmet in his hand.

Achilles and he had already had the first of many quarrels, a banked fire now, because of what he'd heard from Caesar and what Machiavelli had said about "fools who don't know enough to realize you're playing the Devil's game by His own rules."

Perhaps they were, but the black bird had come and Maccabee had returned to them, with Achilles, and this was Agamemnon's fortress.

"Go up there," Machiavelli had said in a sensual tone not fit for the words it bore, "and you'll make the last link: you'll be stuck on the beach, fighting your unwon war forever—all that was lacking for it was Achilles and you. It'll happen so fast your head will swim: you'll all be on the beach, with your mad Agamemnon, who's been collecting Achaeans all these centuries. He'll fight it until he can get it right."

"So? Big deal," Achilles had said.

And Diomedes had looked at Machiavelli, realizing that the Devil's pawn was short a certain bit of information: Patroklos was not on the rolls of Hell.

And if he were, there was still Alexander to consider.

So they were here, dismounting the giant bird, with Agamemnon to face and the 10th and all Caesar's forces, including physeters, sneaking up the hillside in their wake.

He'd wanted to find all this; if it meant ten years on the beach, then that was what it meant.

But what Welch's voice had told them, of heroes turned to statues to wait unknowing, of Agamemnon madder than he'd ever been before, of Aziru in the hallway and Scaevola eternally battling his way up an infinite number of stairs from dungeons of infinite expanse, could not be allowed to continue.

Not under Achaean administration. Not under the aegis of Diomedes' people. This time, as he had not last time, Diomedes was here to say no when no would do some good, to put a stop to matters for his soul's sake.

Achilles widened his stance, a halogen torch in one hand, shining it over faces grim and stony on the battlements.

"Got great intelligence, I'll give you that," said Achilles to no one in particular, while Maccabee pulled his robe close about him, shivering in this ancient courtyard full of death.

Diomedes ignored Achilles. He called out: "Agamemnon! Come forth! It is I, Diomedes! And Achilles! And bring your guests, whom you must treat as such—every one, not just Alexander and Nichols, but Antony and Aziru, Scaevola and the rest. Anyone detained with treachery or guile, bring out unharmed. Or all the Achaeans will know you for a man unfit to counsel. You will no longer be a king. You'll be reviled in Hell. You'll—"

On the great front steps, men or statues moved, and doors opened.

Through them and down came Agamemnon in a golden mask, his steps heavy, his bull's chest heaving, a standard in his hand.

"What's this?" Agamemnon cried querulously. "Slander from a brother of the wars?"

Achilles spoke then, "Give us our people, or we'll trade you ten lives to one. Not spoils this time, except in Hell's terms."

Somewhere in the shadows of the court, an engine started: the com truck moved up and, its headlights blazing, parked beside the chopper, motor idling.

Agamemnon kept coming, things behind him shuffling in and out of shadows, men and women who were human gathering on the steps.

When the king in the mask was ten feet from them, he stopped. His thick-wristed hands were twisting on his standard. His voice was muffled when he spoke: "Achilles. Diomedes. It *is* you. Let us not quarrel, but rejoice ..."

"Alexander," Achilles said implacably. "And the others, chief. Now."

Maccabee, who was here only for Alexander and should have had enough sense to keep silent, clutched his robe at his throat and stepped forward, saying, "You've done evil, in God's sight. And He sees, even here. Return our—"

Agamemnon began to thump his standard on the flags. And the sound it made reverberated from the walls and towers of the citadel, and stones began to crack.

"Evil?" Agamemnon howled over the deafening echoes. "Evil? To keep everyone safe until we were all united once again? To set the scene to right the wrongs, to play the war out, and do it right?"

Achilles, Diomedes saw, was reaching for the pistol at his hip.

Behind, as Agamemnon thumped and screamed, stones were beginning to fall from the turrets and men to pour from the citadel's great inner doors. Diomedes saw Alexander, behind the shield of Herakles, helping someone: Antony.

And Nichols, behind him, had Aziru's arm over his shoulders.

Seeing this, the com truck wheeled toward the emerging men with a screech of tires, and Maccabee darted forward with more strength than Diomedes would have thought he had.

In the chaos, Agamemnon never faltered: he howled and he thumped his standard and, around him, the citadel walls came tumbling down.

Diomedes saw Achilles raise his service pistol, take aim.

But it couldn't happen. Diomedes couldn't let it happen. He reached out, touched Achilles' wrist, and shook his head. There was witchery here too foul already.

Achilles ported his pistol.

Agamemnon was screaming that, since Achilles and Diomedes were here, they could wage their war again and win it, and Agamemnon would never face the labrys-axe or a vengeful wife again.

And with every thump of Agamemnon's standard, those trapped within the citadel walls were getting closer to that reality:

The walls were tumbling down, and beyond them, a moonlit, wine-dark sea could be seen.

Ships like ghosts were appearing, and the sandy shore of Ilion, and this citadel was changing as its stones came apart, into an Achaean encampment while, farther back on night's horizon, another citadel took shape.

Diomedes had no time to question his decision, or wonder what would happen if Welch called Caesar's forces into play and physeters vaporized the outer gates and all the 10th entered.

Would there be Romans and Egyptians on the beach? Would Kleopatra be the Helen, this time?

It was too horrible.

Diomedes jumped for Agamemnon just as the crazed leader took one hand from his staff to tear the golden mask from his face.

"This!" Agamemnon howled as Diomedes hit him in the ribs with the full force of his headlong charge and both went down together. "This face, I cannot live with it! Refight the war, and we can change the future, which is my past! Bold Achaeans! Diomedes, give your counsel in my favor!"

They hit the ground together, rolling, Diomedes grabbing for the standard as rocks fell close at hand, rocks as big as men and some shaped like them, rocks that bounced off the helicopter's armor and dented the com truck picking up Alexander and his party.

And when he'd wrestled the standard from Agamemnon and finally sat on his adversary's chest, breathing hard and bleeding, with the standard pushed against Agamemnon's throat to keep him on his back, Diomedes saw two things:

He saw the face of Agamemnon, one eye dripping onto his cheek, that cheek open to the bone.

And he saw the eight ball, rolling to stop with a message uppermost that Diomedes couldn't help but read.

The eight ball said, *If it ain't broke, don't fix it.*

And wily Agamemnon, spying it, pleaded, "You see, Diomedes? Your destiny lies with me. . . ."

But it didn't. Agamemnon was wrong. Behind Diomedes' back, the sounds of angry physeters spitting hellfire could be heard.

8.   Of Pawns and Kings

The tanks came sweeping in, new and dreadful groundborne fleet, upon the shifting landscape in the shifting twilight, now Ilium, now Mycenae, now Asia, now Greece; and pounded the remnant of the lowermost walls to rubble, bursts of fire and smoke in the dark of a madman's mind.

Hatshepsut had no doubt of the hazard. She kept talking, using nightsighted binoculars to direct fire past the citadel as well, wherever she saw targets through the general murk, wherever there was anything of Ilium to aim at; and shells went thumping in off the heights down to the beaches, where eyed ships blew to fragments and the fleet of Agamemnon foundered yet again on that shore, this time come to defend. But it had no such weapons, and Achaeans died in droves. Egypt thrust off the Sea People again, this time from Ilium, and Hatshepsut stood up in Curtius' jeep and got a look at the wreckage through the smoke—it was absolute. Like the citadel. Even while the very landscape shifted and changed, and the shadows of a taller, greater citadel loomed on a hill somehow grown wider. Picking targets in this lunacy was a chancy proposition. But the ships lay smouldering, smears of fire in the nightglasses. Some shells had hit, of the two tanks she had turned that way.

So Odysseus might have perished in this almost-night. Back to the Undertaker—mission aborted. And Automedon and Paris alike. Hector with Hecuba and Helen and Cassandra, wise Nestor and fool Thersites.

So her own omens advised her. And they came whispering again: *That's one of two. One calamity down, the other unavoidable now.*

"Where does that leave me?" she wondered, not to Curtius, herself and her driver parked off on a small height with a vantage both toward the walls and toward the ghostly dark sea that had appeared under the reddish night.

Without guarantees, the voice whispered into her ear.

"*Animadvorte dextram!*" Curtius had never lost his antique accent, but that was easy enough to catch, the young Roman pointing to the right and reaching after the mike himself, forgetful of kings, to direct the fire of the number two tank off to shadows moving down that shore in the fireglare.

Hatshepsut braced her foot against the seat and applied a pair of fieldglasses to the situation down on the beach, not particularly interested in minor harassments; the tanks were handling it. The tanks had a vantage that could handle most everything— the citadel too, if they could get their own clear of it. But ardently she wanted out of this place, off this shifting hillside and away from seas which materialized with fleets already ashore. There was no guarantee someone hereabouts did not have artillery; or even air support; and she had no particular liking for a valley like this with hills about it like so many fortresses. The whole business was mad, mad as Tiberius, whose villa she could all but see for a moment, in the outlines of that shadow-against-the-sea, before it shifted again to something else; before—Osiris and Set! the whole hill elongated, and became something altogether different, a long, long slope toward that shadow-keep that melted away like mirage as a sickly gray dawn spread itself from behind them.

"Set take it!" she yelled into her mike. "Number four and five!"—and sent them up to secure the highest ground the lumbering monsters could manage, and sit there; while around them thunder broke; and shells crashed; and the ground shook as if some single great piledriver were thumping away, rearranging the hills, creating illusion and taking it away again as dawn came up meteoric and swathed in cloud.

It was Diomedes' show over there on the Mycenae-hill, where unnatural dawn had broken, dispelling dark fantasies of larger fortresses, showing a citadel partially collapsed, partially whole, high up a long, long hill. His show, and Achilles', and Maccabee's. Shock troops, which had done some good, getting the chopper over that wall, getting its guns to bear on that higher gateway—if that *was* what had wrecked the citadel up there, if there had *been*, gods to help them, no such thing and the night and the river-mists had conjured it out of the fogs which now lay thick beyond—

Had there been a sea? Were they smokes which went up out of that mist, and wreathed the sky beyond, obscuring what lay farther in this gray, chill dawn?

Had she dreamed ships, and fired on illusions, and had they all gone mad, attacking a citadel half-shrouded in fogs and seeing ghosts and giants up there?

But the Romans were still advancing from below, their engines long masked in the hammering

fire of the tanks, whose fire she had called in against
that western wall, but never where it obstructed
the road. And against the eastern, where it was
breached. Where the copter sat like a black ungainly bird, exposed in gray and unlooked for daylight, where small figures moved within range of
her glasses.

It occurred to her as she watched that among
other Hellenes who might be the better for a trip
to the Undertaker, Diomedes would be a prime
candidate. She did not take kindly to indignities,
particularly public ones. But she had not ordered
him shot on the spot: policy. She had not ordered
him assassinated after: she was taking a wait and
see. Mostly, she had reckoned after the fact, he
was a large rowdy man whose subtleties stopped
at his predjudices and whose wisdom met the same
limits. And he had interesting connections. *That*
saved his life, that he proved to know the pilot of
that sleek and very useful bird that had come
thwup-thwup-thwupping into this misty sky from
Osiris-knew-what regions of Hell. With Maccabee
aboard.

That was interesting. So was the sight the field
glasses picked up now, amid all the chaos, through
the rent in the walls. Which was the selfsame
Diomedes getting up off a man who looked much
the worse for wear, and threatening him with the
flat of a spear-blade.

The Hellenes were all quite mad and omen-
ridden. There was, for instance, Alexander himself
standing there quite stolidly in this unnatural dawn,
watching this display of threat with his arms folded.
And the newcomer Achilles, standing there beside
him, a slight man in night-camouflage who probably had his pockets all full of interesting tricks.

Julius' Achilles. Julius' Alexander of Macedon.

She had read her history. And her poets. And patterns shaped themselves.

One order to a tank to turn about and place one well-aimed shell, just there she subvocalized an instruction, like clearing her throat, and got the attention of a certain part of her apparatus, muttered the range and got the precise coordinates, just to see if it were possible.

Then another force came sweeping up the hill, a jeep topped the rise, with its headlights glowing in daylight as it came up toward the Lion Gates and the wreckage of the walls. There were other jeeps, spotters off along other lines. One with this unit. Behind it a large number of Romans and the German guard and the Macedonian cavalry were coming up that slope while someone had gotten that gate open to give the vehicles and the horses a clear road—right into the courtyard to stop a moment and exchange a word and a gesture that indicated upslope as first the Macedonians and then the Romans went tight-formation for that gate and kept coming through.

Pharaoh held her breath.

She had it in her power to shift the course of Powers in Hell, and knew it. They were all three there on that hilltop, in that courtyard. So were all their forces. She was here, in command of firepower enough to reshape the landscape. And Julius was—

—*friend?* The Pharaoh had none. Lover? She had had those beyond counting.

Damned lucky, that was what he was. She let that jeep keep going, as it intended to do. And said nothing at all to that voice which came to her sometimes.

Those tanks did not see well by day or by dark, despite their nightscopes. It was their great limitation. They could make fatal mistakes of all kinds.

Friendly fire. And the greatest danger to stability in Hell would be dispersed.

But she had ruled in stability. And Julius had taught her Roman games. Crapshooting.

"*Alea iacta est,*" she said to no one in particular, not even thinking it was Latin.

"What die?" Curtius asked her, her driver, out of his long silence beside her.

"Something about Rubicons," she said, and sat down, hard beside the young Roman. Pretty lad. He had ridden his horse down to Hell. Or the Romans had simply cut their throats, boy and horse together, to stop the earthquake. Curtius never told the story. But once in her arms, he had dreamed that the ground was moving.

I take that for a compliment, she had said, and worked the shivers out of him. But he was not a good lover. A sweet boy who had gotten too hard and given too much and who had offered up his life before he had known what he was giving away, being only eighteen. Now he was multiple thousands of years old. And there was Hell's own understanding behind those eyes that turned her way as she sat down, the two of them isolate on this hillside, but not, thank the gods, understanding of what she had contemplated.

Had she given that order, she would have killed Mettius Curtius quickly, from behind. It would have been kinder, and she still had affection for him.

As it was she simply gave him a sphinx-stare, the sort she had given her councillors and her vizier-architect when his life hung in the balance.

"You mean we can't go back from here?"

Another sphinx-look. *All Hell can't go back from here, Roman, and no, this necklace isn't listening, but I wouldn't say that aloud for any persuasion. Something here the Devil could manage and another*

*thing he failed at and I wish I were myself sure
which side is which, or how many times Niccolo's
doubled. He's the one I'd like to ask. Or gods know—
Julius himself. Never underestimate him.*

*Why didn't I give that order, dammit? I'd have
made it away in the confusion. Before the damned
Romans got it sorted out. And Niccolo. He'd manage. He always does.*

Luck? Mine or Julius'?

As on the lower part of that hill the Macedonian
cavalry went racing up to add itself to Julius'
forces, and held its pace after that to that of the
infantry. A gift, doubtless. Kingly generosity.

There was nothing kingly in the figure which,
snuffling, sought again its mask, and wrapped itself in its robes. Alexander, who had dealt worse,
and drunk himself stuporous after, compelled himself to watch it all, his Germans standing at his
back; Achilles did, for his own reasons.

And over by the black machine, another matter,
another figure which had wrapped itself, and sat
down there in the dark, enigmatic as the mad king
when it found its feet in this dreadful dawn, in the
dust of the passing Romans, and walked toward
him, all shrouded in robes and sheet.

He had the Uzi in the crook of his arm. He
swung it warily in this direction, figuring that
it belonged to Diomedes, or to Achilles, but not
trusting it, not believing, in fact, that this improbable man in black—his red hair covered with a
helmet and smeared with dirt like his face—

Zeus! not Achilles. Not Achilles. This—slight, nervous man who reminded him most of Zaki at his
most exuberant.

And who brought this *thing* in over the walls
like a god in the plays, so that he all but looked for
the ropes and the cranks. It had none. It only spat

out this sheet-wrapped apparition which rose up and came toward him like some leper in a bad dream, like the lepers that lined the roads in the eastern lands and begged alms and terrified passers-by with threats of ill luck.

But it flung back its wrapping. It stood there with tears running down its bearded face. And the king, the *basileus*, stood there quaking with dread. It was Cocytus where a man met his ghosts. It was guilt which confronted him.

"Alexander," Maccabee said, reaching out to him. The voice was unnatural and hoarse, fitting this place. "I'm back."

It wanted to touch him. He let it. And it was very pale and very weak, but it felt solid under his own hands. "Judah?" he said. Such ghosts were *lamiai*, which came to take the blood of the living, or to draw them down to the tomb, of which there were many about. But he would not strike it. He had too much of guilt for that.

He smiled at it, and it smiled back. And did not strike either. So it would wait a while. He put his arm about its shoulders and walked with it, over to join the man who claimed to be Achilles.

Illusions and illusions.

The little Jew Zaki came scrambling from where a Roman jeep had let him off, and came running hard toward them.

Do you believe everything you see, wise little Jew? Do you trust such gifts? Ask the Luwians. Ask Hector and Priam.

But he felt strangely emptied of concern. As if, Maccabee having come to harm him, some kind of fate was on him, and a clarity which heretofore only came with the wine or the god. He looked up the hill, the long hill which had changed in the night, and changed before the dawn, and recalled that that long expanse had been a mere courtyard, and the doors much closer where he had left Antonius and the rest.

"We are mad here," he murmured to the ghost beneath his arm. "We have descended to the underworld and it is the House of the Axe we've come to."

But speaking in the Hellene tongue, he said it *laby-rinthos*.

"There!" Curtius said, pointing, and Hatshepsut adjusted the glasses and took in her breath, focused on the same sight, for a straggle of figures poured out from the shattered walls of the citadel-that-had-been, high above the advancing Roman lines, shapes whose partisanship could not be guessed—naked as they were born, but likeliest Hellenes, seeming harmless. With them was—oh, yes, by that way of moving, that gesture, unmistakably Antonius—supported by a horde of—Isis and Hathor! pale, half-naked women as they headed downhill toward the Roman advance vehicles.

"*Ave magister equitum*," Hatshepsut murmured in sarcasm not lost on Mettius Curtius, as she lowered the glasses and handed them over for his edification. "The hero Antonius, arriving down the hill. He's out, Alexander's got him clear after all. Another gift. A true benefit, gods know."

Dante Alighieri peered at the printout which echoed off the screen, tore it off and circled numbers and fussed, chewed his pen and made more notes, popped another antacid and scribbled again, there in the warren of stacked books and references and printouts.

"Oh, dear," he said, and reached for the antacid bottle again, forgetting that he had just done so. He spilled the whole bottle and tablets went rattling and bouncing everywhere in this office off-limits to sycophants. "O dear, O dear."

The link remained silent, an ominous silence from the field.

But things were not quiet elsewhere. There was an Egyptian colonel visiting at Assurbanipal's villa. There was a damned lot of attendance on that officer. It made one nervous.

And the numbers, without Julius to provide the newest ones through their carefully arranged codes, were increasingly dangerous to use. Dante knew this. He sweated every time he had to use a code, for fear of the results.

It was not fair that an innocent like himself had been swept up in this madness. An innocent, purely by a clerk's error, condemned to this dreadful situation. He worked—ever so hard. He sought favor of the powerful. He had no wish to involve himself in their wars and their upheavals, and every sense that he had gained in this place was screaming alarm, that he was compromised, that they all were, and that Julius must come home to save them.

It was Julius who had snared him in. It was Julius that no one could say no to. It was Julius who tamed all these fierce spirits and rendered the household liveable; and if Julius was lost, if somehow Julius failed to return to them, they were undone.

There was only Sargon, and the Emperor, and a boy left besides himself. And the countless sycophants.

The Lion of Akkad was no small defense. But he was one man. And sometimes when Dante looked at that almond-eyed, bearded and brooding countenance, the least small chill went down his back.

Augustus still maintained his hold here. But only by virtue of the Lion's good will. And the Lion was no Roman nor Italian, but a visitor from Upshore, and inland, where Rameses maintained his own garrisons.

From Assurbanipal's villa, at the least, where even now that Egyptian colonel and a small company were in temporary residence.

It was decidedly Antonius, staggering down the hill in the murk of this unnatural and cloudy day, in the uncommon company of half a dozen women in various states of undress. It was also, Julius saw, his lost driver Aziru stumbling along behind, all but naked himself and looking as if he had had a long night of it . . . so two of his were accounted for, on this climb that, by some trick of eyes or land or, gods help them, Hell itself, had gotten longer than they had planned.

"Mouse," he said, and Mouse veered that way, understanding these things unspoken, turning the jeep crosswise across the path of the fugitives.

"He hasn't suffered," Klea said thinly, from the back seat. As if she were disappointed in the fact, after this trek and so many lost.

"Come now," Julius said. He was no little wroth himself. And yet if Klea was going to be, it was his part to play the peacemaker. To save Antonius for himself—later. "It's *Antonius*, not Oedipus." Meaning the old plays and Antonius' notorious theatrics. Always comedy. Always the joke. *Stay off him, Klea, he's mine, I know what to do with him, how to get the best out of him, he's better than you know, Klea. One more time, forgive him.* And then he wished he had not conjured by an Achaean name. As Antonius came panting and staggering his way up to the jeep.

"Thank gods," Antonius said, collapsing against the side of the jeep ahead of Aziru and his white-limbed mob of painted courtesans.

And Aziru, a moment later, came reeling up to
them with his face all haggard and haunted, and
nothing but a towel to wrap himself, feminity in
hue and cry after him. "Gods," Aziru murmured,
and flinched from the female hands that reached
out and tried to stay him and Antonius, the women
all half afraid of the jeep and half desirous of
climbing into it or anything else that looked re-
motely like cover. Antonius climbed aboard with
them all wailing and grabbing at him; Aziru
clutched his towel with one hand and tried man-
fully to haul himself over the side. "Out!" Julius
yelled, swinging to free his own arm from impor-
tunate women. And "Out of here!" Klea cried, and
let off a pistol shot which half-deafened him, at
which the pale creatures howled and wailed and
recoiled as Mouse gunned the motor and spun off
in quick retreat.

Julius looked back at the tangle in the rear, Klea
jammed indignant into the corner with her re-
volver in hand, Antonius clinging to the seat and
Aziru clinging to his towel despite the awkward-
ness of his position, one leg still over the side.
Antonius turned an anguished look in Julius' direction; the look on Klea's face would have stopped
a gorgon dead in her tracks.

"I'm sorry!" Antonius cried over the roar of the
motor and the rattle of gunfire. "Dammit, *Cai*, I'm
sorry! I—"

Julius gave him one of those looks too. At which
even Aziru lay quietly in his predicament, and
nothing moved in that back seat. Julius looked
past them then, where a line of legionaries and a
scatter of horsemen had come up the hill after
them, halting with the solid deliberation of infantry and the skittish restraint of cavalry at tight
rein—*someone* back there with the riders had sense.
"Get us out of here," he told Mouse, figuring it

was time to head down that hill again, regroup and figure out what they had for assets and what for liabilities.

And Mouse dutifully got them out, a drive right across the front of the lines to the flank opposite the horse cavalry, blowing the horn for a retreat.

Something hit the fender and rebounded; another something whisshted past with that unmistakeable sound that no Old Dead ever forgot, even if he had not died of it. Snipers in the ruins up there had position on them. Had let Antonius and the rest escape, to draw the lot of them into range.

Julius slouched down as he could and got a burst of fire off, screening the legion as it began its retreat, doing the cav's job.

Then the misty light flashed off movement high among the ruins, and the way that light came back, off the gold and steel boss and bronze rim of rectangular leather shields, the steel fittings of leather helmets, shadows turning up at regulation interval up there on the rim of a shattered rooftop—
"Edepol!" he yelled, grabbing the side as the jeep swerved and the jeep took a violent onesided bent for a few feet til Mouse got it under control. They had lost a tire, still going like blazes.

But that was the thunderbolt of the 10th on those Roman shields up there; that businesslike gray and brown advance was nothing hasty.

"Iacite!" a familiar bellow rang out, and there was a sound like a hammer blow soon after.

Javelins. So much for the enemy snipers on the wall, unfortunately at a lower elevation than a Roman infantry unit.

"Pull around," he yelled at Mouse, and the jeep with its improbable cargo swerved in a scatter of gravel and headed back across the hill, Mouse blowing the horn as they went: *about, about, advance.*

But there was no more fire. No more commotion

at all up there on the height of tumbled walls and exposed support columns. They pulled to a halt, there with the cohorts of the 10th ranged there behind them, stolid and unmoving.

In time, as he had figured, though the legionaries stayed their roof position up against the clouds and the haze, Scaevola came walking on down the hill, shield on the right arm—unmistakably Scaevola. With two legionaries for a guard. And the 10th kept its lines trim and steady as Scaevola walked up to the jeep, a red wash all down his right leg.

"H'lo," Scaevola said. And staggered and grabbed onto the fender as his escort grabbed for him. " 'M all right," Scaevola said as Julius went over the side to take hold of him. "O gods. Got any messages?"

"Dammit, no!"

"I'm sorry, I don't think I can—"

"Mouse!"

"Damn—" Mouse scrambled out, Aziru and Antonius trying to help from their vantage, along with the legionaries, hauling him right in over their laps, Aziru ramming the tunic skirt up under Scaevola's armor-edge where it did something to stop the flow of blood that was suddenly everywhere. Mouse ran round again to get to the wheel, Julius flung himself aboard, and they headed off, bad tire and all, bouncing and slewing on the angle of the slope to the Lion Gate, down toward the road, as he rummaged after the first aid kit and into it.

Damned thing, no more modern than the damned jeep. He turned about, knee in the seat, and tried to get a syringe filled with all the bouncing. Dropped the damned kit in the process. There was a lot of blood. It was all over the floor. Scaevola was out, his head lolling loose against Klea's shoulder as she tried to hold him against the bouncing. Julius just rammed the needle in and shot the plunger home. Right or wrong to do, he had no sure idea. But it was something. "Hold the damned wadding tight!" he yelled at the Amurrite. As they hit another dip and the tire gave way altogether. But the black copter was ahead of them on the downhill and the medics and all its equipment, if they could keep enough blood in the man.

There was no surety, in death, that they would not lose him altogether. Like Marius. Like a hundred others he mourned. And this one there was no replacing. This one was, for all his outspoken bluntness, and by way of it—an honest and a loyal man.

The jeep came squealing in to a jolting halt on the pavings in the shadow of the copter, and the Lion Gate; and Julius was over the side almost before it had stopped moving. "Wounded!" he yelled in English, which was *lingua franca* down here; and the suspicious occupant of the copter put his head out. "Dammit, we've got a casualty!"

"*Cai,*" Antonius said. In a way that sent foreboding over him. Even before he turned around and saw the way Scaevola was lying, and his whiteness, and the fact that he was dead weight Klea was hard-put to hold onto. Scaevola's eyes were still open.

"Damn," he said. And: "Damn." And bruised his fist against the fender of the jeep.

When the medics had come up and got Scaevola off his passengers, and offloaded him onto a stretcher, the boy just glowed the way bodies did when a living hand let go of them down here, and began to burn, which took the stretcher with it and ruined a piece of gear they might need, gods knew. But it was a small enough gravegift.

No deathmask, no rites, not even a handful of

dirt cast over him. It could not help. Nothing saved you down here from whatever they had decided to do to you.

"Give him back," he muttered at no one in particular, and bruised his fist a second time, and wandered off toward the hill, toward a blurred view of legions standing under Baculus' command and Hatshepsut's more distant surveillance. "Dammit." He rounded on Antonius. "That's your command up there, you want to see about it now or sometime tomorrow?" And to the medics: "Get up that hill. *Move.*"

They moved. He walked off a distance and not even Klea followed him. There was nothing particularly to say.

But his eye fell on Machiavelli standing off to the side and rested there a very long time. Machiavelli did not move. Or flinch. It was an order which passed and one which made the man very uncomfortable. But there was no refusal either. No demur and no disclaimer of responsibility.

On your life, little Niko. On your dislike of pain, Niccolo. Because I don't care. There's a point I don't care and you really don't want to see that side of me, do you, my shadow, thou voice of other voices? Ever seen a man crucified—guest of mine?

Machiavelli inclined his head ever so slightly, at the last moment at which he would have accepted that surrender. Machiavelli had a fine sense of such things. And pushed them as far as he dared. Almost too far, very close to too far, this time.

And with that look on his face, with that same look, Julius turned around and stared at the redhaired chopper pilot, who gave him a wry look, a casual stance; at the King of Macedon, who was standing there beside a bathrobe-clad and barefoot Judah Maccabee, who sat on a bit of tumbled masonry; but Alexander was on his feet and his face was pale and angry.

We're all here, are we? Julius thought, and wondered where in Hell and from what deep hole of it Administration had pulled this last and dangerous joke. *If* it was Administration that had done it. There were accidents and calamities aplenty in Hell and some of them befell the Devil himself.

A meeting on a death. Omen?

Or was that crawling up his backbone mere common sense, asserting itself late in the game. It was one thing to imagine such a meeting with one's lost elements. It was quite another to face it, already knowing Alexander.

That was the difference. *Knowing* Alexander. He had not known him, then, when Machiavelli— Machiavelli!—had come to him with his proposal and an antique ring, and touched on his romanticism and his curiosity, and, oh, yes, even that darker, survival-oriented curiosity which at that time had sounded no warnings, but only wondered, in that way it wondered about every anomaly in Hell.

A personality had its flaws. Always. And here was the young fool who had defied Sulla and chattered his teeth loose with the ague the while; and baited Agamemnon; and won a decoration in Asia; and killed a friend in his drunkenness; and spared Roman enemies he knew would kill him, because he would not, *would* not, be Sulla; or crucify Rome on the cross of his own security. Young warrior, and young king, and old cynic from a world which had outgrown kings, which had grown too complicated, a Gordian knot of a world which no longer yielded to sword-cuts.

Achilles? *This?* There was hope in a man who took to modernity with such zeal—but none in the cocky, push-me-if-you-dare stance. While in Alexander there was a kind of desperation, a weariness as if the flesh were wax and melting under too much fire inside and too much strangeness about him.

One of us who doesn't give a damn; one who gives too much, and needs too much; and where am I in this triad? One who's seen too much?

A chill, small hand touched his and clasped his fingers. Klea, Kleopatra. Patro-klea-patro-klos-hephaistion. Or *anima* to their *animus*. Yang and yin. Achilles would likely know that word. And slowly Maccabee got to his feet and held onto Alexander's arm in the same way—*don't be rash. Don't do a thing you'll regret. Don't say a thing of ill omen. There's too much at stake here.*

"You're a surprise," he remarked to Achilles. "Where have *you* been? Difficult even for hell to swallow you up unnoticed for all this time. Jockeying this thing around, is it?" A nod of the head at the chopper. "Not in any records that crossed my desk." *I didn't know about this, Alexander-my-friend. No more than about you. But you were in hiding. Where did this one learn his skills?*

A lift of Achilles' right shoulder, a tilt of his head. He took off his helmet and swiped the back of a grimed hand across a grimed face, making a bright streak. Brighter still when he flashed a grin. "Hey, I got this order to deliver this fellow, I don't ask."

"Who from?"

Another shrug. "Pentagram, where else?" A second grin. Between which the eyes were dead-cold. "General, sir."

Julius lifted his chin the minutest degree. Alexander took a deep breath and a step forward, which stopped when Julius fixed him with a stark, straight look: *Let's don't be a fool right off, shall we, Macedon-*

ian? At Achilles he smiled his political best. "All right, son, just what *did* happen here?"

Achilles' frozen grin went to pure ice. He always had had trouble with CO's. Another lift of a shoulder, this time of an elegant, begrimed hand: the other held the helmet. The red hair was knotted at the nape, long and non-regulation; and gods, Julius gritted his teeth and knotted his jaw and decided not to make an issue of it now or later, the issue of which issue he could foresee with no oracle at all. Manipulated, by the gods, by a cocky and all too brilliant little bastard with a permanent chip on his shoulder.

Achilles had passed as a woman while draft-dodging, he recalled, for about a year. And got a king's daughter With Child, a quarrelsome bastard son (O Brutus), who himself finished off what little Achilles left of Hellas.

This present ticking bomb just shrugged off toward a standing corner of the wall, as if that answered questions. "Agamemnon's indisposed. Diomedes is sitting on him. Figuratively. Sir."

"To prevent his murder," Alexander said. The Great King's nostrils flared, white-edged. "Julius, we are in danger here." Alexander held up the eight ball. "It gives no good omens."

Achilles laughed, a soft sneeze, and wiped his mouth as if that hid it.

"Neither does anything else in this place," Kleopatra said; and offended Alexander further just by being there. But she let go Julius' hand and walked over to Alexander, laying a small hand on his arm and saying softly: "I am what you know. No rival to anyone here. Trust me. Trust Julius." She stopped short of Achilles. "What have you done with Agamemnon?" While Maccabee stared at her with knotted brow and stormclouds gathering. And Alexander's face flushed with hectic color.

She dropped the hand. Wisely. But it was her Alexander was focused on, her face Alexander (thank the gods) looked *down* to meet. "Great King," she said. "What will you do with Agamemnon?"

Alexander drew a deeper breath. As if he had suddenly come back to himself, and stopped wandering unanchored. "He will swear loyalty to me," Alexander said. "And lend us his resources. With the physeters and this—" He waved a hand toward the copter. "And Mykenai in hand—we will make our supply lines. And *you*—" He spoke sharply to Achilles. "If Achilles you are, Peliadês, you will swear me an oath too, and do no harm to Agamemnon. If he betrays us, then I give him to you. But until then he has my protection."

"And mine," Julius murmured, not to lose his own handle on things. The Great King was at it again, kinging it. Besides, it was Klea's little play, and it looked to be working.

Allies, *prodi*, himself and Alexander. There was something about three contenders and an apple. Unless two would ally they were locked in stasis till the sun froze.

Allies, indeed. Achilles would be an uncomfortable bedfellow. All knives and sullen, suspicious pride and vanity. A right *pretty* fellow all scrubbed up, doubtless he was, and touchy as hell.

Right now Achilles was still smiling; his mouth was, at least. "Fine," Achilles said, and drew a larger breath and stuck his hands in his belt. "Deal me in. Piece of it, huh? Me and a general and the great damn king of all Asia. Fine."

"Don't push it," Julius said. "Yes. Deal. And you know why. Hang around and *learn* something. I'm sure that's what you're here for." With another smile fit to boil butter. "Isn't half this damn camp? Alexander, drinks. In my tent. If you will."

"I have my gear," Achilles said, with a nod toward the chopper. "In there."

"I suppose you brought your own groundsupport? Or does that chopper stay?"

A guarded and nasty look.

"Hell of a flight you made," Julius added. "Down the tubes with those rotors . . . *hell* of a flight."

"Hey, I'm good." Nasty smile too. "Fly just about anywhere. Sir. I got the fuel. But my backup's just going to have to run it out of here. Unless you need it."

"I take it he's a real hotshot too, that backup of yours."

"Sure is. Hey, let me get my stuff. Drinks, you said."

"Sure," Julius said. "Brought a tent, did you? But we'll use mine."

Achilles tossed his helmet to the other hand, slapped it on and walked off to the copter, swagger in every line of his back.

Klea made a sound between hiss and whistle, between her teeth. And Alexander's face was a study in outrage.

"That is a *lie*," Alexander said in clipped, fine tones. "That *boy* is a lying dog."

"That *boy* is damned dangerous," Julius said. "I'd worry less if I thought he was lying. That *boy* has friends in strange places. And I'm altogether afraid he may be what he says he is. How did he get here? How did he get that machine here? Maccabee?"

"I remember nothing of it," the Israelite said quietly, worried-looking. "That is the truth."

"I don't doubt it in the least." Julius cast a sudden straight look at Alexander. "As kings go, he ruled a village. He commanded a half a legion. Because *we're* wider in perspective—was he? He's a damned boy, you're right, and he never lived to be more than that. *Ambition*, Alexander. How would you and I be, stopped before we were twenty?"

"Gods," Alexander muttered, with an expression of distaste. And scowled more deeply. "This business of souls is your fancy, not mine."

"It's true," Kleopatra said. "That's the third. The youngest. The unfinished one."

"What do you know of it?" Alexander snapped. "Woman."

Kleopatra lifted her head, jaw set in an expression which was hers. And for some reason the color fled Alexander's face. As if he had seen a ghost. Or recalled some memory.

"I know," Klea said. And Alexander set his hand on Maccabee's shoulder and drew him a step away.

"My men will have Agamemnon under guard," Alexander said.

"Before we get to that tent," Julius said, "before then, Alexander, know that you and I are both in charge in this camp. Share authority. What does it matter to us? I yield to you, you to me, to no one else."

"I give you nothing!"

"They say that boy's immune to arrows. Are we? I don't like my back unguarded."

"Let Klea guard it."

"She does, marvelously well. But it's my hand I'm offering you. Do you know that gesture, Macedonian? Had you friends? Or has a king—friends?"

Alexander stood stock still. His mouth was a firm line, his face pale and flushed at once. And sweating, despite the wind. Then he went and offered his hand, forearm to forearm, a painful, defiant grip.

Julius matched him, and held, and stared him in the eye without looking down any more than he had to. The pressure from the other side slackened, became merely solid, and the gaze of Alexan-

der's eyes close at hand was an unwanted naked-
ness. On both sides. There were few situations
where Julius was not in control; few situations
could send either of them, he guessed, into panic
retreat. But this was as close as he had come in a
long while.

It twisted at his gut when Alexander suddenly
laughed, and startled him into doing the same, as
if they had both caught the same hellbound joke
they played on each other in their dilemma, merely
by existing; and they let each other go, quickly,
because all Hell was uneasy while they were that
close to each other.

Three of them, *pro di immortales*, and the ground
went unstable where they walked, tremors going
all the way into the webs of Administration.

They were in mortal danger. All three and all
they touched. That much was absolutely certain.

"Ssss." Hatshepsut lowered the glasses yet again,
one knee in the seat of the jeep. Her Voice was
whispering to her again, at least one of them was,
telling her that it was damned well time she got
herself back to the main unit: leave the tanks where
they sat for the moment. So someone else was
thinking in terms of artillery. And those surround-
ing hills.

About the vision she had had, the fortress which
appeared when there was *not* that general suffu-
sion of pale gray light in the clouds, and where
there were not those reeking vapors going up from
Cocytus' strange landscape—she had not reported
that. She reckoned that Curtius would, when they
got in. Curtius was a sharp lad, and left nothing to
chance.

Herself, she gave away no coin that might be of
value, and meant to deliver that one personally,
first to Julius.

Machiavelli second. Niccolo and she had certain things to discuss. "Let's get out out here," she said to Curtius, who started up the jeep and turned off down the hill.

There were worlds to conquer, she thought, if she could get out of here. But by Osiris and Set there were realms hereabouts which had no little to do with them. One started where one stood, if one wanted to rule the universe, and this hillside and yonder tumbled ruin was as apt a starting point as any.

9.   Gift Horse

When they were all very drunk, Alexander and Achilles left Caesar's tent.

It was nearly morning, yet Maccabee and Diomedes still waited.

Waited on the beach, or so it seemed before Alexander blinked and the camp reasserted itself over a seaborne, hellspawned mist.

"Gods," Diomedes stretched, rising, hand to the small of his back, as Homeric as he'd looked the day Alexander had first seen him. "We thought you'd never come out of there."

And behind his back, Paradise began to rise, so near and yet so far.

Achilles shrugged. "So what? We got it hashed out. We've got all the damned time in the world."

Maccabee gained his feet more slowly, still the pale ghost from Cocytus. Alexander blinked back winey tears and stretched out a hand to his friend, forgetful that he was still holding the eight ball.

Maccabee, olive blanket held tightly at his throat, took the ball gently.

"What does it say?" Diomedes asked, while Achilles stared squint-eyed at the half-tumbled citadel of Agamemnon in the distance and at the slope toward the sea.

"It says," Maccabee replied, bringing the ball close to his fair-stubbled chin, " 'See Minos.' "

"C Minus? My ass," Achilles snapped. "A Plus, if you ask me."

But Alexander had seen something run out of the citadel and down the slope toward the shore, something so beautiful and so sad that he clutched his heart and Diomedes, sober and observant, stepped in to support him.

"You tremble," said the Argive under his breath. "What is it?"

Then he followed Alexander's gaze and saw the living omen on the beach, the wild beast running, tail flagged and head high, toward the rising light.

And the light that was also a part of that omen gilded the massive hindquarters and shone in the flying mane of the horse who ran free on the hard-packed sand, and who trumpeted his existence to the world.

"Bucephalus," Alexander whispered, tears streaming down his face.

None of the ancients had to explain to one another the significance of a wild horse running toward the light, or of the fact that the horse was, without doubt, Bucephalus.

They followed the horse, the omen, the godsend, their destiny as, above their heads, Paradise continued to rise.

SPECIAL BONUS EXCERPT!

**Proceed if you dare
as the Damned Saga
continues . . .**

Here is an excerpt from Crusaders in Hell, *the next installment in the HEROES IN HELL™ shared universe series, coming in 1987 from Baen Books:*

GILGAMESH REDUX
Janet Morris

"To the end of the Outback, and back again."
    —Silverberg: "Gilgamesh in the Outback"

"The lord Gilgamesh, toward the Land of the Living set his mind," chanted Enkidu, hairy and bold, trekking beside Gilgamesh up to the mountain peak.

And Gilgamesh interrupted: "Enlil, the mighty mountain, the father of all the gods, has determined thy fate, O Gilgamesh—determined it for kingship, but for eternal life he has *not* determined it. . . ."

These lines, from the epic sung as *The Death of Gilgamesh* for ages, shut both men's mouths.

But in the inner ear of Gilgamesh, the poem continued, fragments sharp as spear points in a wild boar's heart: "*Supremacy over mankind has Enlil granted thee, Gilgamesh . . . battles from which none may retreat has he granted thee . . . onslaughts unrivalled has he granted thee . . . attacks from which no one escapes has he granted thee . . . in life. Be not aggrieved, be not sad of heart . . . On the bed of Fate now lies Gilgamesh and he rises not . . . he rises not . . . he rises not.*"

On the top of the mountain peak now stood the lord Gilgamesh and his servant—his friend—Enkidu, and Gilgamesh wondered if Enlil inhabited this peak even in Hell.

It was silly, it was foolish, to have climbed this

mountain in search of more than he could ever find in Hell. For that was where Gilgamesh now was, who had sought Eternal Life and now sought Eternal Death, the peaceful sleep that had been promised him while all around him were the lamentations of his family.

In life. So long ago in Uruk.

For a time the presence of Enkidu had soothed him, but now it did not. Below and behind them was the caravan they had joined, because Enkidu had seen a woman there he craved, and because the caravan was well supplied with weapons that were to Enkidu like toys to a greedy child: plasma rifles, molecular disruptors, enhanced kinetic-kill pistols that fired bullets tipped with thallium shot whose spread was as wide as Gilgamesh's outstretched arms.

Cowards' weapons. Evil upon evil here at the end of the Outback. Such was behind Gilgamesh, down on the flat among the covered wagons of the mongrel caravanners with whom, for the sake of Enkidu, he'd fallen in.

Before him, on the far side of this mountain whose peak Enlil did not inhabit, was a shore and a sea an island off that shore, an island belching steam and gouts of flame from its central peak—the destination of the caravan Gilgamesh had left behind on the flat: Pompeii was the name of the island, and whatever awaited there, neither Eternal Life nor Eternal Death was among its secrets.

Gilgamesh knew this because he was the man to whom all secrets had been revealed in life, and some of that wisdom clung to him even in afterlife.

"To the Land of the Living," Enkidu took up his chant once more in stubborn defiance of the murky sea and burning isle before them, "the lord Gilgamesh set his mind."

As if it made any difference to Fate what Gilgamesh wanted, now that Gilgamesh was consigned to Hell. Enkidu's mind had been poisoned by the woman with the caravan, by nights with her and the thighs of her and the lips of her which spoke the hopes of her heart: that there was a way out of Hell.

So now Enkidu sought a way out of Hell through tunnels; through the intercession of the Anunnaki, the Seven Judges of the Underworld whom Gilgamesh had seen in life; through perseverence and even force of arms. Myths from the lips of a woman had seduced Enkidu and put foolish hopes in the heart of Gilgamesh's one-time servant and beloved friend—hopes that were, with the possible exception of intercession by the Anunnaki, whom Gilgamesh had seen and knew to exist, entirely apocryphal.

If Enkidu and Gilgamesh had not so recently quarreled and parted, if Gilgamesh had not missed his friend so terribly when they did, the lord of lost Uruk would have argued longer and harder with Enkidu. He would have refused to join the caravan. He would have stamped out Enkidu's vain and foolish hope of escape from Hell.

He should have done all those. But there was no one in the land like Enkidu, no one else who could stride the mountains at Gilgamesh's side, whose stamina was as great, whose heart was as strong, whose hairy body pleased Gilgamesh so much to look upon.

There was no companion for Gilgamesh but Enkidu, no equal among the ranks of the damned. Thus Gilgamesh put up with Enkidu's foolish hopes and hopeless dreams. Enkidu was not the man to whom all secrets had been revealed.

Only Gilgamesh was the man. Only Gilgamesh had known the truth in life. The truth has less value, here in afterlife. It had no more value than the slain carcass of a feral cat or a rutting stag or a rabid demon—all of which Gilgamesh had slain while hunting in the Outback. It had no more value than the skins he cut from those carcasses as he had in life. It had no more value than the flesh beneath the skin of those animals, dead while he dressed their carcasses, dead while he ate—if he must—their flesh.

But not dead. Death was rebirth here. Death was forever elusive. Death was merely a hiatus—and a shortcut to the teeming cities of Hell's most helpless damned, among whom Gilgamesh could not breathe.

In Hell's cities, Gilgamesh felt like the lion caged to please the king. In Hell's cities, his limbs grew weak and his spirits low.

This city before them now was no exception. It dried the chant in Enkidu's throat. It dried the blood in Gilgamesh's veins. Pompeii, the caravanners whispered, had come whole to Hell, so purely iniquitous were its very streets. Its dogs had come. Its dolphins had come. Its whores had come. Even Pompeii's children had come to Hell.

And it was a city, so the tales ran, where everything was as it once had been—where outsiders were unwelcome and never settled, where a language neither Greek nor English was the norm.

Gilgamesh looked at Enkidu out of the corner of his eye. Enkidu had brought them here, from the clean violence of the Outback, because of his loins and his lust for modern weapons.

Gilgamesh had never asked Enkidu if the former servant got pleasure from his copulation with the woman, or only frustration, as was the lot of so many men in Hell. Men whose manhood was too dear, too often proved, too important to their hearts, often could not consummate the act.

Gilgamesh and Enkidu had met because of one such woman, centuries ago in life.

He shook away the cobwebs of memory, so common lately, and said to Enkidu: "See, the city of ill repute. Let us leave the caravan now, Enkidu, and return to the Outback, where the hunting is good."

"Gilgamesh," replied Enkidu, "the animals we hunt do not die, they only suffer. The skins we take ... are these not better left on animals who must regrow them? And the haunches we eat, which distress our bowels? Let us go with the caravan into the city, and explore its treasures. Are you not curious about that place, which came to Hell entire?"

This woman was destroying Enkidu, rotting the very fiber of his mind, Gilgamesh realized, but said only, with the patience of a king, "We will not be allowed into the city, Enkidu, you know that. The caravan must camp on the shore and its people go no farther."

"Ah, but the lord of the city will come to us and then, hearing that you are Gilgamesh, lord of the land, king of Uruk, he will surely invite us there ... to see what no outsider has ever seen." Enkidu's eyes were shining.

Gilgamesh had never been able to resist that look. He said, "If you will put away this woman— who will not be allowed to travel with us to the city in any case—and separate from the caravan thereafter, Enkidu, I will announce myself to the lord of the city and demand the hospitality due the once king of Uruk—and his friend."

"Done!" cried Enkidu.

High above the caravan, in a helicopter hidden by Hell's ruddy clouds, an agent of Authority named Welch reviewed the background data that had brought him here, on his Diabolical Majesty's most secret service.

Welch had become a member of the Devil's Children, Satan's "personal Agency" among a dizzying proliferation of lesser agencies, without ever meeting Old Nick face to face. Agency was special, privileged, demanding and unforgiving of failure.

Agency was not, however, infallible, and the briefing material before Welch on the chopper's CRT was no better that Welch's own spotty memory could provide. Worse, perhaps, since bureaucracy in Hell functioned but never functioned well.

Tapping irritably at a toggle to clear his screen, Welch mentally recapped the "secret" anaylsis he'd just read:

Mao Tse-Tung's Celestial People's Republic had spread quickly along the tundra of the Outback, stopped only by Prester John's border to the south and the Sea of Sighs to the west. New Kara-Khitai had already been invaded by the collectivizing hordes of the CPR, led by Mao's Minister of War himself, Kublai Khan.

Communist troops in the Outback didn't bother Authority—as Mao had said, revolution wasn't made in silk boxes. The misery Mao's CPR fanatics brought with them like bayonets on the barrels of their ChiCom rifles would have been allowed to spread unchecked, at least until it overswept Queen Elizabeth's domain and the West was Mao's entire—*if* Mao could have been content with that.

Unfortunately, Chairman Mao had greater ambitions. He sought to export revolution to every socialist crazy who could say Marghiella, and that included Che Guevara (or what was left of his soul since Welch had called in an airstrike on Che's main Dissident camp north of New

Hell). If the export of revolution had stopped with rhetoric, perhaps Authority could have looked the other way.

But Mao was using drug money to fund his ideological allies—from Che on the East Coast to the Shi'ite bloc landlocked in the Midwest. Once his revolutionary exports reached New Hell, reached as far as the very Mortuary itself, then something had to be done.

Narco-terrorism wasn't to be tolerated. The poppy fields of the Devil's Triangle reached from Idi Amin's southern frontier to the Persian holdings in the Midwest, and over to Mao's capital, the City of the Fire Dogs. From Dog City, "China White" made its way south and east by boat and caravan, dulling the sensibilities of the damned.

Communism was one of the Devil's favorite inventions, and that made Welch's assignment harder. He couldn't simply nuke the emerging Western ComBloc back to the stone age—Authority wouldn't permit it. His assignment was to stop the flow of drugs East, especially into New Hell, where the Dissidents were attracting too much attention. So it was overflights in this Huey, piloted by a hot-dog Old Dead, Achilles. It was a covert crusade against drug smugglers.

And it was going to take one Hell of a long time to show any results.

Welch sat back from the computer bank in the belly of the Huey and reached sideways for his pack of Camels and a swig of beer.

Machiavelli had done this to him: vendetta. More precisely, Machiavelli had done it to Nichols, Welch's one-time ADC—sent Nichols out on a search-and-destroy mission aimed at a specific caravan master who did business out of Pompeii; sent him with an Achaean relic for a pilot and Tamara Burke, whose sympathies in life and afterlife were questionable. (Whether she'd been KGB or CIA, even Welch wasn't sure.)

Rather than let Nichols spend the rest of Eternity fighting Mao's considerably greater resources, Welch had pulled every string he could think of to secure command of this mission—even called an air strike on Che's base camp to clear his deck in time to board Achilles' Huey.

Welch shouldn't have been here, fighting the Yellow Peril out in the boonies when Agency had bigger fish to fry, not when he had so much unfinished business with Julius Caesar's crew back in New Hell. But he owed Nichols this much and more: Welch's miscalculation on their last mission had gotten Nichols killed.

If Welch had been doing his job right—before and directly after Nichols' death at Troy—he wouldn't have owed the soldier anything. But Welch had come back from the Trojan Campaign with a case of something very like hysterical amnesia. It had been Nichols who found Welch, sloppy drunk with Tanya—Tamara Burke—in a New Hell bar and offered aid and comfort.

Aid and comfort in Hell were hard to find. Aid and comfort coming from a junior officer rankled. Welch had been the case officer on the Trojan Campaign; Nichols had been one of many weapons Welch had employed there.

So it was all backwards, to Welch's way of thinking. He had to get things back into a perspective he could live with—or die with. In Hell it didn't much matter, but case officers thought in terms of human coin: debts owed, favors done, responsibility and trust.

Trust was a big one: whether betraying it or ratifying it, it was the fulcrum on which all operations turned.

This mission, on the face of it, was simple, if

Achilles' assessment was correct: strafe the caravan with the Huey's chain gun until nothing moved; firebomb what was left once they'd made sure that Enkidu and Gilgamesh were among the dead . . . or the missing.

That was a little addendum to the main mission: separate Gilgamesh and Enkidu, and send or bring both Sumerians back to Reassignments.

There was nothing in the orders about how, though, and Achilles was right: death meant the Trip; the Trip ended you at the Mortuary (except, sometimes, if you died on the battle plain of Ilion, a couple of dimensions away from here . . .) and then at Reassignments.

Even Tamara Burke had voted for the easy way, until Welch had put her down with a carpetbag full of feminine accouterments and detailed her to infiltrate the caravan and seduce one of the Sumerians.

Tanya had a field phone, tracer jewelry, and a chopped Bren Ten that could be heard to New Hell and back if she had to shoot it. And she was an experienced field collector, as well as a proven seductress.

But the look she'd shot Welch when they'd let her out a hill away from the caravan had been scathing. Only Achilles was pleased with that.

So now it was Welch and Nichols in the belly of the chopper, alone but for their data collection equipment and each other, bathed in sweat and running lights and trying to keep their equipment cool as they waited for a signal from Tanya that the caravan had picked up its load of drugs and was headed toward the hinterland. The low-shrubbed boonies. The damned no-man's-land of buffer-zone that was so undesirable even the commies hadn't claimed it. Yet.

"You know, something about this doesn't feel right," Welch said to Nichols, arching his back in his ergo chair so that he could put one foot up on the padded bumper of his "mapping" console, that could show him how much spare change Enkidu had in his pocket or how much ammo was in one of the caravan guard's Maadi AKs. "Tanya should have called in by now. The caravan should be loaded up and on its way out by now. And I can't find the right heat signature for Gilgamesh and Enkidu to save my soul."

"Umn," said Nichols with illuminating volubility. "Me neither." Nichols was still hunched over his tracking console, stripped down to a black t-shirt that showed the screaming eagle tattoo on one muscular arm. "Think maybe they've gone off on their own? The OD's, I mean?"

The OD's: the Old Dead—Gilgamesh and Enkidu. One of Nichols little rebellions was a feigned inability to pronounce either name. "Tanya would have let us know," Welch said, because it was his job to say that, not because he really believed he knew what Burke would do in any circumstance that might come up during field work.

"Yeah?" Nichols was more blunt, the sneer on his square face eloquent as he shifted to lock eyes with his superior. "What if Achilles and her have cooked up a little something of their own? That's lots of money, lots of power, lots of anonymity, down there." Nichols gaze flickered to his feet on the deck, below which was the caravan, camped on the shore in sight of Pompeii. Nichols didn't like Achilles and the feeling was mutual.

Achilles liked Tanya, though. Anything with a dork would follow Tamara Burke anywhere, sniffing and wagging its tail and leaving its common sense behind. Welch ought to know.

"What are you getting at?" They knew each other too well for Welch to take umbrage at the "Sirs" missing from Nichols badinage. When you were sweating it out in a com truck on the battle of Ilion or in Caesar's private office at a New Hell Villa or in a chopper flown by one of the biggest egos in Hell, you wanted a man like Nichols to have your best interests—and the success of your mission—at heart.

"A little recon. If you don't mind. You don't need me here right now. What these babies ain't sayin', you can handle." Nichols' chin jutted toward the electronics displays.

Maybe it wasn't necessary, but it was logical. And it was what Nichols did better than he did anything but exponentially increase body count.

"Okay, you're go," said Welch absently in their familiar shorthand, and unwound from his chair to give the order to Achilles on the flight deck. He could have patched into Achilles' helmet-circuit from here, but if there was an argument—and there almost always was with Achilles—he didn't need Nichols hearing it.

Standing, Welch had to slump to avoid hitting his head. Stooped over, he said: "Finish my beer for me. And take more than you need down there. Including this." He reached into his hip pocket and pulled out one of the miniaturized black boxes he'd requisitioned for his recent sortie into Che's camp. "You get into trouble, or just want extracted, push this button." He turned the match-box sized oblong in his fingers until the red nipple on one side was facing Nichols. "I'll be waiting."

"You expecting this kind of trouble?" Nichols frowned at the black box before he took it.

"I'm expecting a damned good reason why Tanya's not checking in, yeah."

Damned women, you could never tell what they had in mind. But it wasn't so much that he didn't trust Tanya, it was that Welch knew Nichols. Nichols had a disdain for the Old

Dead that might cause him to underestimate the opposition.

No matter who the antiques were, the opposition here was really Mao. And Mao was nobody's friend, nobody's fool. Welch promised himself that, when he got back to New Hell, he was going to get Machiavelli transferred to Sanitation Engineering.

Up on the flight deck, listening to the inevitable "better idea" that Achilles had, Welch made a mental note to include the Achaean in Machiavelli's Sanitation squad. Then he pulled his 9mm of his hip and, flicking suede lint from its barrel, said levelly to the pilot, "You fly 'em, I'll call 'em. Understood?"

The chopper pilot began landing procedures without another word.

Nichols had scrambled thirty feet away from the Huey before he looked back. Even knowing where it was, he couldn't see the damned thing. Stealth technology had come a long way since Nichols died, not in the Med during the Big War, but on an island off America's coast in the aftermath.

Didn't matter. Nichols shook his camouflaged head. Didn't mean a damn thing, Welch was right.

But it made him queasy, looking back at the electro-optically distorted field which masked the chopper so well you could have walked right into one of its rotor blades and gashed your head open.

Okay, he thought, so Achilles knows his job. Ought to give him one point. But Nichols couldn't do that; his gut knew better. And Nichols, unlike Welch, remembered every minute of the Trojan Campaign—up until he'd died during it. They'd scaled the very gates of Hell on that one, and Welch, his partial amnesia and his officer's attitude, just wasn't applying enough good old-fashioned suspicion to the events that had brought matters to their present turn:

Nichols had died in Troy, but been held in limbo, somewhere, awaiting Achilles' pickup—for this mission. On whose orders? To what end? Welch, meanwhile, who would have gotten Nichols out of limbo if he had used a P-38 to do it, was afflicted with convenient amnesia and watchdogged by Tamara Burke, whoever and whatever she was. If this was all coincidence, Nichols was a Persian eunuch.

If it was just luck, it was bad luck. And Nichols didn't like bad luck; if he had a god, it was the one that got you out of wherever alive, stepping three inches to the right of a cluster bomb that would have blown you to perdition; ducking your head to swat a mosquito just when the round that would have smashed it to jelly sped by.

Nichols knew damned well that Achilles was trouble—always had been, always was, always would be trouble, for friend and foe alike. He'd mucked up the first Trojan War and tied the commanders in knots during the second. If Caesar and Alexander the Great couldn't get around the jinx that Achilles put on any mission he was attached to, what chance did he and Welch have?

You couldn't talk to Welch about Achilles, beyond operational talk—Welch didn't believe in luck. Welch took everything personally. Which was fine, most times—it made him an officer with whom Nichols was proud to serve. But it made him touchy about certain things, like what he didn't remember about Troy.

And Welch didn't remember one very important thing about that mission: he didn't remember that, when Achilles came flying into the middle of an already-complex situation, nobody—not Caesar's crew, not the opposition down there, not his passenger Judah Maccabee, not Agency itself, and most especially not Welch—would admit to dispatching him.

Achilles was a damned wild card and even the Myrmidons hadn't had a real cheery survival quotient, according to what Nichols had heard, serving under him in life.

But Achilles knew his ECM. He could cajole stunts out that Huey like Nichols had never seen—or heard.

Blinking hard and listening hard, Nichols could barely focus on the chopper as it lifted, purring no louder than a happy cat. Stealth, you bet. Better than it had any right to be, like Achilles was better than he had any right to be, Nichols was willing to bet, doing somebody's bidding. Like maybe that of the Pentagram faction that was supporting the dissidents.

Achilles and Tamara Burke: neither of them had put a foot wrong the whole time they'd been in Hell. He and Welch had called up their jackets, and there wasn't a single negative notation or disciplinary action in either of their files. Too damned perfect not to be trouble.

But you couldn't convince Welch of that, not without proof. Tanya failing to check in wasn't proof, not in the mind of a guy who'd been laying her flat while Nichols was on ice somewhere for . . . how long? Long enough, that was sure.

Nichols checked his webbing and what he'd hung on it: he could probably have done the whole job himself, with what he was carrying. He had an Alice over his back with a SADEM— Special Atomic Demolition Emergency Munition—that would end any argument, except how he'd come by it. He had every electronic gizmo Welch could come up with. He had a det cord bracelet around his wrist and a high-pressure chemical delivery system next to the survial knife in his boot.

Recon had a tendency to turn into more than that, every now and again, and Nichols wanted to be ready.

Crouched among bushes bending violently with the chopper's take-off (even Achilles couldn't alter physics), Nichols checked his weapons-belt—front line kit was ninety rounds of 7.62 NATO in life, and that was what Nichols took with him on a mission like this, whenever he had a choice.

Then he started scuttling through the bushes on the slope, beyond which he could see the caravan making camp. Get there without being seen, find Tamara, make sure she didn't have a problem she couldn't handle, and give her Welch's message that she was to maneuver one of the two Sumerians to the pick-up sight and bring the OD onboard, nothing more.

Welch didn't see any reason to kill the two Old Dead, probably because Achilles was so intent on just that. So it had become a command decision, an internecine struggle on which depended command authority in the field.

Personally, Nichols didn't think you could teach Achilles nothin'; he didn't even see a reason to try. Nichols could get the Huey back to New Hell, if the one lesson Achilles might possibly understand became appropriate. Hand on his M14, Nichols prowled, pumping himself up for a covert entry where there was no night or cover to shield him, and plenty of nervous sentries around a caravan expecting to pick up a fortune's worth of drugs.

He had a suppressor on his customized auto-rifle, because that was the way you did this sort of mission, and he kept checking it as he scrambled down the rocky slope. He also had a button in his ear and a mike on his collar, so that he could voice-actuate communications with the chopper.

The odd sky, here where Paradise seemed skewered in place among clouds too dense and too low not to generate ground fog, threw him back in time and place, among the lush fauna of his volcanic, mountainous shore.

Jungle it wasn't, not the real sort, but it was close enough and Nichols had been Sniper Research, despite interdepartmental hassles, for a while when he'd been alive.

He was trembling with chemical hype from his nervous system by the time he reached the edge of the caravan, stopping on an overhang spawning a waterfall that generated some serious white noise, this close. Stopping to take a look-see, wriggling on his belly over rocks and past rocks and over lush grass, getting closer. . . .

"Yo, Nichols!"

The sudden sputter of Achilles' voice in his ear-piece made Nichols flinch. His foot dislodged a rock, which hit another, that tumbled down toward the water, and fell over the falls. . . .

"Not now, droolface," Nichols muttered into his collar, where his mike was. Idiot or spoiler, he was going to kill this guy, no matter what it cost him, and get him Reassigned somewhere where bugs were the only things that flew.

Below, the stone cascading down the waterfall, then bouncing, had flushed something unexpected: short guys in black outfits came running out from under the falls, gesticulating, chattering to each other.

Damned monkeys, or worse . . . no wonder this place sent his mind echoes of Ho Chi Minh trail. Bunch of Asiatics, hiding behind the waterfall. . . .

Nichols looked again, with all the acuity his trained eye could muster, and this time the waterfall didn't look natural. But it sure was convenient, and well-engineered. Nichols would give Mao's boys that.

Recon meant you were supposed to get back alive to detail enemy troop strength, he reminded himself as two parts of his being conflicted.

Sniper Research meant that you shot whatever you found out there, so that you could do your damned research uninterrupted. . . .

Head count, in this situation, was approximate, but Nichols was willing to bet that behind the waterfall he'd find lots more ChiCom troops—smugglers for the sake of the Revolution, in this case—and a tunnel entrance that would explain why no previous unit with this assignment had been able to find the transship route that Mao was using.

Whistling soundlessly, Nichols rolled over onto his back and very carefully, scanning the terrain around him, wiggled his arse until he'd gotton upstream far enough that he wouldn't kick any more stones into the water.

Then he began unwinding the det cord bracelet on his wrist, combining it with other necessaries from his kit until he had a time-detonated explosive device that ought to block the tunnel entrance, as well as stop the flow of water, when it blew.

He sat there a few seconds, considering his handiwork. You had to use the faults in the rock strata, judge it just right. . . . Deciding it was right enough, if nobody messed with it, he fixed his little trap to blow if a careless foot stumbled onto the det cord, which had enough RDX in it to be trouble by itself, and went on his way.

He'd known he'd find a use for all this stuff he was packing: you don't deplane with ninety pounds on your back and haul it over enemy terrain for nothing. He'd canniblized one of Welch's black boxes, but Welch's wouldn't mind.

It was going to be such a nice, satisfying bang. If the ensuing explosion didn't stop the drug traffic from Mao's fortress in Dog City, it was going to slow things up: rerouting, redeployment of personnel, rebasing ... all these things took time, men, resources.

Content that he could give Welch what the officer needed to report a successful mission, with or without Tanya and the Sumerians—and without setting up a semi-permanent staging area here which they'd have to man—Nichols scrambled down the slope and headed west.

He had no intention of getting caught in the act, or anywhere near here. What he'd left behind was more important than what remained for him to do: score one for on-site decision making.

It took the better part of two hours to circle the camp, find Tamara Burke's wagon, and slip over to it from the rear. He knew he should have reported what he'd done, called in and let Welch know. But then Achilles would know. And he didn't trust Achillies worth a damn. Or the com line he checked in on.

Welch who didn't like "excess" casualties, might have given him an argument, Nichols knew. Welch had a message for Tanya that underscored that forgiveable, but very real, flaw in the Harvard man's nature.

The camp was easy enough to negotiate— nobody here asked questions when strangers came around, especially strangers with backpacks in unfamiliar, non-standard, camouflage.

Finding Tamara's wagon was no problem— they'd scrounged it for her; there wasn't another like it in the caravan. Tapping on it with the butt of his survival knife, Nichols had a moment to worry.

He didn't like those sorts of moments, wherein possible problems that might never occur popped up like phantoms and scared him witless. But he sat out the flash of anxiety stolidly—he knew how to manage field jitters. You just kept telling yourself, "So what?" and they passed.

Because there was no answer to that question, beyond the simple answer: you handled whatever came your way.

It was taking her too long to answer, and he risked a low, "Hey, Burke, you in there?"

From somewhere, a desperate scramble became a barking dog, launching itself at him.

Reflexively, Nichol's service pistol came to hand. The dog was big, brindle, a decent target. He was deciding, as he watched it bound toward him in a slow motion his adrenalin-prodded physiology provided, that a two-shot burst would beat a headshot in his situation, and drawing a bead, when the gold silk of the wagon parted hurriedly and Tanya Burke said, "Don't you dare, you bastard." And: "Ajax, down!"

Ajax slid to a slavering, unhappy halt and, paw-before-paw, stretched out on the ground, whining.

"What are you doing here, Nichols?" Tamara Burke demanded angrily.

Everything about her was too damned perfect. She was too pretty, too rumpled, too obviously roused from sleep.

"You alone, Burke?" Suspicion kept Nichols alive.

"At the moment." The woman crossed her arms over breasts whose nipples were rising in the cold under her thin chemise.

"You didn't check in," said Nichols uncomfortably, his eyes still riveted to her breasts, pressed firmly by her arms.

"This is the first sleep I've had," she said with a strained, game smile. "Enkidu . . . well, I'm doing my job, what I was assigned to do." She shrugged. "Gilgamesh doesn't like modern equipment, and he's not the only one around here who's suspicious, so I ditched the lot."

"That was dumb." Nichols wanted to get out of here, give her the message and be done with it. But the woman was showing signs of strain, real or feigned, and he had to know which.

"I knew you wouldn't leave me. I can't guarantee anything . . . they went up the mountain, Gilgamesh and Enkidu. They haven't come back. I think Enkidu will, though—for me. He promised." She darted a look at the dog, then at their immediate surroundings. Content that no one was paying undue attention to them, she leaned closer, her knees now up against her chest.

Nichols leaned in too, and put a hand on one bare knee. "Welch wants one aboard the chopper—he doesn't care which. Doesn't want to kill 'em. Can't imagine it's more than ethics, though, if things get tough—" He safed his service pistol, still in his hand, and held it out to her, butt first.

It was a sacrifice she obviously didn't understand, or appreciate.

She shook her head; her hair flew around her face; she bit her lip: "No, Nichols, if Gilgamesh found that. . ." Then the rest of what he'd said sank in. "Look, I haven't seen anything more incriminating than lots of pack animals with nothing to carry. We might be way off base here. And what do you mean, 'wants one aboard the chopper'?"

"Let me explain," Nichols suggested. "We don't have much time."

The timer on the explosives was set for ten minutes from now, if he didn't intervene with a

272

radioed signal. And he didn't think he would. These primitives were going to read it as a minor earthquake; they were out of sight of the blast, anyway. And, whether Achilles was somebody's spoiler or not, this misson was going to go perfectly, or Nichols was going to know the reason why.

When luck had given him a handle on the ChiCom problem at the waterfall, pajamas and all, he'd known he was going to win this one.

All that remained in question was whether Tamara Burke, here, and her Sumerian boyfriend lived through it or got back to Reassignments the hard way.

Nichols didn't really care which. It would be interesting to see the look on Achilles' face, however things turned out.

He returned his attention to the business at hand: briefing Burke; getting out unseen; using the extraction beacon Welch had given him from a safe LZ as far as possible from the waterfall and the imminent destruction there.

A few minutes later, headed upslope on the far side of camp, he heard and felt the explosion and his heart lifted. Behind him, the caravan folk were running around nervously and dogs were barking, but there was no attempt to mount a show of force, no sign that foul play was suspected.

He'd have liked to have some drugs to show, but he had an ex-waterfall, a blocked tunnel, and a new hole to show, and likely some dead guys.

And, most important, it had worked: nobody had found and disarmed Nichols' explosive ordnance; nobody had stopped his show. Now he just had to make the other side of the hill and wait for pickup. Sometimes, Hell wasn't any worse than life had been. At least, not life as he remembered it.

*   *   *

273

Enkidu was among the chaos of the caravan when the bird descended on a roaring gale from Heaven.

He had been talking with a dog, down on his knees, barking at the round-eyed hound who barked at him, a dog belonging to the woman of the caravan whose wagon was painted red and gold, draped with golden silks.

This dog had been barking, "Enkidu, beware! Danger! Intruder!" and Enkidu, who had been like a wild beast in life, who had been lord of the forest and ravager of its game, had barked back, insulted. He, Enkidu, was no intruder and at the dog's bark he had taken offense.

So they had been readying to battle it out there and then, Enkidu and this impolite dog who called him an intruder, when the bird began its descent and the silks on its owners wagon blew wildly.

If Gilgamesh had been with Enkidu, things might have gone differently. Enkidu would not have been down on his knees in the dirt, barking loudly about how he would bite out the throat of this impudent dog as surely as he, Enkidu, was covered with hair. Enkidu would have been standing upright, like a man, and thinking canny thoughts, like a man.

But Gilgamesh had gone to the edge of the Sea of Sighs to greet the magnificent boat with its dolphin's prow and scarlet sail that had come from Pompeii. Gilgamesh had gone aboard the boat to secure passage to the city for them both, leaving Enkidu to wait alone.

Long hours had Enkidu waited, and then gone back up the shore to where the Caravan made its camp. Gilgamesh, king of long-lost Uruk, would come and find Enkidu when he was ready. And then Enkidu must put the caravan woman by, forget her ivory thighs and pomegranate lips, and go with Gilgamesh onto the boat and into the wondrous city beyond.

Until then, Enkidu had it in his mind to make love to the woman upon her flocked couch. But the dog of the woman had scratched at his spiked collar with a clawed hind foot and bristled his brindle fur and barked harsh words at Enkidu, while his mistress stayed inside her wagon, as if she heard nothing of the argument taking place outside.

So now, as people scattered and hid their faces in the dirt while the dog tucked his tail between his legs and his furry body underneath the wagon, only Enkidu remained in the clearing to brave the buffeting wind and howling cries of the black bird that descended upon them, scattering dust and scraps and detritus in every direction.

Enkidu put a hairy arm over his hairy brow and squinted at this manifestation, wishing that Gilgamesh, to whom all secrets had been revealed, was beside him to read this omen.

Since Gilgamesh was not there, Enkidu did as he pleased in the face of the unknowable: he straightened up his great body, like a wild beast protecting its territory in the forest.

Enkidu spread his legs wide and crossed his mighty arms and leaned into the gale come from this black bird from Heaven—or from some other Hell—and then he waited.

Enkidu did not need Gilgamesh to tell him what was right. Enkidu did not need the cowardly dog who whined behind the wagon wheels. Enkidu could protect this woman, this dog, this caravan, this territory, by himself.

Privately, Enkidu wished he had a weapon, for the bird was twice the height of Gilgamesh and as long as three caravan wagons. But he did not have a weapon, because Gilgamesh despised the weapons of the New Dead and Enkidu loved

275

Gilgamesh, whom the gods had decreed was wiser than he.

Not even Gilgamesh, Enkidu thought as the belly of the bird opened wide, would have known this bird by name or what words to say to gain power over it.

Nor was Gilgamesh, Enkidu reminded himself, wishing he was not wishing his friend was here to tell him what to do when a man came out of the belly of the bird whose awful breath was blinding and whose terrible roar was deafening.

Because the bird's roar was so loud, Enkidu did not see or hear the woman come out of her silk-topped wagon until she touched his arm.

He looked down at the woman whose red lips said, "Enkidu, come with me. Ask no questions." Her hands tugged on Enkidu's mighty arm, pulling him toward the bird out of which the man had come.

And that man was running toward them, gesticulating, yelling: "Tamara, come on! Bring him or forget him. Time's up," in English.

The woman jerked hard on Enkidu's arm and pleaded with him, saying, "Enkidu, my hero, you are not afraid of that chariot without horses, are you? Come with me, where wonders abound, if you are brave. But if you are a coward, kiss me goodbye and stay behind!"

Her blond hair whipped around her face in the gale as her pale eyes searched his for an answer and behind them, the once-proud dog began to howl.

"But Gilgamesh . . ." Enkidu shouted back as the man stopped and waved again, a man dressed in the colors of the land and with furrows on his brow, a man as tall as Gilgamesh and as bold, for he had come from the belly of the bird.

"Enkidu," pleaded the woman, releasing his arm and running toward the other man. Halfway there,

276

she halted and looked back: "Enkidu, come! Let me save your life!"

The man beyond the woman wore weapons about his person, fine weapons of the most powerful kind. In one hand he held a plasma rifle; around his neck hung far-seeing goggles.

His other hand was outstretched, beckoning Enkidu with a gesture all men understood. Then he grabbed for the woman and jerked her abruptly toward him.

Words were exchanged between them and the man dragged the caravan woman away, toward the belly of the bird while, all around, the caravanners huddled in fear and none lifted a hand to help her.

Behind Enkidu, under the wagon, her dog began to keen.

Enkidu ran toward the black bird with wide strides, strides that ate up the distance and brought him to the bird's side as the other man and the woman reached it.

There the noise was too great for speech and the wind too fierce for open eyes. Squinting, Enkidu saw the woman clamber up into the dark belly of the bird and reach back with her white arm, her fine fingers outstretched to him.

Her mouth was open. She was calling his name. She wanted him to jump into the belly of the bird with her.

And while all the people and the dog with whom he'd just argued were watching, Enkidu made his decision. He went up to the bird. He touched the bird's side, and found it to be metal. He grabbed the bird's feet, and found handholds there.

He climbed into the bird of metal, into the dark and stinking shadows of its belly, and there he took the woman in his arms.

"Nice job, Tanya," he heard the man who wore the colors of the land say. "Better get him away from the window. He's not going to like the rest of this."

The woman from the caravan cooed at Enkidu and pulled him gently toward a couch among a magical wall of temple lights while, outside, the noise became unbearable.

Enkidu jumped up from the couch and ran to the place where he'd entered the belly of the bird, but there was no opening there. He ran along the wall until he came to a window, and there he paused.

Outside, the ground was becoming tiny and on it people were falling. From their bodies, blood was pouring. From the wagons, flame was spouting. From his vantage in the belly of the bird rising up into the sky, Enkidu could see it all.

And he could separate the sounds now, those he heard: one sound was that of the bird rising toward the sky, but the other sound was more terrible. The other sound was that of chain guns and cannon, of automatic-weapons fire strafing the caravanners' camp below.

When the bird had risen high enough, Enkidu glimpsed the island where Gilgamesh had gone. It was beautiful and magical and colored like a rainbow; in its center the mouth of a demon belched smoke and fire.

Enkidu felt remorse that Gilgamesh was not with him, in the belly of the bird. But the caravan woman was telling him how lucky he was to be alive, and how many wonders he would see when the bird reached its destination.

"And weapons, Enkidu, such as you have never had in your hands," said the woman called Tanya.

"But what of Gilgamesh?" said Enkidu. "My friend Gilgamesh was to come back for me, and we were to enter the city together."

"You're lucky you're alive, buddy," said a man whose torso was black to the top of his arms.

278

"Stay away from drug runners in the future. As for your friend, Gil,"—the man bared the perfect white teeth of the New Dead—"Reassignments'll decide when and whether you hook up with him again, because that's where you're going, Mister—Reassignments in New Hell." As he said this, the man took out a pistol and began fondling it. Behind him, Enkidu could see the shifting lights and glowing oblongs, like windows into other worlds.

"Reassignments?" asked Enkidu with a frown.

Nichols!" protested the woman from the caravan at the same time. Then she put her hand upon Enkidu and began to soothe him, promising all and everything she could do to make life better for him in a strange new land.

When Gilgamesh was put ashore by the dolphin-prowed boat of the Pompeiians, he looked everywhere along the beach for Enkidu and did not find him. So Gilgamesh trekked up the shore, toward the caravan's encampment, where Enkidu surely must have gone.

Joy was in Gilgamesh's heart. He was anxious to find Enkidu and tell him of the wonders he had seen. Behind him, the boat awaited, compliments of Sulla, Pompeii's ruler, to bring both heroes over the water to the city.

Gilgamesh had learned that Pompeii had not always been an island; parts of its shoreline were now submerged, a danger to ships. This Sulla was a Roman who had designated the city a colony for his war-weary veterans. There were many heroes on the island, and people of magical inclination like Greeks and Etruscans as well.

Quickly did Gilgamesh stride the distance to the camp, imagining the joy in Enkidu's face when he told him of the warm welcome they would receive in the city.

And when Gilgamesh told him another thing: this Sulla had said to Gilgamesh, "Gilgamesh, great king of Uruk? What are you doing so far from home?"

In the eyes of this Sulla, a Roman of soldierly bearing with a head nearly bereft of hair, had been no treachery, only a politician's caution.

Startled, Gilgamesh had replied: "What do you mean, Sulla? Uruk is lost to the ages. I have not seen its streets or slept in its fortress since I . . . died there." A sadness was in his voice, thinking of lost Uruk, the city of his life.

At that, Sulla queried him piercingly until, satisfied that Gilgamesh spoke the truth, he said, "I believe you, Gilgamesh. There is a false lord in Uruk, then—or another lord, at any rate. My men are tired, biding on this island, of small squabbles and small adventures. Should you and your friend, Enkidu, decide to return to Uruk, to regain your rightful place there, I might be persuaded to help you." And then a canny glimmer came into the eyes of Sulla. "Of course, we would have to know just where in the land this Uruk lies."

So Gilgamesh had replied truthfully that he did not know where in all the land Uruk was situated, that he had never come upon it in his wanderings.

And the Roman had told him then of the fabled treasures of long-lost Uruk, and offered again to help him find his home.

Such good news did Gilgamesh have for Enkidu, that he did not notice the quiet until he was upon the very camp itself.

There he saw scattered bodies, ruined wagons, and such destruction as made him cover up his eyes.

Taking his hands away, Gilgamesh ran through the camp, calling out for Enkidu.

But Enkidu was nowhere in the camp. It was as if the ground had swallowed him up, as if the demons had taken him, as if he had never been. Body after body did Gilgamesh turn face up in the dirt, but none of these were Enkidu.

After many lamentations, when Gilgamesh was exhausted in his grief, he sank down beside the ruined red-and-yellow wagon of the woman Enkidu had loved, and there he waited.

Perhaps Enkidu had gone hunting. Perhaps he had not come back to camp at all. Perhaps he would come back, if Gilgamesh waited long enough.

With a throat raw from lamentation, Gilgamesh sat there in the dust and watched the bodies of the dead around him disappear: some burst into flame, and those moved as if alive while they burned; some became like water and soaked into the soil; some melted like tallow over a flame; some simply disappeared.

While he was waiting for Enkidu to return, thinking of the dolphin-prowed ship at anchor, ready to take them to the island of Pompeii, Gilgamesh heard a sound.

A cry. A whine. A mewling sob of pain.

Up rose Gilgamesh, searching out the source of this heart-rendering cry, and found a dog, underneath the woman's wagon, bleeding from his neck and from his right forepaw.

Gilgamesh knew this dog, whom the woman called Ajax, although Enkidu had told him the dog did not recognize that name. He said, "Dog! Ajax dog, I am Gilgamesh to whom all secrets have been revealed—I can heal you if you let me touch you. Do not bite me, dog."

The dog raised his muzzle and bared his teeth as Gilgamesh reached for him. Then he sighed a heavy sigh and put his head down on his unwounded paw so that Gilgamesh could touch him.

When Gilgamesh touched the dog, it quivered and then it closed its eyes. When Gilgamesh cleaned the dog's wounds and dressed them with unguents from the woman's wagon the dog cried but did not bite him. When Gilgamesh bound the dog's wounds with strips of yellow silk from the wagon's curtains, the dog wagged its tail.

When it was clear that Enkidu was not returning to the caravan, the king of Uruk picked up the dog called Ajax in his arms and carried it to the boat waiting to take them to Pompeii.

So did Gilgamesh set sail for the magical city, with a wounded dog for his companion, and from there, perhaps, to trek to long-lost Uruk. And because Enkidu was no longer with him, Gilgamesh stroked the dog and told it everything he would have told Enkidu of the adventures awaiting them.

Gilgamesh did this with a heart that was heavy, but not unbearably heavy. Enkidu had gone off with the caravan woman, this was certain: neither of their bodies were among the slain.

Gilgamesh, like Enkidu, was not alone.